CW00520509

# THE
# ROSE
# GIRLS

# BOOKS BY JENNIFER CHASE

JENNIFER CHASE

# THE ROSE GIRLS

bookouture

Published by Bookouture in 2023

An imprint of Storyfire Ltd.
Carmelite House
50 Victoria Embankment
London EC4Y 0DZ

www.bookouture.com

Copyright © Jennifer Chase, 2023

Jennifer Chase has asserted her right to be identified as the author of this work.

All rights reserved. No part of this publication may be reproduced, stored in any retrieval system, or transmitted, in any form or by any means, electronic, mechanical, photocopying, recording or otherwise, without the prior written permission of the publishers.

ISBN: 978-1-80314-933-2
eBook ISBN: 978-1-80314-932-5

This book is a work of fiction. Names, characters, businesses, organizations, places and events other than those clearly in the public domain, are either the product of the author's imagination or are used fictitiously. Any resemblance to actual persons, living or dead, events or locales is entirely coincidental.

*For the hardworking cold-case detectives who never give up the fight*

# ONE

The rain poured and the wind blew relentlessly, but the old man didn't slow his pace. Dressed in a dark, waterproof trench coat and wearing a wide-brimmed fishing hat, he took one steady step at a time, helped by his bamboo walking stick. He stood up straight. He'd never missed a daily walk in almost forty years, so he pushed on through the weather and went deeper into the woods. It didn't matter that he was eighty-two years old; he purposely kept away from town and preferred his privacy, even if that meant walking in the rain at night.

The daylight had dwindled and the dark clouds cast gloomy shadows over the small rural town of Coldwater Creek. With a population of fewer than a thousand residents, it remained one of the most densely forested and picturesque communities in all of Sequoia County, California. It was the only town that fell across two county lines.

The water cascaded over the old man's hat, running down his face through his straggly gray beard, but he still didn't show any signs of retreating. He kept to the side of the rural road when he heard a car approaching. The headlights momentarily blinded him. The car, a small four-door blue sedan, swerved across the lane, barely missing him. He raised his cane in annoyance.

The old man stopped and watched as the car continued past, still weaving side to side, and then it slowed until it came to a complete stop. It sat idling. The tailpipe expelled swirling clouds around the car. The windows were heavily fogged up and the condensation blocked out any view of the occupants.

The car began to shake back and forth, the engine still running. As the old man neared, a hand slammed against the back window, slowly sliding down the glass and making an eerie, squeaking sound. He stood still like a statue, watching the events unfold in front of him as the rain poured down around him.

Without warning, the passenger door burst open and a young teenage girl wearing jeans, a pink sweatshirt, and white sneakers fell out onto the ground. She flailed around the rough, wet pavement and the bushes that grew along the roadside, trying to regain her balance. She was breathing heavily. Frantic. Several shiny silver bracelets dangled from her right wrist. She was kicking her feet trying to get away from the car, and as she twisted and turned the old man saw that her eyes were wide in terror. Her long dark hair was wet against her face. She didn't speak or scream. It appeared that the air was trapped in her lungs from overwhelming fear. When she finally got to her feet, she stumbled down a hill and disappeared into the blackness of the dense woods.

The sedan gunned its four-cylinder engine and moved forward, still with the passenger door open, and then slid in the mud to the side of the road and parked. After shutting off the engine, the driver of the car extinguished the headlights. The area was plunged into darkness.

The old man opened his coat, reaching for the Colt .45 revolver strapped in a holster on his belt. He rested his hand on the well-worn bone handle and waited. He peered at the vehicle with his failing eyesight. The license plate was obscured with mud and the letters and numbers merged together, making it impossible for him to read.

Within seconds, the driver's door opened and a man emerged. He was wearing a heavy-weather coat with the hood pulled up around his head. His black boots hit the ground and he moved with certainty and ease—almost as if this was something he had done many times before. He grabbed a flashlight from inside the vehicle and turned the light on. He shut the driver's door then went around the car to close the passenger door, before making his way down the hill following the trail of the girl.

The old man watched the flashlight beam sweep back and forth through the forest until it disappeared. He strained to hear voices or approaching emergency vehicles, but the only sounds were the rain hitting the ground and the wind whipping through the trees bowing the branches.

The old man stood, contemplating what to do. Finally, he walked up to the car. He hesitated, not wanting to get involved in other people's problems, before planting his walking stick in the mud, and reaching for the car door handle to pull it open. He glanced back in the direction the girl and man had disappeared, before turning back to the car. He leaned inside and saw a small white rag on the passenger seat and blood streaks across the dash and the interior door. There were clothes in the back seat wadded up in piles.

No paperwork.

No registration sticker.

The odometer showed digits over one hundred thousand miles, but he couldn't read the exact number. On the floor, threadbare carpet mats showed the car's age and extensive use.

The old man stood up straight and shut the car door. He looked down at the forest path; dark and eerily quiet except for the wind and the patter of rain at his feet.

# TWO

*Sunday 2015 hours*

"I love you too," said Detective Katie Scott as she ended the call. She smiled as she drove, thinking of her fiancé, Chad.

She slowed her speed as wind gusted fiercely across the road, rocking the unmarked police sedan back and forth. Rain pounded the car roof and thrashed across the windshield until the wipers were barely able to keep up.

"That's so sweet," said Detective Sean McGaven, Katie's cold-case partner who was sitting beside her in the passenger seat, smiling. His voice was almost drowned out by the rain.

"I second that," said forensic supervisor John Blackburn from the back seat.

The three had been representing the Pine Valley Sheriff's Department at the annual forensic and investigative conference in Las Vegas and were on their way home. "Now you guys don't be jealous." She smiled.

"You know we are," said John.

"So what town is this again?" said McGaven, trying to look out through the rain.

"It's Coldwater Creek."

"Oh." McGaven craned his neck, looking for a sign. "At least we're in our county now. Right?"

"It's a shortcut. The sooner we get through this storm, the better," said Katie, wanting a hot shower and to sleep in her own bed. The three-day seminar had been enjoyable and informative, but now it was time to get home and get back to work. There were cold cases waiting.

"So you say."

"I've been through here before. Trust me, it's much quicker than the main highway," she said.

Katie slowed her speed and drove around a large branch in the road. It was dark; no streetlights and no buildings in sight. She pressed the accelerator.

"Hope we get home in one piece," said John with light humor as he pushed his duffel bag up on the back seat as a cushion and decided to relax with his feet up on the empty seat.

"Funny," said Katie, watching the road. She knew that the turnoff was about twenty miles and it would save them quite a bit of time.

"Don't I know it."

Katie sighed, picking up speed and activating the high beams. Soon, she began to relax as the rain subsided and the roads grew more familiar. She had taken this route many times when traveling, but not for more than a year. During the day it was picturesque, with farms and land as far as the eye could see, but at night it seemed dark and ominous.

Katie saw headlights approaching, the high beams blinding through the rain. "What the hell?" She tried to shade her eyes while keeping watch on the road.

The car moved toward them and seemed to increase speed. Katie tried to maneuver the police sedan to the side of the road and slowed her pace as the small four-door vehicle continued to race at them.

"Look out!" said McGaven.

Katie hit the brakes and swerved to the right. But the oncoming car didn't change course, causing the police sedan to skid in the mud before taking them down into a small drainage culvert. The car's brakes screeched before they came to a violent stop.

The headlights dimmed.

"Everybody okay?" she said breathlessly.

"Yeah," said McGaven.

"I'm okay," said John, rubbing his forehead. "But that's going to leave a mark."

Katie's heart still pounded and she felt a bit dazed, wondering why the airbags hadn't deployed. She turned to make sure that McGaven and John were indeed okay.

Looking at his partner, McGaven said, "You okay?"

"I'm fine, but no thanks to the airbags."

"Can you back out?" said John.

"I don't know..." Katie turned the engine over and it roared to life. "That's a good sign." When she put the car in reverse and pressed the accelerator, the wheels squealed and spun. She stopped and then tried it again with the same result. Turning the engine off, Katie slammed her hands on the steering wheel. "We're officially stuck. I'm so sorry." She felt guilty that her shortcut turned out to be a bust.

"I don't think they'll have roadside service around here anywhere," said McGaven.

"You're probably right," she said.

"There must be a garage somewhere in town," said John.

"Maybe." Katie looked at her watch and it was almost eleven. "But they'll have been closed for a while by now."

"What do you want to do?" said McGaven.

"Let's see if we can call for service in town. Maybe the police dispatch can send a tow truck?" she said.

"At least it's stopped raining," said McGaven. He began

searching his phone for a direct number. "And we do have a cell phone signal."

Katie looked around, unnerved. Something bothered her. It was the fact there were no streetlights, no lights of any kind coming from houses or nearby businesses, making the atmosphere extremely unsettling.

More than an hour later, Katie saw headlights approaching; it was the tow truck that had been dispatched from the police station. The cab was painted red and yellow with big letters saying "Sal's Towing and Garage" on the side. Hazard lights flashing red and blue from the top and back of the truck lit up the entire area.

"*Finally*," she said and opened her door, stepping directly into the mud. "Uh..." Katie managed to climb around the car and up to the road. Her shoes and pants were now wet and muddy. She saw a tall man with a dark beard wearing navy blue overalls jump out and make his way around the front of the truck to meet her.

The rain had stopped, leaving the air heavy with the aroma of pine trees. There was a hint of mugginess to the air, making it feel warmer than it was.

"I take it you folks called for a tow truck?" he said.

"Hi, yes. I swerved to miss a deer and ended up here," she said.

McGaven and John joined Katie.

"I'm Sal," said the truck driver, shaking everyone's hands. He took a closer look at the sedan and climbed down near the hood. "Hmm." His lean body was fit and amazingly agile as he investigated the damage on the car.

"Can you pull it out?" she said.

"Of course, but it doesn't look like you're going to be driving anywhere soon."

The last of Katie's hopes dwindled. She had been so looking forward to getting home tonight, but it was becoming more and more apparent that that wasn't going to happen.

"What's it going to take to fix it?" said McGaven.

"I'll have to get it back to my garage, but your tire and front bumper need to be repaired. Other than that, I don't know the extent of the damage until I get it up on the racks—and that will be in the morning." His steely blue eyes examined the position of the car. Unzipping his jacket he tossed it into the truck, revealing a myriad of tattoos on his bare arms.

"What can we do to help?" asked John.

"Just step back up there while I get the truck in position," he said. Looking curiously at all three of them, he said, "Do any of you need an ambulance or medical attention?"

"No, I don't think so," said Katie.

McGaven and John shook their heads.

"Okay then. I'll get your car out of the ditch and hooked up in a jiffy."

They watched while the tow truck driver made good on his word. He pulled the sedan out of the ditch and was able to get it hooked up and secured in twenty-five minutes.

McGaven and John retrieved their luggage.

The tow truck driver walked up to Katie. "Do you all have a place to stay?"

"No. We were driving straight through to get to Interstate 35, heading back to Pine Valley."

"That's still a ways. How about I drop you at the Wild Iris Inn? Otherwise the nearest motel is more than thirty-five miles from here."

"That would be great. Thank you," she said. She felt annoyed at herself for landing in a ditch, but it was an accident and there was nothing else that could now be done.

"You'll like the inn. Mama makes great food. I'll call ahead to let them know you're coming."

"Thank you. We really appreciate your help," said McGaven.

"It's so late. Will they still be open?" asked Katie.

"Of course. Nothing ever happens around here—this is just the little bit of excitement we all need. They'll be delighted to help you all out."

# THREE

The tow truck finally drove off with the police sedan safely secured after dropping Katie, McGaven, and John at the Wild Iris Inn. Sal said he would contact them first thing in the morning with a diagnosis of the car. The three of them stood in the lot for a moment, staring at the ancient-looking house in front of them, decorated with a gold plaque reading 1892. There were lights on and several cars parked in front, but it was completely silent, almost as if it were just a backdrop on a film set.

The house itself, the size of a small manor, had a pale pink exterior with intricate white lattice trim along the edges of its roof. It covered two stories, with a pretty bird's-eye tower set at one side. Three chimney stacks stood out along the rooflines. One of them had plumes of smoke puffing out.

"Well, here we are," said McGaven.

"It's like we've stepped out of a time machine," said John.

Katie looked around, noticing the number of garden gnomes

and small cheery flags with flowers and smiley faces decorating the entrance. Again, something bothered her, but she filed her feelings away. For now, her priority was to get some sleep and start again tomorrow.

"Well," she said, "let's get our rooms." She walked up the stairs to the porch followed by McGaven and John. Pulling the screen, she was about to open the door when it flew open before her and a matronly woman wearing an apron greeted them. Her dark hair was braided down her back and her eyes were kind. The well-weathered wrinkles around her eyes and mouth made her seem like a motherly type.

"Hello, please come on in," she said. "I'm your host, Sadie Ramos, but most people just call me Mama. So sorry to hear about your troubles, especially on a night like this, but don't worry, you're safe and dry here."

Katie smiled and said, "Thank you. We don't want to cause you any inconvenience."

"Oh, nonsense," she said. Then looking at McGaven and John, she asked, "Do they talk?"

Katie laughed. "I'm sorry. I'm Katie, and this is Sean and John."

"Pleased to meet you all."

"So, can we get three rooms?" said Katie.

"Oh, I'm afraid that won't be possible."

"What do you mean?" said McGaven. "Sal said you had room for us."

"Oh yes, of course. I do, but it's just one room. There are other guests here getting out of the rainstorm like yourselves, and two rooms have some repair issues with the bathrooms that won't be fixed until Tuesday."

Katie sighed.

"But, don't despair," Sadie said, squeezing Katie's arm. "I do have the suite on the top floor—with a spectacular view. It has a king bed, a twin bed, a pullout sofa, and a big bathroom. It's large. There's plenty of room and privacy for the three of you. Will that suffice?" She watched the three expectantly.

Katie looked to McGaven and John. "What do you think?"

"I think that we have no choice," said McGaven.

"He's right," said John.

Katie and McGaven had shared a cabin before, and even shared her house during a case, but it seemed a bit weird that all three of them were going to stay in one room in a little town out in the middle of nowhere. But it was just one night.

"Okay," she said.

"Oh, wonderful," the woman said.

They followed Mama as she climbed the wooden staircase to the second floor. Paintings adorned the walls on every side. Most were landscapes, some still-lives of food and wine, and all were in dark wood frames. The stairs creaked under their combined weight as the three detectives carried up their luggage. Once at the landing, instead of going down the hall-way, they continued up another half flight of stairs to where there was a door with no identifying number or name. It almost looked like it could have been a closet.

It was cramped at the entrance. Katie looked over to her tall partner, catching his grimace as he pulled his duffel bag closer to his body, trying to shrink into the small space. Katie was tired —exhausted even. Her lower back ached and her legs were heavy.

Mama retrieved the key from her apron pocket and inserted it into the door, rattling it in the mechanism before she disengaged the old lock with a click and entered the dark room.

Katie glanced at her colleagues. They both had the same confused expressions. She knew how they felt. It did indeed feel like they had stepped off a time machine and were awaiting their fates.

The lights went on and Mama said, "Come in, come in."

Katie was first as she stepped over the threshold into a large area. Mama had told the truth; the room was big and appeared to be in three sections, not including the closets and bathroom. It hadn't been heated, so the cool air made Katie shiver.

"Wow," said McGaven as he followed his partner.

"That's an understatement," said John, marveling at the room.

"There are extra pillows and blankets in the closet, as well as extra toiletries if needed," said Mama. "I'll bring you up some snacks and drinks in a few minutes. Do you want me to start a fire to take the chill out of the room?"

"Thank you, no, we'll manage," said McGaven.

Mama walked to the door after setting the key on a side table. "Let me know if you need anything else."

Katie walked to the entrance. "Thank you so much. This is great." After closing the door, she turned to her colleagues. "Can you believe this?"

"It's like the twilight zone," said McGaven as he dropped his bags in the corner near a bed.

"I don't care how we got here, but I'm going to crash out," said John. He put his duffel bag near the couch.

"Don't you guys want to flip for the king-size bed?" said Katie.

They both mumbled at once. "No, it's yours."

"You sure?"

"Yep," they said.

"Great." Katie wasn't going to argue.

John began building a fire in the ornate fireplace. There were small logs and newspapers, which he carefully layered before lighting it. A slow flame began and continued to build into a nice crackling fire.

After Katie had put her bag in the bedroom nook, she took a look around at the freshly painted shiplap walls. There was a large paisley-printed chair in the corner next to an antique nightstand and lamp. A small pad of paper and a pen rested on top. There was a dark painting on the wall of what looked like a pond or a lagoon in the moonlight, and another of a vase of pink and purple flowers above the headboard. The bed was made up with crisp white linens, four overstuffed pillows, and a duvet. It looked inviting and she couldn't wait to slip under the covers.

Katie walked back into the common area. Here, original wood floors had been carefully sanded and stained, and the two rugs that covered them made the room more comfortable. A small desk and chair as well as a bookcase rounded out the room. There was a large open wall that had two doors to the closet areas. She saw in the smaller bedroom nook a small bed with several pillows and a quilt with a red, white, and blue theme.

"You guys okay?" she said.

"Yeah," said McGaven. "As long as John isn't too much of a snorer."

"Funny," he said. "Last time I heard it was you that sounded like a lawn mower."

Katie felt the coolness of the room begin to slowly warm from the fire and tiredness overcame her.

In fifteen minutes, everyone was ready for bed. Mama had returned with bottled waters, breakfast bars, and the news that breakfast was served from 0800, the same time they would be able to find out the fate of their vehicle.

A silence washed over the room except for the occasional sound of the fire popping and sputtering.

Katie brushed her teeth and washed her face. After slipping into a T-shirt and leggings, she climbed into the wonderfully comfortable bed. She had already called her uncle, Sheriff Scott, to let him know that they wouldn't make it home tonight and that the department's vehicle was in the shop. He would take care of her retired military K9, Cisco, until she returned.

Katie then sent a quick text to Chad, letting him know their predicament and that she would call him in the morning.

As she settled into the clean sheets, she finally began to unwind, feeling her muscles begin to relax. It was quiet. Peaceful. It took less than ten minutes before she drifted into sleep.

# FOUR

Katie was woken abruptly the next morning by an urgent knock at the door. She sat up in bed, glancing at her cell phone for the time. The person knocked again, more loudly. Rubbing her eyes she threw back the covers and with bare feet she hurried to the door. McGaven and John didn't move from their beds.

Katie took a couple of deep breaths, trying to fully wake up. She opened the door. A man dressed in a police windbreaker with a heavy hood, a scarf, combat boots, and military pants stood there, looking at her curiously. His face was pale and his expression solemn as his dark eyes scrutinized her.

"Can I help you?" said Katie. Her voice was hoarse as she fought her sleepiness.

"Detective Scott?" he said.

"Yes," she said slowly.

"And Detective McGaven, and forensic supervisor Blackburn?" He leaned forward as if looking for them.

"Yes, they're here."

"I'm Chief Roy Baker."

"Nice to meet you, Chief, but I think you might have the wrong room."

"I don't think I do."

"Is this about the car?"

"No."

"What's this about?"

"I just got off the phone with Sheriff Scott and he told me you were here."

"And?" Katie was intrigued but still didn't know what the chief of Coldwater Creek could possibly want with them this early in the morning.

"There's been a homicide," he said.

"What does that have to do with us?" She had a nagging feeling of what he was going to say, but tried to act like she had no idea.

"Coldwater Creek hasn't had a homicide—ever. Only a couple of accidental deaths over the years. Nothing we couldn't handle. But this..."

"I'm sorry, Chief, but I don't think I'm following here." She was fully awake now.

"Coldwater Creek is partially in the jurisdiction of Sequoia County—your county."

"And?"

"And, I called the sheriff to ask for assistance in this case and to send me his best detectives. I was pretty shocked when he said you were already here." He tried to force a smile, but his thick mustache didn't move.

Katie looked back in the room and saw McGaven sleepily emerge from the covers. John was already sitting up on the couch, listening to the conversation.

"You mean to say Sheriff Scott already agreed to have us investigate this homicide in your town?"

"Yes, Detective." He sighed. "I have only two officers—one full time and one part time. We're not equipped to conduct an investigation of this nature. I know how important crime scenes are, so I want to do this right, from the beginning. That's where you come in."

"Where are your officers now?"

"I have one guarding the scene making sure that its integrity is kept intact—and keeping the busybodies away." He seemed to be trying to assure Katie that they were following all the correct procedures.

"I see... and where's the victim?"

"She's near Bates hiking trails and campgrounds."

"Do we have an ID?" Katie's mind sprang into action.

"Yes. It's Ivy Miller. She's... fifteen years old."

Katie was stunned. Her heart ached for the young girl, her life ended before it had even begun. "Well... I... need to call my sheriff and—"

"Do what you need to do. I'll be waiting downstairs. But I suggest you make it quick," he said and abruptly left. She listened to the thud of his boots as he made his way down the creaky stairs to the ground floor.

# FIVE

Katie rode with Chief Baker in silence. McGaven and John rode with Officer Brock Daniels following behind them. Katie had called her uncle to verify what he wanted her to do and was told they were to help in every way they could to investigate the murder in Coldwater Creek. How long they were going to be in the tiny town was unknown at this point.

They drove past a historical marker pinpointing the Coldwater Creek Forest area and named after Clifford D. Bates, circa 1895. It was the second marker she had seen since they had arrived. The other was at the inn. The town had some history and significance, which made her think that there would be a certain amount of tourists wanting to visit. Katie turned her attention to Chief Baker.

"Who found the body?" she asked.

"Lana Stanley, who was walking her dog, Coco, as she usually does in the mornings."

"Did she know the victim?"

"I know what you're thinking. She knew the victim, so that

might make her involved somehow. But, Detective, everybody knows everybody here."

Katie thought about it. It was true that often rural crime scenes were discovered by hikers, joggers, or dog walkers. She also knew that in a town so small where everyone knew each other it would be difficult to get unbiased answers from people, and separate any facts from rumors.

As they drove toward the scene, Katie realized they were close to where they had been pushed off the road last night. But the surroundings looked so different in the morning. The rain had stopped sometime in the middle of the night, but the road was still wet and the sky gray and overcast. Between clusters of trees that stood along the sides of the road in rich variations of green, she could make out houses scattered here and there on large parcels of land. It was as if a veil had been lifted overnight and she was now venturing into a new town.

Katie glanced across at Chief Baker as he drove. She could tell that he was tense and obviously felt the burden of solving this case to be a heavy one. The chief's weathered hands gripped the steering wheel with purpose, his jaw was set tightly, and his frown was obscured by a subtle five o'clock shadow and his thick mustache. She wondered where he had been when he had received the call about the murdered girl. It was a big story for the small town, and one that wouldn't go away anytime soon.

"Anything you want to ask me, Detective?" said the chief as if he had heard her thoughts.

"Not right now," she said, wanting to see the crime scene first.

"Is this situation too coincidental for you? I mean, you happen to break down in the town and by the next morning we need your assistance for a homicide..."

"It is a pretty huge coincidence. But I haven't really had time to think too much about it until I see the crime scene." Katie knew that there was more to the chief than what she saw in front of her, but she had a gut instinct that he would tell her more about himself, and the town, when it was time.

"We'll both have questions," he said. "Officer Lane and I have been investigating some burglaries and vandalism, which has been taking up most of our time."

The chief slowed the police car down and turned right onto a gravel road. A sign read "Bates Hiking and Camping," with a well-worn logo that was slightly askew. Another patrol car was up ahead near the entrance to the hiking trails, parked between a dense cluster of trees. The vehicle had its trunk wide open, revealing yellow tarps and a duffel bag within.

Katie immediately began to survey her surroundings. She was already trying to figure out how the killer could have come and gone—and why this particular area was of interest. It wasn't what she was used to at a homicide crime scene. Usually there would be several patrol cars, not to mention detectives' cars, first responders, and a CSI van. The lack of support available for this small-town murder hadn't really hit Katie until they had actually rolled up.

"Here we are," said the chief.

Katie stepped out of the car and took in the environment.

Officer Daniels pulled his police vehicle in next to the chief's and parked. McGaven and John quickly exited the car to join Katie.

McGaven handed her a pair of gloves. "What do you think?"

Katie sighed as she pulled on the gloves. "I think... we need to see the crime scene." She wasn't sure what to expect or what challenges they were going to face. "Let's go." She began walking down the muddy trail.

McGaven followed her. John would stay at the scene with the officer until the detectives reported back.

Chief Baker followed but kept a respectful distance.

Katie set a slow pace, looking carefully about her. The

denseness of the forest reminded her of Pine Valley, with the early morning air fresh after the rainstorms of the night before and the fragrance of pine all around. Usually it was comforting, but today it was unsettling. Everything was still wet from the storm, making her concerned about the condition of any forensic evidence there might be. Some sections of the trail were drier underfoot than others due to gravel mixed in with the soil.

She finally saw the other Coldwater Creek officer, pacing back and forth at a break in the trail. The young cop looked up and saw the detectives approaching. His cropped brown hair and boyish face made him appear much younger than he must have really been—he was clean-shaven and his uniform looked expertly pressed.

He jogged up to Katie and McGaven, looking from one to the other. "Detectives?"

"I'm Detective Scott, and this is my partner, Detective McGaven."

"I'm Officer Lane, Brett Lane," he said, nervously shaking the detectives' hands.

Katie's hopes were slightly dashed as she realized that the officer was a rookie. That could pose some difficulties. "Officer Lane, did you secure the crime scene?" she said.

"Of course. No one has been anywhere near the victim."

"Did you interview the witness?"

"Witness?"

"The person who found the body."

"Yes, of course. I spoke with Lana and then told her to go home. If we needed anything more, we would contact her."

Katie glanced at McGaven and raised her brows in a code that meant they were in for quite the investigation. She turned and saw the chief behind them on the trail, staying behind and allowing them to do their jobs.

"Take us to the victim," she said.

Officer Lane nodded and led them farther into the forest.

Their footsteps were noisy as they trudged down the gravel-covered path deeper into the wooded area.

Katie surveyed the area as they went, realizing that as it had been raining so hard last night the killer might've had some difficulties moving about. But the denseness of the forest would perhaps have helped by providing shelter from some of the storm.

The young officer stopped and gestured to where the body was located. He then remained where he was, keeping his distance but clearly eager to watch the detectives in action.

That was when Katie first saw the girl. She sucked in a breath and slowly moved toward her. Ivy Miller was sitting down, leaning against one of the massive pines. Her bare legs and feet were straight out in front of her. Her head lolled slightly to the left, and had been covered with a clear plastic bag tied firmly around her neck. Her mouth gaped. Her wet long dark hair was pasted to her bare chest and shoulders.

Katie let out a breath. "Office Lane!" she called.

"Yes?" he said, walking toward her.

"Did you cover the body with this blanket?" Katie tried hard not to yell at the young officer. She knew why he did it, and completely understood, but it could ruin potential evidence.

"Yes, ma'am." He looked down. "I couldn't let her sit naked like that for everyone to see."

"I know it's difficult, but it would have been better to put up barriers blocking the view of the body rather than covering her. We have to be careful not to disturb any potential forensic evidence. You understand, right?"

"Yes." He didn't look Katie directly in the eye. It was clear he was embarrassed by his mistake.

As frustrated as Katie was, she didn't want to let her anger show—they would have to move forward because the oversight had already happened. "Don't worry, it can't be helped. The blanket may even have helped to preserve evidence against this weather."

Katie bent down and moved in close to examine the body. She gently folded the blanket back to reveal that the girl's arms were resting in her lap, palms up. The girl was completely naked and her clothes were nowhere in sight. Immediately Katie noticed the tattoo on the inside of her lower left arm; it was an intricate ivy vine with a small pink rose in the middle. The colors were vibrant, making Katie think that the tattoo must have been recent. There were three thin silver bangles on her left wrist; otherwise, the teen had no other pieces of jewelry or visible identifying markings.

Her hands were bloodied, as if she had struggled with her killer, and her right index fingernail was torn deep, leaving the remains jagged and bloodied. Several scratches were visible across her chest.

Katie turned to McGaven. "There was a struggle—looks like she fought with everything she had. We need to get her hands bagged for any evidence, this blanket too."

"Do you think the tattoo means anything?" he said, still looking at it.

"Not sure. It appears fairly recent, but we'll know more once we're back at the lab."

McGaven made notes as Katie continued her preliminary search.

Katie always had a difficult time looking at victims' faces— in the eyes especially. It was as if they were condemning her for not getting here sooner. There was a voice in Katie's head in an endless loop that said, "How could you have let this happen?" but it was that same voice that would urge her to push harder to find out who had murdered a teenage girl and left her body out in the forest. Waiting to be found.

Katie saw that the blood had pooled in the girl's lower body and the extremities where Ivy sat, which meant that she hadn't been moved from another location after her death. Rigor mortis had already set in, causing the muscles to stiffen. Her arms and legs were toughening up, making them respond to any movement like that of a rubber mannequin. The overall body had a bluish sheen due to fluid-filled blisters rupturing during the decomposition process, and the loosening of skin was now beginning to show—it appeared that she had died last night.

"What?" said McGaven noticing his partner's pause.

"She wasn't dumped here. This is where she died." Taking another breath, Katie continued to examine the bag and twine wrapped around the girl's neck. "Look at this twine. It's wrapped several times and tied in unusual loopy knots."

McGaven leaned closer to take a look. "It seems like a bowline."

"Isn't that the type of knot used in rescue missions?"

He nodded. "Like when you tie a rope to something solid and then wrap it around a drowning victim, say, in order to secure them. It's easy to do and is also helpful in camping for securing tents and shelters."

Katie glanced around her. It made sense to her that the killer must have known his way around these rural areas—there were few footprints along the main path. It was most likely why he had chosen this spot. She carefully moved the rope a little, revealing purplish marks on the girl's neck. It seemed consistent with being strangled. Katie couldn't see if there were any other marks on her face through the plastic—she wanted it removed properly and documented at the coroner's office.

Something occurred to her. Katie suspected that everything the killer had done to pose the body would have been for a purpose. It was possible there was something that they weren't seeing right away. She looked in the direction the body faced. Something didn't seem right. It was as if Ivy was waiting for someone to come along. The killer had made sure that the girl faced the trail so anyone walking would see her.

*Was there a message?*

*What did the killer want the body to convey?*

Katie bent down again and carefully moved the body, pulling the girl's left shoulder and torso forward in order to see her back. "Gav," she gasped. "Look at this."

McGaven was immediately at her side, staring at Ivy Miller's back.

A crude flower resembling a rose had been carved into the middle of her lower back with one slashed word next to it: "*MORE...*"

# SIX

Katie and McGaven watched as John began to painstakingly document the scene. The young local officer helped, following John's orders. The police chief had notified the medical examiner's office and was waiting for them to send out someone to transport the body when the search and discovery was finished.

The area around the forest was quiet. The wind had dropped completely and the sky was dark and overcast. The rain didn't fall, which meant the air was muggy and stifling. But Katie knew that that could change at any moment. She wanted to pay special attention to everything—things were so rarely what they first seemed in her line of work and she didn't want to make assumptions based on her previous experiences. Every crime scene was different—just like the shards of a shattered glass; no two pieces were exactly alike.

The two detectives searched the forest in the immediate area for clues and the killer's potential entry and exit points. Katie carefully made her way back to one of the hiking trails. The rain had washed much of the dirt and gravel down the path, leaving patches and uneven areas behind it. She looked closer, seeing footprints along the side. One set was small and shaped like a running shoe and the other had a heavier more defined tread, indicative of something like a work boot.

"Gav, we need to mark these," she said. "I'm not sure if it's related to the murder, but I can't imagine anyone else out here last night. It seems to fit the pattern of Ivy and her killer coming out here. By the gaps between the prints, it looks like they were running."

McGaven was carrying small orange flag markers that he had received from Officer Lane. "This will have to do," he said. He handed a few to Katie. She carefully stuck several of the flags into the ground around the two sets of shoeprints.

McGaven dialed John's cell number. "We have shoe impressions about a hundred yards from you."

"Working my way there shortly," he said.

Standing up, Katie took a three-hundred-sixty-degree scan. The trees, bushes, and uneven mounds of dirt caused by the rain meant that the killer and victim could only have come from the area of the parking lot—there were no other routes.

Katie moved up the hill toward the road. It was the same one they had been traveling on before the accident, and there was an area where a car could pull over and be completely off the main thoroughfare.

She stopped just short of the parking area. There were deep tire impressions that appeared to have skidded, leaving behind a muddy residue.

"What do you think?" said McGaven.

"Does it look to you like a car pulled over here," she said, gesturing, "and skidded to a stop?"

McGaven moved closer, carefully staying clear of any usable impression evidence. He bent down, studying the area. "It's totally possible. But it could have been anyone."

"True," said Katie. She loved the way her partner questioned everything. It made investigating tougher, but it also made her work diligently to get to the truth. "But, add everything together. A car stopping here, skidding to a stop, two sets of footprints heading into the forest."

"And the murdered body of a local teenage girl."

Katie frowned. "Those tire impressions couldn't have been here longer than hours, not days. They would have been muddied or completely washed away." Again she marked the area with the flags for John to document and process.

A white truck came around the turn and slowly drove by the detectives. The driver stared at Katie and McGaven. He had a grayish beard and was wearing a baseball cap. The truck sped on.

"Curious guy," said McGaven.

"Jot down the make and model of the truck and description of the guy as best as you can."

McGaven quickly took the notes. "You think it might be a killer coming back around to admire his handiwork?"

"I'm not taking any chances."

Katie walked up to the road, and looked up and down it to see if there were any other driveways or back roads leading off it, but there was nothing within the vicinity. As she walked back to the area where the tire marks were located, she noticed some round holes near the roadway.

She bent down and ran her index and middle finger over them.

"What is that?" he asked.

"I'm not sure. But there are some perfectly formed holes right here. It doesn't look like something an animal would make. And there might be another footprint here, but it's too muddy to tell."

McGaven marked the area. "Just in case."

Katie looked at where the vehicle had stopped and estimated that the holes would have been next to the car doors.

"What would make those holes?" said McGaven.

"They are perfectly formed. About... half an inch."

"A hiking pole? Some kind of tool?"

"Maybe."

"Someone could have been changing a tire. It would be about the right distance."

"Let's see what John has to say, but I want accurate photos with a measuring device."

"We seem to have quite a few clues and forensic evidence. That's a good thing," McGaven said.

"More than usual, and that's what concerns me."

*MORE...*

# SEVEN

*Monday 1105 hours*

Katie and McGaven rode with Chief Baker back to his office, which was located downtown next to several small businesses including a diner. The businesses reminded Katie of when she was a kid. The neatly maintained sidewalk in front of store-fronts, each with its own style and theme, gave the town a special homey feel. There were colorful awnings with stenciled names above their doorways. A flower shop, antique store, hardware store, and bookstore, besides the diner, made it appear that you had stepped back in time. It made Katie smile as she remembered Pine Valley growing up.

People from town were strolling around, running errands and stopping to chat with one another, so it didn't appear that anyone knew about the murder yet. However, it was only a matter of time before they did and the horrible news of Ivy's death would probably spread like wildfire through this small, close community.

Officer Daniels was already back, his cruiser was parked out front. John would ride back with Officer Lane when he was finished at the scene.

The detectives got out of the chief's car and headed into the office.

McGaven's phone rang. "Detective McGaven. Yes. Thank you for calling back. What's the prognosis?" He gestured to Katie that he would take the call outside.

Katie nodded and followed the chief into his office. It was small. There were three desks littered with paperwork, mostly junk mail, magazines, and various pieces of paper sticking out of a few file folders. A California Penal Code book lay open on one of the desks. She guessed that desk belonged to Officer Lane and he was studying up on it.

There were small framed family photographs on two of the desks. Katie guessed the smiling woman with two children was the chief's wife, and the other of a smiling woman out in the wilderness was the girlfriend of Officer Daniels. He wasn't in the office. She wondered where he was. Speaking with a person who might be important in the homicide investigation, she hoped.

"Please, sit down," said Chief Baker to Katie. He moved a stack of files from a metal chair and pulled it next to his desk.

Katie wanted to get straight to work, but she knew that she needed to get some information from the chief. She took a seat and tried not to show her impatience.

"I can tell that you and your partner know how to run a crime scene. In fact... I'm very impressed. Your sheriff did lend us his best detectives." He sat down, pushing some paperwork out of his way. "I'm surprised he would."

Katie's first instinct about the chief was that he was an honest man who really cared about his town. He was also smart enough to know when he was out of his league.

"Thank you, Chief. We appreciate you saying that. I do

have some questions—as I'm sure you realize, we need to get this investigation going while it's still fresh."

"Yes, of course. Ask away."

"Have the parents of Ivy Miller been notified yet?"

"Yes. She lived with her grandmother."

"I see," said Katie. She knew what it was like growing up with a relative and not your parents.

"Her grandmother, Sydney Barrett-Miller, took her in when she was about ten years old. Her daughter, Ivy's mom, ran off a few years ago and has never returned. Sydney will be making the identification at the morgue later today."

That made Katie tense. She had a strong feeling this case was going to be a tough one. "Do you know Ivy's closest friends? Where she liked to hang out?"

"I'll do you one better," he said, rising from his chair. From a small bookcase, he retrieved a recent yearbook. It was the Coldwater Possums high school yearbook. He thumbed through several pages and passed the book to Katie. "There's Ivy and her two best friends, Nikki Prager and Dawn Cromwell."

Katie immediately recognized the victim in the posed photograph that must have been taken in the quad of the school. Ivy was smiling broadly, her eyes sparkling and her long dark hair blowing away slightly as she leaned sideways against her two friends, holding a single rose. They were all posing for the camera and it was obvious that they'd been joking and having fun. Ivy seemed full of energy and excitement with a full life ahead of her.

Katie looked more closely and spotted the three silver bangles on her wrist. Her blouse was tied in front and she wore a pair of blue jeans. She was shorter than her two friends, but it was clear that she made up for it in her energy and infectious smile. One thing that struck Katie was she looked happy and content.

She studied the faces of Ivy's friends. They were both

blondes, Nikki with short cropped hair and Dawn with a French braid. They were wearing jeans and cutoff T-shirts. It was clear that they were close and shared a bond. Then Katie thought about the slashed word on Ivy's back. *MORE...*

"Chief, we need to get the addresses for Ivy's house, for her friends' houses, and also any area they might frequent."

"Of course," he said immediately. "We can get those for you no problem."

"I don't want to alarm anyone unnecessarily, but we need to make sure that Ivy's friends are both safe as soon as possible and take extra precautions until we know more about the circumstances of her death."

The chief stared at her.

"There was a word carved into Ivy's lower back," she said in explanation.

"A word? What did it say?" he asked.

Katie took a deep breath. "It said, 'More.'"

"More? What does that mean?"

"I guess it means that there's no way of knowing if this is a one-time murder or if there could be... more."

"I see." His expression was clouded with horror, his eyebrows pushing downward.

"Have there been any problems at the high school? Any reports of trouble? Kids ditching school more than normal, stuff like that."

"No. Nothing at all."

Katie sighed. "John will be preparing the crime-scene evidence and chain of custody for transport back to the Pine Valley sheriff's office." She glanced around the room with its basic furnishings and supplies. "The equipment and testing from our department there will be what's needed to start getting some answers."

"Sheriff Scott informed me of this. There's no doubt it's the best way forward." The chief's overall expression was tense, his jaw tightly clenched, but his eyes gave him away.

McGaven entered the office.

"Any news?" she said.

"Good news and bad news," said McGaven. He sighed. "The car is fixable, but it won't be ready until tomorrow."

"Oh." Katie was disappointed. Then again, there still was so much to do. She wondered how long they would be required to stay in Coldwater Creek.

"Don't worry," said the chief. "You're all more than welcome to stay at the Wild Iris as long as is needed."

"Thank you. Let's see what we can do today. The clock is ticking," she said. "Can we speak with Ivy's grandmother?"

"Of course. I'll give her a call now."

He looked up a number and dialed it.

McGaven raised his brows in question at Katie.

"I'll fill you in on the way out," she said.

Katie noticed an old map on the wall next to a current one. Both maps were professionally framed under glass. The older one was obviously a reprint of an original dated 1901. She studied the layout of the old town and its buildings. Part of the area was very rural and she wondered if it had many cabins.

"Chief," she said.

He had just hung up the phone.

"Are there rural cabins or homesteads in this area?" she said, gesturing to the dense forest.

"A few. We do have some people who don't like to be bothered with the rest of the town."

"Do they live off the grid?"

"Not completely, as far as I know. They usually have supplies brought in or shipped in monthly or quarterly."

"Do you check on them?"

"We have on occasion, but there's no need. And they don't

want to be bothered." He studied Katie. "Care to share what's on your mind?"

"Oh, nothing. I just wanted to get a better picture of this community," she said. Katie actually wanted to know about any secluded places. In her experience, people who distanced themselves from the rest were usually hiding something.

"I see."

"What's this building?" she said, pointing at a large square building on the edge of town.

"Back in the day it was a grain-storage facility."

"What is it now?"

"It used to be used for storing emergency equipment for forest fires, snow, and flooding. But now we house that kind of stuff in a more stable metal barn."

"I see." The chief didn't seem to be ready to offer much history or information about the town. That might make it more difficult for her to get a clear read on the nature of the community. But she would soon find out enough about it.

McGaven took a closer look at the map. "Can we get a copy of this?" he said.

"Absolutely. We'll get whatever you need and forward it to your room at the inn."

"Chief, let's go talk with Ivy's grandmother," said Katie.

He grabbed the keys on his desk and headed out the door.

"Where's Officer Daniels?" she asked.

"Following up on some leads. Nothing to get excited about yet," he said.

Katie looked at McGaven. She didn't say anything, but she had an instinct that said she wasn't yet getting the full picture. If the chief had wanted her to know the details, he would have told her.

# EIGHT

Katie was surprised to find out that Ivy's home was in an upscale neighborhood more reminiscent of a suburban area near to a large city than a small county town. The house itself appeared to be one of the larger ones in the area.

Chief Baker drove up to the estate and parked on the street.

"Wow," said Katie quietly, surveying the house and grounds.

"Mrs. Barrett-Miller is quite the Coldwater Creek socialite," said the chief.

"It seems that she could live anywhere. Why here?" said McGaven. "I don't mean any disrespect."

The chief laughed. "None taken. You'll have to ask her yourself about why she stays here."

As she exited the car, Katie noticed the large and perfectly manicured front lawn and neatly kept bushes outlining the property. Even after the rain, the yard looked tidy and well cared for. She almost expected two full-time gardeners to be hard at work, trimming, clipping, and sweeping, but there was no one to be seen. The walkway leading to the front door from the sidewalk was an intricately placed flagstone design, with dark green moss growing in between each piece. It added a pleasing architectural element to the front of the house.

The house itself was a two-story modern with upstairs dormers. It was painted a dark turquoise blue with white trim lending it more of an East Coast feel. It surprised Katie to see how much the house looked out of place. She had expected to see ranch-style homes, log cabin designs, and modest cottages. It was what she was used to seeing in the county areas. She wondered what made this house so different than the rest of the street. And why?

It was quiet. No movement from the neighbors, no barking dogs, no sound of kids, and no cars driving by. The area around them appeared almost two-dimensional, as if they were stepping onto a movie set rather than onto a real property.

Katie felt uptight being in another jurisdiction, where there were many unknowns, and had to push to maintain her focus on the murder investigation. Inside there was a grandmother who had just lost her granddaughter in the most hideous manner. It was imperative to find a suspect.

McGaven was quiet, obviously lost in his thoughts as he surveyed the area.

Two tall vases of flowers with a small balloon attached rested on the front porch. It seemed word of the tragedy had already circled around some parts of town.

Katie stepped up to the double front doors and rang the bell. Her throat tightened. She kept her eyes focused on the door and didn't look at the chief or McGaven as she waited.

The locks disengaged and the door opened.

An attractive woman in her early fifties stood staring at them. She was impeccably dressed in a long-sleeved fuchsia blouse and pressed black slacks. Her gold dangling earrings with matching bracelets were difficult to ignore. Her long dark hair had been swept up in a loose bun; her makeup had been carefully applied and seemed more fitting for an evening party than the daytime.

"Hello, Chief Baker," she said. It was clear from her slightly red eyes that she had been crying, but was trying to keep her composure.

"Thank you for seeing us, Sydney," he said. The chief turned to the detectives. "This is Detective Katie Scott and Detective Sean McGaven from the Pine Valley Sheriff's Department."

"Nice to meet you," the woman said. She stood still on the doorway and scrutinized the detectives for a moment.

Katie thought that there was some familiarity between the chief and Ivy's grandmother with the way they interacted, as if they had a secret. "We're so sorry for your loss. Thank you for letting us come over today."

She nodded and opened the door wider for everyone to enter. "Please come in."

Even though it was obvious that the interior was going to be as grand as the exterior, the inside still gave Katie pause. She felt herself thinking again that the home seemed out of place in Coldwater Creek. It was reminiscent of a high-tone place in a wealthy area, not a small rural town in one of the densest pine forests in California. It wasn't that it mattered; it was just an observation that was slightly unsettling at first glance.

Inside, everything matched the modern style. Beautiful rugs covered wood floors and high-end antiques were perfectly positioned throughout. The entryway wasn't large, but it opened up to the second story, giving a grand, estate-house feel. A wide staircase with wrought-iron railings led gracefully up to the second floor. There were vases in various hues of blues and greens set along the shelf of a long elegant table with intricate carvings. Beautiful old tapestries of different outdoor scenes from around the world hung on the walls instead of the usual paintings or photographs.

"You have a lovely home," said Katie. She could tell that the conversation was stilted and the situation was uncomfortable for all, but she and McGaven had a job to do.

"Thank you, Detective," Mrs. Barrett-Miller said. "I suppose you need to see Ivy's room?"

"Yes, please. It would be helpful to know more about her and what she was doing in the week leading up to her..." Katie couldn't finish her sentence. "But we have a few questions first. Would you have a moment before we see Ivy's room?"

"Of course," she said, but it was clear that she didn't want to talk. "Please." Mrs. Barrett-Miller walked to the large open kitchen, indicating that the detectives could have a seat at the counter. She took her position to face them.

The kitchen was almost big enough to support a restaurant. There were plenty of beige and white granite counters and two islands. The stove was oversize, with six burners and a grilling area. The room was meticulously clean and didn't have any personal items or even a bowl of fruit on any of the counters. Katie doubted that there was much cooking done, however, based on the specialty food containers she could see in the recycle can.

"I cannot imagine how difficult this is for you, Mrs. Barrett-Miller. But we need some information to help navigate us in the right direction. So that we can investigate your granddaughter's death properly," said Katie. She wasn't sure if the chief or one of the officers had already taken the woman's statement.

"Please, Detective. You can call me Sydney."

"Thank you, Sydney. One of things we do is try to retrace the last days. Can you tell us what Ivy was doing yesterday?"

"What she usually does on the weekends. She's always with her friends—Nikki and Dawn. What exactly she was up to, you'll have to ask them." She sighed, looking anywhere other than at any of the officers. She was preoccupied with her hair, fussing with it between her fingers.

Katie looked at the chief as he kept his hands in his pockets, staring at the floor. "I see. Would you know the places she usually liked to go?"

"If they aren't at each other's houses, they would go to the bowling alley and Snack Shack in town. Many of the teenagers like the place," said Sydney.

Katie looked again at the chief, expecting him to ask questions or fill in the blanks.

"I'll make a list," he said.

"Did Ivy mention if anything was bothering her? Or, had her mood changed recently?"

"No. She was cheerful and full of life. That was Ivy all over, though. People always wanted to be around her because of her zest for life and positive influence."

"Had there been any problems with her friends or anyone you know of at the high school?"

Sydney appeared to think about that question, but she shook her head. "No. I can't think of anything. Everything seemed as usual."

"If you think of anything or remember something that Ivy had said, please call us or the chief."

"Of course. Her room is up the stairs." Sydney gestured. "It's the second door on the right. Everything is exactly as it was when she left yesterday—as if she were..." She took a deep breath and seemed to struggle to keep her composure.

Katie had been going to ask more questions, but decided that they needed to see Ivy's room and move forward. She led the way through the house and climbed the beautiful staircase. McGaven followed and appeared to be eager to get on as he almost passed her before they reached the top.

Katie gave her partner a sideways look, raising her

eyebrows, which meant that she was surprised by the house and had questions for almost everything about it.

She moved over the landing and looked to the right. The doors were all closed. Slowing her pace, she came to the second door on the right as instructed but hesitated as her hand touched the knob. It wasn't clear to her why she felt the need to stop.

Turning the handle, she pushed the bedroom door open. Immediately, a fragrance of a floral mixture hit her nose. She guessed it was mostly made up of notes of rose and lilac. The thick off-white carpeting that covered the floor felt soft beneath her feet. Reaching for the nearest table lamp, Katie switched it on. The room lit up.

McGaven followed her in and quietly shut the door. "Nice room," he said.

Katie nodded. It was almost more of a suite than a bedroom. It had a sitting area, a large bathroom vanity, closets, and wall-to-wall mirrors. The oversized four-poster bed had sheer fabric draped artistically around the top. The linens were of a pale rose color with various-sized pillows piled at the back. The bed was tidy and made, with a stuffed polar bear sitting in the middle. There was a nightstand to either side, each set with coordinating lamps.

A tall built-in bookcase stood in the sitting area with an overstuffed paisley-print chair and a coffee table set invitingly beside it. Books and papers were scattered across the surfaces. Several books were stacked on the floor beside the chair.

Clothes had been left lying across the back of the chair and several pairs of shoes were scattered about the floor leading to the bathroom.

"Well," said Katie. She pulled on gloves before she touched anything. "This doesn't seem like a typical teenage girl's bedroom. There are no posters, for one... Maybe in wealthier city areas, but it doesn't seem typical here."

McGaven followed her example. "Well... let's see what shakes out."

"I'll start over here," she said, indicating the bed. "We need to look for anything that might tell us what she's been up to and who she might have been meeting."

"I don't see a laptop."

Katie glanced around. "I bet it's here somewhere. Think where a fifteen-year-old girl would hide her most prized possession."

"What about a journal?"

"I have a feeling that she would have used a computer instead of a paper notebook."

"Why?"

"Teenagers now keep everything on one of their devices, not on paper. And her tattoo looked recent and I bet that her grandmother didn't even know about it—but I bet she searched for the perfect pattern and found out all about getting a tattoo. Teens today are very tech savvy, for the most part. They can use tons of software programs that will help hide computer files from any prying eyes."

"Great," said McGaven. "I can't wait until I have kids." He began searching through the paperwork in the sitting area. "I don't see a cell phone either, but she probably had that with her —maybe John will find it on her body." He continued to search.

Katie looked behind the many pillows and cushions, searching to see if there were any hiding spots. She remembered that when she was a girl she would hide things in her favorite stuffed animals—usually notes or photos. The cute polar bear stared at her. Hesitating for just a moment, she picked up the plush toy and discovered that it had a secret hiding place in its back. She quickly pulled apart the Velcro strip and a small flash drive fell out. "Bingo," she said.

"Maybe it's her backup for her journal?"

"Good point. Let's keep looking."

Katie searched the rest of the bedding, mattress, and underneath the bed. Nothing. She picked up each lamp and felt the bottoms. Nothing. Opening the small nightstand drawers, she rummaged through them, finding only the usual things—cough drops, wireless ear buds, blank notepaper, two pens, nail file, gum, lotion, a charging cable for a cell phone, and a creased romance paperback with dog-eared pages.

Looking around the room, her attention then focused on the bookshelf. Most possessions seemed like those of a teenage girl, but the floor-to-ceiling bookcase seemed out of place. The books were neatly positioned in what appeared to be mostly alphabetical order—each volume varied in size and cover types. Some of the books were textbooks, self-help, craft, and how-to books. There was only a couple of shelves that had reading a teenager would normally enjoy, with romance, mystery, and contemporary stories stacked on them side by side.

"Find anything?" said McGaven.

"I don't know," she said as she knelt down on the rug to examine the bookshelves from the bottom up. "You?"

"Nope. Lots of magazines and torn-out articles and advertisements for various products like makeup, teen relationships, and clothes. Lots of clothes."

"Any tattoo salons or phone numbers?"

"Not yet."

"See if there are any notes or writing on the magazine pages."

Katie ran her fingers over the book spines. The shelves themselves were quite shallow and seemed to be more appropriate to a much smaller area. She pulled a few books forward, looking behind them, but there was nothing—not even dust. It appeared that they had been dusted often. Not something that a teenage girl would do. There were more important things to think about: friends, boys, and combination of both. Or maybe Sydney had a cleaner.

She noticed a certain type of dust on the carpet on the far side of the bookshelf. Dabbing her gloved finger and examining it, she thought it looked like sawdust.

"Anything?" said McGaven. He had stopped what he was doing once he'd noticed his partner studying something intently.

"I'm not sure. It looks like some type of sawdust."

"Sawdust? That doesn't make sense."

Katie looked at the carpet, trying to spot any more of the dust, but there wasn't any. "Well, if it's sawdust, then it would mean it came from wood or..." She stood up and ran her hand along the underneath of the shelves. Then she pushed her fingertips along the side framework. There were more dusty grains. Looking closer, she saw two drilled holes that appeared to be part of a hinge or a locking device.

McGaven joined his partner. His six-foot-six-and-a-half-inch stature was able to check out higher up the framework. "Same here," he said. "But it's only on the left side."

Katie kept looking at the construction of the bookshelf and saw some inconsistencies. The framework was different on the left side than the right. The right side had what appeared to be an extra-thick frame. "Wait," she said under her breath. "I think I've solved this..." She tried to pry the framework. It didn't initially move until she pressed in two places at the same time. There was a loud click.

Katie and McGaven looked to one another in surprise.

"I think you're onto something."

They wrestled with the framework around the unit before they found more release mechanisms by pressing down in various areas. They had been cleverly hidden from anyone who didn't know where to look for them. The bookshelf made a distinct release sound and popped forward, opening from the left and revealing a doorway.

"Wow, when I was a kid I thought a secret passage would

have been cool. I didn't think they were actually real," said McGaven.

"It looks like there was once a lock that might have been removed recently," said Katie, examining the frame. Several thoughts coursed at once through her mind. Was the lock for keeping someone out—or in?

McGaven inspected the area of interest. "I think you're right."

"Take a peek downstairs and see what the chief and Sydney are doing."

McGaven went to the bedroom door, quietly opened it, and slipped out. He came back quickly. "They're talking down in the living room. Sounds lighthearted enough."

"Good, let's see where this goes."

# NINE

Katie slowly pulled the bookcase's huge hidden door. It barely made a sound, just swung out into the unknown. A slight whiff of stale air escaped.

She was very surprised because she had never seen any such thing in real life before. It appeared that this had been installed when the house was built. It would have been next to impossible to build something like this after the fact.

"I've never seen anything like this before," said McGaven.

Katie looked down at the floor and could see the faint dust caused by the door rubbing up against the frame. It made sense. Turning to her partner she said, "Do you have a flashlight?"

"Nope. Just from my cell phone."

Katie swiped her finger on her cell phone screen where there was a flashlight application. The light was bright as she aimed it into the dark abyss. "There should be some type of light—wouldn't you think?" She felt for a switch.

"Wait," he said.

"Why?" Katie turned to her partner.

"Let's make sure that it's safe and the stairs are all there."

"Good point." Katie directed the light beam into the dark hole. It was just a narrow passage with wooden stairs leading downward and turning slightly to the left. She couldn't see beyond the dogleg turn. She carefully took a step down, then another, until she felt that the stairs were safe for their weight.

"Right behind you, partner," said McGaven.

His voice sounded different, like they were inside a box.

Katie led the way and continued down the staircase. The air was stagnant but there weren't any bad odors. In fact, she could capture the slight scent of flowers. She could feel her heart rate pick up in beats. Not liking the close quarters, it made her edgy and strangely tingly in her arms and legs.

As she made her way around the corner, she stepped into a ten-by-ten room. There were no windows and it looked like some kind of door on the far side that didn't have a doorknob or handle to get out.

"Is this some kind of panic room?" said McGaven.

"It could be." She looked around, making a three-hundred-sixty-degree turn. "Would you say this is in the middle of the house?"

McGaven studied the walls. "It could be. I'll have to see if I can get the building plans and see what we can find out."

Katie nodded. "Judging by the holes for the mechanism upstairs, do you think Ivy was ever locked in here?" She didn't want to admit that she felt there was something sinister about the place.

McGaven didn't immediately answer as he looked around.

The room was basically empty. It consisted of a raw wood floor, white-painted drywall with dings and nicks, and a plain ceiling with recessed lighting in each corner.

Katie spotted a touch light switch, which was located about a foot off the floor. That struck her as odd, but she flipped it. Instantly the area lit up, leaving the room without shadows. In one corner on the floor was a couple of dark blue seat cushions, a pair of white sandals, a small notebook and pen, and a gold tray with burned-down incense ash on it.

"Well, this is interesting," said McGaven. His voice sounded like it was coming from everywhere. "She may well have been, but there's no proof."

It made Katie twitch. "A private place for…"

She scooped up the notebook, hoping to find something useful. All it had within were drawings of different variations of an ivy vine and flowers. They were detailed and done by a talented artist. She assumed it was Ivy who had sketched them. The secret room was an intriguing discovery, but Katie wasn't sure right now if it was enough to push the investigation forward. It was merely a dead end.

"What do you think?" said McGaven, eyeing his partner as he waited for some type of hypothesis.

Katie looked down at her cell phone and noticed she had a very low battery. "I'm not sure yet. I need more information. Can you take photos with your phone? My battery is low."

"Sure," said McGaven. Taking out his cell, he began to snap quick shots of the room.

"I'm going to retrieve this sketchbook and log it into evidence, along with the flash drive and anything else we find."

"Sounds good."

"Hey," she said. "Are you okay with this?"

"With what?"

"This. Being stuck here in this town and trying to investigate a homicide under… under weird conditions."

"I'm fine. Don't worry about it. I mean, I really miss Denise, but we're not going to be stuck here forever. Right?"

Katie smiled. She loved the way that McGaven could always see the positive in things. "Right."

After shutting off the light and leaving the pitch-black room behind, they climbed the stairs and returned to Ivy's room.

Everything in the bedroom was just as they had left it. The bookcase door was secured and clicked into place. For some reason, Katie thought that something might be different when they entered Ivy's room again, as if they'd time-traveled, but it was just her imagination running overtime.

"I'll finish looking through the magazines and books," said McGaven.

Katie took a few moments browsing through the bookshelves again. Several questions plagued her. "Gav, why would a fifteen-year-old girl have a bookshelf with these types of books? Like home improvement, a million things to do with yarn projects, investing in rental properties, and the economics of World War II."

"Don't know. Maybe they were for class projects or they were gifts?"

"Maybe. But they're all adult-oriented and specialist."

"Meaning?"

"That... I don't know—yet."

Katie continued her search in hopes of finding a cell phone or other personal items. She went through the girl's closet, checking in purses and various zippered bags, as well as pockets. Nothing. Continuing, she looked through the bathroom drawers and cabinets, but didn't have any luck.

Katie returned to where McGaven was finishing up his search. He held some pages from a magazine. "Got something?"

"Not sure. But there were some numbers on top of this page: 5546."

"Let's bring it in as evidence with the flash drive and sketchbook." She stared at the bookcase and a title caught her eye. *The Mystery of the Secret Room* by Margaret Brand. "Oh, wow. I remember these books from when I was young. I think I read every single one of them."

"What books?"

Katie went to the bookshelf and pulled out the volume.

"These are teen mysteries. But I read them when I was about eleven and twelve. I wouldn't have thought they would be what a fifteen-year-old would read. And I don't see any others from the series."

"Maybe it was her favorite?"

Katie opened the book and flipped through the pages. A neatly folded piece of paper fell out. She picked it up and carefully unfolded it. The paper had come from a printed stationery set with yellow and pink flowers across the top. On it was written neatly in black pen: *You can look but will not always find more...* She showed it to McGaven.

"Is it a warning or a something from a fortune cookie?" he said.

"It means something to Ivy. Maybe a quote from a favorite character in the mystery novel? It definitely meant something to Ivy because she kept it.... Maybe it means that it's something you see all the time, but there's more to it."

"Interesting."

"Let's get back to Chief Baker. I have some questions for him."

# TEN

*Monday 1550 hours*

Katie and McGaven hurried down the staircase carrying the evidence from Ivy's room. They could hear Chief Baker talking with Sydney in the kitchen area. It sounded like they were making idle chitchat.

The detectives followed the sound of their voices and returned to the large kitchen.

"There they are," said the chief who was now smiling. Katie thought it seemed inappropriate given the circumstances. They'd been searching a dead girl's room, after all.

"Sydney, would you happen to know if Ivy's cell phone or laptop has been found? I'm assuming she had one," asked Katie.

"She always had her phone with her," said the older woman, "and I don't know where her computer would be if it's not in her room."

"If you happen to come across them would you let us—or Chief Baker—know? It could help us to find out what was going on in the last twenty-four hours of her life."

"Of course," said Sydney looking to the chief. Her body

language had changed from happy and relaxed, and now seemed tense and anxious.

"Oh, and," said Katie, "we're having to take a couple of Ivy's things from her room and we'll be logging them in as evidence. They will be eventually returned to you."

"Of course, take whatever you need." She didn't look Katie in the eye and seemed preoccupied using her painted fingernail to scrape back and forth at a nonexistent spot on the counter. Again Katie thought that Sydney was almost strangely composed and not like a grieving family member. She sounded like a gracious hostess at a party, not a distraught grandmother.

"Did Ivy like the outdoors? Hiking? Camping?" Katie wondered again about why Ivy would have been out in that area.

"Not at all. She told me again and again that she'd rather have a good book or a magazine than wander around outside. Kids today love their technology and staying inside."

*What would have made her go out to somewhere she hated to be? Especially on a dark night in a rainstorm.*

"Where is Ivy's mother?"

"I have no idea. I don't know if she's alive or dead. Rebecca left about two years ago and I've not heard from her since." It was the first time that she showed sadness as she looked down.

"And her father?"

"Don't know. You see, Rebecca was always a troubled girl, always looking for something more than what we could offer her. It breaks my heart to say it, but she didn't have much use for a family unless it suited her—so on a whim she would take off, usually with friends or a new man she had met. That was a pattern that lasted her whole life until she finally left. I tried and tried to get her counseling, or any kind of help—especially for Ivy's sake—but she always declined, always promising that things would be different next time. But... the last time I spoke with her was in this kitchen about two years ago." She looked away from them all as if the painful memories were too difficult to bring back. "At the time, Ivy begged me to help her mother, but now..."

There was a silence for a moment as they all thought about what had happened to Ivy.

Having to intrude at such a terrible time was the part Katie hated the most. The circumstances were still raw and this woman didn't know where her daughter was and her grand-daughter had been brutally murdered, but Katie needed to ask about the discoveries in Ivy's room. "Sydney, what do you know about the secret stairway and room that leads off Ivy's?"

At first Sydney had a blank look upon her face, then she seemed to realize what Katie was talking about. "Oh, of course. You mean the storage area behind the bookcase?"

"Yes," said Katie. She thought that was a strange way of describing it. It would be very impracticable to use it as storage, with its steep, narrow staircase and the room below with no proper ventilation.

"The original owners of the home were known for quirky ideas that they incorporated into the design. I guess maybe they saw too many movies."

"Did Ivy know about it?"

"Of course, but I don't think she cared. It's dark and dingy and Ivy had a wonderful bedroom with plenty of privacy. She would spend her time reading and drawing. She said she wanted to be an artist, but knew that she couldn't make much money from that, especially at first. She talked about studying computer technology and taking business classes at college." She picked up a dish towel and began wringing it in her hands.

"Sydney, you will get through this—there are so many people who care about you. And we're here for you," said the chief.

There was another moment of sadness. Ivy would never take those classes now.

Katie stirred herself. "Thank you for your time, Mrs. Barrett-Miller. If we need anything else, please call us anytime."

Katie and McGaven headed to the front door and waited there for the chief to join them. Katie was thinking furiously about what Ivy's grandmother had said. She was already trying to put together the pieces of what they'd seen.

As soon as they were at the patrol car and away from the house, Katie couldn't wait any longer. She wanted to put everything on the table and to make sure that there wasn't anything being held back.

"Chief," she began, "we need to get some things straight. The best approach for us is total transparency. We're going to need it if we're going to continue to investigate this murder."

The police chief leaned against the car as if he had been waiting for the time when Katie would question him like this. "Absolutely. What information do you feel you need?"

Katie glanced to her partner, who gave her a nod to let her know that he was on board with whatever she was going to say to the chief.

"Like I said, we need transparency. It's as simple as that. We're at the disadvantage of not working or living here. We're working a homicide case, which means time is our enemy right now. We need to move forward—fast. I may be wrong, but I have a suspicion that you might know more than you're saying. Maybe it might not seem like that big of a deal to you, but you know the local people here. For starters, I have the impression you know Sydney Barrett-Miller better than you're letting on."

"I agree with you," said the chief.

Katie took a breath slowly. She wanted to be direct, but also was conscious of not wanting to say something that she would later regret.

Chief Baker stood up away from the patrol car and took two steps closer to Katie. "We may not be as sophisticated here in Coldwater Creek as your detective unit over in Pine Valley, but

I want to solve this murder as much as anyone. But I've known Sydney and her family for a long time." He looked at McGaven and then back to Katie. "Tell me what you need. I'll do everything that I can to get it for you."

Katie let out a sigh of relief. She was not going to meet opposition after all. "We need copies of *all* reports that you have to date—and that includes backgrounds of who you've already talked to, like the dog walker who found the body, as well as Sydney. Along with that we need to have maps of this town. Any information you have about family, friends, the school would be very helpful to help us coordinate our next moves. Given you're tight on space in your office, it makes the most sense to have everything sent to our room at the inn. Oh, and I'd be grateful if you could set up an appointment for us with your medical examiner."

"Done." Chief Baker smiled. "We—meaning this town and me—appreciate that we have the best Pine Valley detectives working this case."

Katie paused for a moment. She was trying her hardest to read the chief and he seemed genuine. Maybe her heightened senses were firing in all directions and she was wrong—but her gut instinct said otherwise. "Thank you, Chief. We also need to speak with Ivy's friends, Nikki and Dawn, ASAP. And, if you can swing it, please put some type of protection detail on the girls. We don't know at this point who we are dealing with or how far this might go."

"Anything. You got it. Oh, and I have a car for you. It's an old police cruiser, but it'll get you where you need to go around town."

Katie felt some relief even though there was much more work to be done. "Thank you. Oh, Chief?"

"Yes?"

"You knew Ivy, right?"

"Yes, of course."

"How would you describe her?"

He thought a minute. "Ivy was a wonderful girl, even for her age. She was kind, considerate, and always had a smile for anyone she came across."

Katie nodded. "Would she ever get involved with someone or something not on the up and up? Maybe a boy who had been in trouble? Or a situation that might be dangerous?"

"I've been in law enforcement for more than twenty years—and I've interviewed those types you're referring to. Ivy was a good girl and I truly think she would always try to help someone in need. Maybe that might've gotten her killed."

Katie considered his words. It was more information than she had so far heard from the chief about anything. "Thanks, Chief Baker. We'll be in touch."

The man gave a solemn nod and got into the car.

"Well, it's a start," said McGaven to his partner before he got into the vehicle.

Katie took a long look around the estate where Ivy Miller had lived her short life. "It's a start," she whispered to herself.

# ELEVEN

*Monday 1700 hours*

Katie and McGaven rode back with Chief Baker to the small headquarters after they had stopped for a quick bite to eat. Katie hadn't realized how hungry she was until she smelled the fantastic burgers cooking at the town diner. She felt more focused and less testy on a full stomach.

Katie looked around the restaurant and noticed that there were only three other tables. It was after 5 p.m. and it seemed that people should start coming in for the dinner hours.

Chief Baker watched Katie with interest.

"Chief, it seems like the restaurant should be filling up," she said.

"Well, we've been noticing a downturn of business here—over the past couple of years."

"Is it because of work?"

"There's been an adjustment in our population of people leaving for better paying jobs in the surrounding cities."

Katie nodded. She scanned the restaurant and the people at the booths and wondered about their stories. It seemed nice in town, but there was always the economic factor that many people faced. "Is there a tourist season?"

"We definitely see visitors in the spring and summer more. It's what helps the small businesses."

They finished their meals and left the diner.

When they pulled up in front of the police station the Pine Valley Sheriff's Department CSU van was parked there.

"How on earth did John get the van here?" said Katie.

"Don't know," said McGaven. "The man's a genius."

"He left me a text message that he was cataloging evidence, to take back to the lab in Pine Valley," said the chief.

Katie knew that John would be overseeing the chain of custody that tracks the movement of evidence through its collection, safeguarding, and analysis lifecycle by documenting each person who handled the evidence, and the date and/or time it was collected or transferred.

Katie was surprised. She wondered who had driven the van to Coldwater Creek. She saw John exit the passenger side and a petite pretty woman jump out of the driver's side. She was dressed in jeans, T-shirt, and dark denim jacket, and sported short spiky blonde hair.

"Of course, Eva, the new forensic tech," said McGaven. Eva had been brought in to replace Jimmy Turner, who had sadly been murdered two months ago. She was supposed to join the team in a couple of weeks, but was brought in sooner due to the case.

Katie stepped out of the police patrol car with McGaven and the chief.

"Hey, there you are," said John. "Thought we were going to have to send out a search party." He was smiling broadly as he approached Katie.

The young woman approached. "You must be Detective Scott," she said.

"Hi," said Katie. "And this is my partner, Detective McGaven."

"This is my new forensic tech, Eva Crane," said John.

"Nice to meet you," said Katie.

"Likewise," said McGaven as he shook Eva's hand.

"I can't believe I'm going to be working with *the* Katie Scott," said Eva, who was clearly excited about the prospect.

That sounded strange to Katie. She had never heard anyone describe her as *the* Katie Scott before. "It's just Katie."

McGaven and John laughed.

"She doesn't know how to take a compliment, but we're helping her with that," said McGaven.

Katie frowned at her partner before turning back to Eva. "It's nice to have you on the team. How did you get here so fast? I'm impressed."

"Well, today was officially my first day on the job and it was supposed to be more of an orientation day. But John called me and had me go to the lab and then bring this beast here." She jammed her hands into her jean pockets. "I knew this was going to be a great job—never knowing what to expect."

"We're very lucky to have Eva," said John. "She graduated top of her class in forensic science and a minor in chemistry— 4.0 all the way."

"Wow, we have a forensic prodigy here," said McGaven.

Katie smiled as she watched them admire the new recruit's achievements, but she knew that Eva was basically in training. She was glad that John had someone to assist him, though.

"Katie," said John. "We've got all the evidence packed and the chain of custody is squared away. We're going to head back so that I can study everything in the lab. Just so you know, we couldn't find Ivy's cell phone."

"Okay."

"Sounds like you should have the car back sometime tomorrow?"

"I hope so, but it looks like we're going to be here for a few more days."

"I loaded an iPad with the crime-scene photos from today—it's secured in the motel room."

"Thank you."

"I hate to run and leave you guys, but we need to get back. It'll take about three hours or so to drive to the lab."

"Don't worry about it," she said, though she almost felt jealous that John got to leave this town while McGaven and she had to stay.

"I'll keep you updated and send me anything else you come across—especially after the medical examiner completes the autopsy report. I'll keep my laptop open for conference calls."

"We'll be here. Talk to you soon. Nice meeting you, Eva," said Katie as she headed into Chief Baker's office.

"Drive safe," said McGaven following Katie.

Katie let out a breath. "I hope she works out. John needs a stable and competent tech."

"For sure."

Chief Baker hung up his cell phone and rose from his desk. "Okay, Nikki Prager and Dawn Cromwell are at Nikki's house. They plan on staying together for at least a few days. It'll make it easier to keep an eye on them. Dawn's parents travel quite a bit."

Katie nodded.

"You can question them anytime this evening. I'll have Officer Lane leave all the paperwork we have so far in your room—it should be there within the hour. You'll find phone numbers and addresses for the girls—along with everyone we've spoken with today."

"Great. Thank you, Chief."

"Oh, and…" he said, reaching into his pocket and pulling out a keychain with two keys on it, "here is the key for the old patrol car you can borrow. It's parked around behind the building."

Katie took the keys. "Thanks. It won't be for long. Hopefully Sal will have our car fixed soon."

"Need a ride back to the inn?"

"It's only a few blocks, right?"

"Yep."

"I think we'll walk back and get a feel for the town."

"Be my guest."

Katie and McGaven left the police office and began to walk. Suddenly, Katie changed her mind.

"C'mon, let's get the car now. I don't want to waste any more time. I want to see what's on the flash drive."

"Okay."

The detectives walked back around the buildings until they saw the sign for Coldwater Creek PD Headquarters. There was a car parked in the only parking space.

"Oh no," said Katie under her breath. "Is that it?"

They walked to the police vehicle. The first impression was that it was in desperate need of a good wash. But upon closer inspection, they saw it was from another decade. Caked layers of dirt encrusted the windshield. Cobwebs were strewn from the body to the side mirrors. The tires looked a bit flat.

"Hey, I feel like it's from the seventies or eighties. Do you think it was used in one of those old cop shows?" said McGaven.

Katie was surprised they would still even have such an old vehicle. "Do you think it runs? Do we put different gas in it? Is there gas in it?"

"I can't believe it."

"What?"

"You're a police car snob."

Katie finally laughed. "I am not. But..."

"Go on, get in and see if it starts."

"Are you sure that you don't want to drive?"

He laughed. "This baby is all yours."

Katie unlocked the door with the key and got inside. An unpleasant musty smell greeted her first, and then the dusty interior. She kept the door open, trying to air it out.

McGaven stood outside peering in. "Maybe we should get it washed?"

"That would be a start," she said. Carefully inserting the key, Katie turned it and to her surprise the engine roared to life. "Wow."

"Yeah, wow," said McGaven.

The old sedan sputtered a few times with dark exhaust fumes wafting out, but the car managed to settle into an even idle. The air cleared.

"Hop in," she said.

McGaven got in and had trouble finding the seatbelt. "At least the chief kept his word."

Katie didn't respond.

"And he did treat us to the best burgers in town."

"You're right about that," she said. "Now, let's go. I want to get back to our room and see what's on Ivy's flash drive before we go talk to her friends."

# TWELVE

*Monday 18 15 hours*

After parking the old squad car out front, Katie and McGaven headed inside the Wild Iris Inn with the flash drive and sketch-book from Ivy's room. The inn seemed mostly vacant now, probably because it was a Monday night. Everyone had already gone home after the weekend.

"What's that amazing smell?" said McGaven as he paused in the main area.

Mama came bustling out of the kitchen wearing her cooking apron. "That's my famous beef stew. I thought you two could use some good home cooking tonight, since I hear you may be staying a few more days. So terrible what happened—such a sweet girl. I hope you catch the killer soon."

"We're following every lead," said Katie. "Thank you. This meal looks great." Having some comforting home-cooked meals sounded relaxing to her. She knew that they had a lot of evidence to carefully sift through and she was anxious to get started.

"I took the opportunity to supply you with some healthy

snacks in your room. You have a small refrigerator up there and it's nicely stocked now. Let me know if you would like anything special."

"That's wonderful. Thank you."

A tall young man with shaggy brown hair partially covering his eyes entered. "Hey, is that Chief Baker's old car out front? It's out of service. I thought it would be in the junkyard by now." He eyed the detectives with curiosity.

McGaven turned to the young man. "Yep. We get to drive that beauty while we're here."

"Cool. You guys the detectives from out of town?" he asked. "Everyone is buzzing about the murder."

"These are detectives Katie Scott and Sean McGaven," said Mama.

"That's us. And you are?" said Katie.

"I'm Lenny."

"Lenny is my son. He's here helping me out with some repairs that have been sorely overdue," said Mama.

Katie started to head up the stairs and stopped. "Lenny, did you know Ivy Miller?"

"I know who she is, or was, but she's five years younger. We didn't hang around in the same circles."

"What about her friends Nikki and Dawn?" Katie watched his reaction closely. "Do you know them?"

"Not really my kind of group." He shrugged. "I've spoken to Dawn a few times. She seems cool. Don't know much about them."

Katie and McGaven headed up the stairs.

"Oh, hey," said Lenny. "For twenty bucks I'll take your cop car and have it washed." He glanced at their holstered weapons.

"Well..." began Katie.

"You have a valid driver's license?" said McGaven interrupting his partner.

"Of course."

"He's a good boy. He'll make sure the car gets clean and back safe," said Mama. "The car wash is about a block away."

"Sure," said McGaven. "I'll have the money waiting here when you get back." He handed Lenny the car keys.

"Great." The young man took the keys and hurried out of the inn.

Katie thought it would be so much nicer to have a cleaner ride. She climbed the last narrow staircase leading into their room. As she inserted the ornate key, her mind raced. She thought about the killer. She wondered if he was hunting for another victim even as they were beginning to sift through the clues. The case and the surrounding circumstances left her off balance. There was little doubt in her mind: there would be more victims until they found him. But she hoped that she was wrong.

Katie pushed open the door. This time, as they entered, it was warmer and there was a slight hint of a fresh cleaning solution. Katie wondered if Mama did the housekeeping as well as prepare the food.

"Okay," said Katie. She retrieved the iPad that John had left and other items from the small safe in the room.

"Let's see what's on the drive," said McGaven.

Katie went to the overstuffed chair next to her bed to retrieve her laptop, but it wasn't there. Her overnight bag was the only thing sitting on the chair. "Hey, did you move my laptop?"

"No. Why? Can't you find it?"

"That's strange. I swear I put it with my bag before we left." Katie walked around the space and spotted her laptop sitting on a small end table next to the extra roll-out bed where John had slept. The bedding was neatly folded with a pillow on top. She picked up her computer.

"Oh good, you found it," he said.

"I didn't put it over here."

"Maybe John moved it."

"Maybe. Still weird. You would think he would have left it on the table with the iPad."

The detectives sat down at the table. Katie opened her laptop and turned it on. As they patiently waited, she inserted the flash drive into the USB port. It opened up but needed a password.

"Crap," said McGaven. "Password."

"You didn't think it was going to be this easy, did you?"

"No, but I was hoping."

She pushed the laptop to her partner. "You are more computer savvy than I am."

"Okay," he said as he took the computer. "I'm not a code breaker, but people, even teenagers, are usually creatures of habit. Addresses, favorite pet, and last four digits of your phone number or social. Most people want something easy to remember." He had found the social media page for Ivy, where there was a wealth of information about her favorite things.

"Like birthdays or special dates."

"Yep," he said tapping away on the keyboard.

Katie sighed and leaned back in her chair. She put her focus on Ivy's sketchbook, and again, thought how artistic she must have been to have produced such drawings. She looked up. "Anything?"

"Nope. But I'm trying."

"What about the house address?"

McGaven typed out the number. "Nope."

Katie thought a moment about her conversation with Sydney. "Maybe her middle name? Or something from *The Mystery of the Secret Room*?"

Her partner kept typing. "No luck."

"What was her mom's name?" she said.

"Rebecca?" He diligently typed out that name. "No, try again."

Katie retraced everything from the crime scene. "Ivy or rose?"

McGaven sighed. "Nope. I doubt it would be random or difficult. Wait a minute," she said. Katie looked down at the page taken from one of Ivy's magazines. The number: 5546. "Gav, try 5546." She could hear him tap the keyboard with the four digits.

"We're in."

"That was easy."

"Not really, but it worked."

Katie scooted her chair closer to her partner as he opened the file directory. Both of them read the screen. "The files are all numbers."

"Yeah, and they aren't registering as dates either. There are fifteen files."

"Have you ever seen anything like that?" she said.

"No. Most people name files with something that makes sense to them. But this..."

"A secret code?"

"Let's see." He clicked on the first one, notated: 54_2_2, which was identified as a photo image.

The file opened. It was a dark photograph and appeared to show a dim room with candles lined up on a tabletop. It wasn't clear, but rather like the camera had moved, blurring the image.

"What is that? It looks like a woman with dark hair," she said.

"Maybe one of Ivy's friends?"

Katie turned her head to see if the photo made more sense. "I think that woman is older. Maybe thirties?"

"Is her hand over a candle flame?"

"I can't tell, but it could be. Open another file." Katie moved closer to the screen.

McGaven clicked the next file: 59_7_2. An image came up, similar to the previous one in its blurry exposure. But this one had a clearer depiction of a woman sitting in front of the candles. Her expression was somber and she was focused on the flame. The candles in the photo cast a weird, distorted light, making everything seem macabre.

"It looks like it's some kind of ritual, or weird gathering" she said. "It's the way she is staring at the flames and putting her hand in it. I can't tell if it's inside or outside. Who took these photos?"

"Why would Ivy Miller have these photos?"

"Don't know," she said. "Maybe the reason why the images are so blurry and dark is because someone is taking these photos without the subject's knowledge."

McGaven clicked on the rest of the fifteen files. Two were completely black. All the images had the same theme and resolution. The detectives took a few minutes on each one. Katie notated the file names and what they could see in the image.

"Let's get a copy of these to John," she said.

"I was thinking the same thing."

"I don't think he has a computer program that would help with the blurring, but he might know where he could use one." Katie took a photo with her cell phone of two of the images. "I want to show these to Nikki and Dawn and see what their reactions are."

"Good idea. What's bothering you?"

"I was just thinking... Where would Ivy get these photos? From whom? Did someone give them to her or did she find them?"

"Maybe she somehow stumbled upon them from someone she knew?"

"Maybe. I want to quickly go through the photos of the crime scene," she said. Opening the files, she swiped through the photos. "We need to get a photo of the tattoo and the rope to carry with us, so that we can begin canvassing the town to try to find out more about them." She snapped a few photos with her phone. She hesitated and then took a close-up image of Ivy with the bag over her head and rope tied around her neck.

Katie and McGaven studied the crime-scene photos for a few more minutes before they left their room to head over to Nikki Prager's house.

"Maybe we'll get some answers," said McGaven.

"They will at least be able to give us more information about Ivy, and maybe that will help us retrace her last days."

"Do you think they'll be able to help us?" said McGaven.

"I guarantee that these girls know something. The question isn't whether they do or don't... but if they will tell us."

# THIRTEEN

*Monday 1955 hours*

Katie was relieved that Lenny had returned the patrol car. It was now clean inside and out, and smelled much better. She and McGaven were soon on the way to Nikki Prager's house to have a chat with the two girls who had been Ivy's closest friends. The chief had already spoken with their parents, so they were up to date that the detectives would be en route to interview them.

"Make a left at Carver Street," said McGaven. "We're looking for 311."

Katie followed his instructions, turning the vehicle slowly as she scrutinized the area. It was a modest neighborhood of mostly one-story homes. Due to the recent rains and how close the neighborhood was to the forest, many of the front yards were overgrown with weeds and small branches lying where they had fallen. It was quite the contrast to Ivy's well-kept home and neighborhood.

"There it is, the gray house," she said. She pulled up along-side the house and parked the car on the street, looking around her as she did so. Katie always took the opportunity to check out the surrounding area, looking at the neighbors, the accessibility, and if anyone had proper security such as cameras and motion lights. It gave some insights into the way people lived—if they were tech savvy, security conscious, or just didn't care what went on around them.

"Ready?" said McGaven as he gave a quick smile to his partner.

"As I'll ever be."

Stepping out of the vehicle, something very familiar caught up with Katie. She wasn't sure what it was, but something about the street reminded her of growing up in Pine Valley—and then Chad entered her mind. It was the close-knit neighborhood. Every yard had indications of kids living there with discarded balls, basketball hoops, and tire swings. She and Chad had known each other since they were kids. How much she missed him and wanted to see him.

Shaking off the thought, Katie looked at the neighbors and tried to ascertain if singles or families lived in the closed homes. She then followed her partner up the driveway and to the front door of the Prager residence.

The front yard was basic: no frills, fun adornments, or planted flowers. It was a simple easy-care landscape. Even the dark gray doormat was unremarkable.

Katie rang the doorbell.

Within a few moments, a tall older woman with dark blonde hair answered. Her solemn face and slightly down-turned mouth showed sadness and sorrow. She wore dark jeans and a light blue sweatshirt. "Yes?"

"Mrs. Prager?" said Katie.

"Yes, you must be the detectives." Her expression didn't change, but she eyed them suspiciously.

"I'm Detective Katie Scott and my partner, Detective Sean McGaven."

The woman nodded and opened the door wider for the detectives to enter.

Immediately the warmth hit Katie. She hadn't realized how chilly it had become outside as the evening had rolled on. The familiar smell of something that had been baking in the oven made her stomach rumble.

"I hope we're not interrupting your dinner," said Katie.

"No, we finished about twenty minutes ago."

"Has there been anyone stopping by and checking on everyone?"

"Officer Lane has been by twice today."

"Was he parked or just drove by?"

"He came to the door and made sure everything was okay, but didn't stay."

Katie wasn't pleased, but reasoned that the entire department was made up of only three officers, including the chief.

"Is Mr. Prager here?" asked McGaven.

"No, he's working late at the office."

"I see. Where would Dawn's parents be?"

"She lives with her dad and he travels a lot for work. So she spends most of her time here."

"Can we speak to the girls?" he said.

"Of course. They're in Nikki's room—it's just down the hall."

"Would you like to be present when we ask questions?" said Katie.

"No, they've done nothing wrong. I assume you want to know about Ivy."

"Yes, we're trying to retrace her last few days," said Katie. It seemed to always sound so hollow and unsympathetic when she explained their investigation and how they conducted the victimology leading up to the incident, but it was how they had to proceed.

Mrs. Prager nodded as if to say that she understood, and

disappeared into the kitchen. Soon, the sound of dishes, pots, and pans was heard as she began to clean up dinner.

Katie looked at her partner and shrugged as if to say, "Okay, let's go." She hurried down the hall to where she could hear two voices and assumed that the door with stickers and some brightly colored decorations attached was to Nikki's room. She knocked.

"Yes?" said a voice.

Katie opened the door to the small bedroom. It was nothing like Ivy's room, which had seemed more like an adult's than a teenager's. Posters of various actors and musicians, some in compromising positions, were all over the walls like mismatched patchwork, overlapping each other. Pages of advertisements and models wearing contemporary clothing ripped from magazines were attached with colorful thumbtacks to the walls as well. The clutter gave the room a dizzying appearance. A double-sized bed, small desk and chair, nightstand, and a small half-size bookshelf were the only pieces of furniture in the room.

The first girl sat at the small computer desk and appeared to be surfing a social media site on a laptop. Katie assumed that she was Nikki as she closely resembled her mother.

Dawn was propped up on the bed. Magazines sat in small piles around her and she was tearing out pages and photos of interest.

Both girls looked up when Katie and McGaven entered. They had differing hair length, Nikki short, Dawn long, but both blonde with pink highlighted tinges on the ends.

"You the detectives?" said Nikki. Her gaze was curious but her eyes were red. Clearly she was saddened by the loss of her friend.

Katie softened her usual approach. "Yes. I'm Detective Katie Scott and this is Detective Sean McGaven." She moved farther into the room as McGaven stayed at the doorway. "You must be Nikki," she said to the girl at the computer. Looking at the other girl, she said, "And you're Dawn?"

"Yes," both girls said.

"We're very sorry for the loss of your friend," said Katie. She couldn't help but notice the pink rose tattoo with a vine on the inside of Nikki's arm. It had a different shape than Ivy's but still a strong resemblance in style.

"Ivy didn't deserve this... I heard that she was suffocated with a bag. What the hell?" said Nikki, stifling her tears.

Katie could tell that the girl was genuinely upset. She decided to begin with something more personal between the girls instead of diving right into the horrors of the murder. "I notice you have a rose tattoo like Ivy's. Did all of you get them at the same time?"

"Yeah."

"What made you choose a rose?"

"You know how you always see roses in a group—together?" said Nikki.

"Yes."

"Well, we've been best friends ever since kindergarten. And we wanted to do something that showed we have a bond. We were always going to be friends. Ivy met this guy, Tyler, I think was his name, who is a tattoo artist. So we all went to him."

"Is this place in town?"

"Yeah, the Tattoo Lounge."

Katie glanced to McGaven knowing he was thinking that they would be chatting with Tyler soon. "I just have a few more questions, okay?"

Nikki nodded.

Katie moved closer to the bed and sat down. "I love roses too. I think the yellow rose is my favorite," she said. "Pink would be second."

"I thought about a yellow rose," said Nikki. She studied Katie for the first time. "I could see you with a rose tattoo."

Katie chuckled. "I never thought about that before." She paused. "I know things seem really tough right now, but as clichéd as it sounds, it will get better. I lost my best friend when I was a little bit younger than you two."

"What happened?"

Katie remembered the event only too well. Even now she had to remind herself to keep her emotions in check. "She was murdered too."

"Oh," said Nikki as she looked down. "I'm sorry."

"So I do know how you feel. But we're trying to find who did this to Ivy. Can you help us?"

"Is it true?" said Nikki slowly. "Is it true that she was suffocated with a bag?"

For the first time, Dawn showed her sorrow as she wiped tears away from her face.

"The investigation is ongoing and we're trying to find out what was going on and who she might have talked to." Katie didn't want to give gory details to the girls.

"So you can't tell us?"

"It appears that she was strangled. But, I'm not authorized to say any more right now. We're doing everything we can to find the killer."

"What do you want from us?" Nikki turned in her chair to face Katie directly.

"Well, I'd really love to hear from you about what Ivy was like. What kind of thing did all of you like to do together?" Katie wanted to begin her interview with general inquiries that the girls would find easier to answer before she had to move on to more direct questions.

"She was our best friend... We've been friends forever. We hang out together and study together... No one can replace her."

Katie waited patiently.

"She was always there for us," said Dawn. "Always. Now, she's gone..."

"Would you know of anyone that wanted to hurt her? Maybe someone who threatened her?"

"No! No one. Everyone loved her," said Nikki. "You don't understand. Ivy was the one that always wanted to help other people."

Katie suspected that Nikki was laboring over something that she wasn't telling. She had suddenly averted her eyes from Katie's gaze. The teen seemed agitated, as if remembering something she didn't want to.

"Whatever you tell us stays with us in confidence," said McGaven.

"Did Ivy have a boyfriend?" said Katie.

"No. Not really. There was a guy she liked. They've never gone out or anything. At least Ivy never told us if she did."

"What's his name?"

"Lenny... I don't know his last name."

"He's an older guy," said Dawn. "I know him."

"You mean Lenny at the Wild Iris Inn?" said Katie.

"Yeah, he's home now from college, I think."

"Do you know him?"

Nikki shrugged. "No, not really. I mean, I know who he is but he's from the upper classes at school and already graduated."

Katie glanced to her partner. She was very aware of her tone when asking questions. Dealing with teenagers could be tricky. "When was the last time you saw him, or heard Ivy mentioning him?"

"I... don't know."

"Ivy hasn't talked about him in a while," said Dawn as she continued to thumb absentmindedly through a magazine. "And we haven't seen him."

"When was the last time you saw Ivy?" said Katie. She watched Dawn sift through the magazines and remembered the phrase in the book: "You can look but will not always find more." She could see in her mind's eye the word *more* on Ivy's back.

"Saturday night."

"Not on Sunday?"

"No, we were going to meet today."

"Do you know what Ivy was doing yesterday?"

"She said something about staying at home," said Nikki as she glanced to her friend.

Katie shifted her weight on the edge of the bed. "We were at Ivy's house earlier. Wow, that's some house, huh?"

"I guess." Nikki kept her eyes focused on the dizzying array of posters instead of the detectives.

"Was there anything special about her room?" said Katie. She studied the girls closely for any look, twitch, or hesitation that they might be hiding something.

"What do you mean?" said Nikki.

"Her room. That bookcase?"

"I don't know." She shrugged.

"Oh, so you two didn't know about *the room*?"

"What about her room?" said Dawn. Now she looked directly at Katie.

"Well, we found a secret door," said Katie. She now had the girls' undivided attention. "It was that huge bookcase. Kinda like a movie, huh. You know what we found?"

They shook their heads, hanging on Katie's every word.

"There was a staircase." Katie now lowered her voice. "It led down to a secret room."

"What was in there?" said Nikki, clearly curious.

"You really didn't know about this?"

"No."

"It was just a small room with Ivy's sketchbook. It looked like she would go there to draw."

"Really?" said Nikki with a puzzled expression.

"So she never said anything about it?"

"No."

"Oh, so you didn't spend time hanging out in her room?"

"We did, lots of times." She looked down. "That wasn't always her room—at least not a few years ago."

"It wasn't?" Katie was surprised to hear that.

"No, her original room was smaller and at the back part of the house."

Katie thought about that and why Sydney hadn't told them this. "Has there been anything different in your routines recently?" she said.

"Like what?"

"Well, like a confrontation with someone or maybe someone following you."

"No, nothing like that."

"Would there be any reason for Ivy to be out last night—at the hiking trails and Bates campgrounds?"

"No, Ivy hated hiking. She liked being at parties outside. I think she went camping once and she hated it—she would never be out there at night on her own. *Never.*" Nikki took a small piece of paper in her right hand and began crumbling it.

"Did she say anything about meeting someone?"

"No..." Nikki became choked up as tears flowed down her cheeks. "I don't know what you expect from us. Our best friend is dead—she was murdered. Don't you think if we knew something—*anything*—that we would tell you?"

"Of course," said Katie. Although, she wasn't so sure. She reached into her pocket and took out a business card. "Here's my card with my cell number on the back. If you think of anything or if you just want to talk, call me."

Nikki took the card. "Thank you." She wiped her tears.

"Just one more thing... do you know where Ivy kept her cell phone and laptop?"

"She always had her phone with her. I know that because her pink cell phone case was hard to miss. She had it on a strap like a purse and it was always over her shoulder," said Nikki.

"Her laptop? We couldn't find it in her room."

"I don't know… It would be in her room."

"Now I want to make sure that both of you are careful. I know that Officer Lane is driving by periodically, but don't go anywhere unless you tell someone. And don't go anywhere alone. Stay in groups, okay?"

The girls nodded in agreement.

"You don't think whoever killed Ivy would come after us?" said Nikki.

"It's just a precaution. Okay?"

"Okay."

"If we have more questions, can we come back and talk?" said Katie.

Nikki nodded.

Katie stood up and headed to the door.

"Detective?" said Nikki.

"You will find Ivy's killer, right?"

Katie nodded. "We're following every lead until we do."

Katie and McGaven left the Pragers' residence and got back into the old patrol car. Her heart ached for what the girls were going through—because she knew full well what it was like.

"Well," said McGaven.

"You were awfully quiet back there."

"I thought it was best that you talked to them. You were great."

"What do you think?"

"Some truth. Maybe some deception. Not sure if it's just a teenage thing."

"There were a couple of trigger questions that caused Nikki to react. One was the tattoos and the other was about Ivy meeting someone. She had a genuine reaction about the secret room."

"I caught that too. You think Lenny might be involved?"

"We can't rule him out. But we need to talk to the tattoo artist."

McGaven glanced at his watch. "It'll probably have to wait until tomorrow."

"Have you heard anything about our car?"

"I got a text from Sal earlier and he said that it might be ready at the end of the day tomorrow."

Katie sighed.

"I also got a text from the medical examiner and our appointment is at 10 a.m. tomorrow."

Katie didn't say anything as she eased the car away from the curb and headed back to the inn. Her mind wandered back to Pine Valley; she had become antsy, wanting to leave town—she was missing Chad.

"What's on your mind?" he said.

"I was just thinking."

"Here we go, full speed ahead."

"What did you think about the crime scene?" Katie forced her thoughts back to run through the area, the body, and the potential motive.

"It seemed to be organized, and a bit of overkill with both strangling and suffocating."

"I agree. Also, she wasn't dumped there. From what we know now, it seems that she was killed and posed there."

"Why? What did they want to accomplish with Ivy posed?"

"I think the better question is: Who was Ivy meeting and why?"

# FOURTEEN

*Monday 2100 hours*

Katie and McGaven returned to the Wild Iris Inn. It was still quiet but the wonderful smell of homemade stew drifted throughout the area.

"Where is everyone?" said Katie looking around. Walking into a deserted place made her senses tingle. She found herself expecting something out of the ordinary to happen—she called it her police intuition.

"Don't know. It's Monday?"

"Wait," she said, spotting a note. It read: *Detectives: help yourself to the stew. Everything you need is in the kitchen. ~Mama.* She turned to her partner. "Well?"

"I'm hungry. Let's do what the instructions tell us," he said, heading to the kitchen.

Katie followed her partner, taking in the furnishings around them. The place seemed cluttered to her, but it was in style with the historic building. There was a lot of thick fabric everywhere. Rugs. Heavy drapes. Blankets draped over the two couches. Table toppers. Chair slipcovers.

"This is what I'm talking about," said McGaven, entering the kitchen. He moved toward the stove.

Katie saw what he referred to. There was a large cast-iron pot on the cooktop next to a basket of freshly baked bread. There were bowls, silverware, napkins, and glasses. "I was hungry, but now I'm starving."

The detectives helped themselves and returned to their large room. Before climbing the stairs, Katie left a thank-you note for Mama.

Once inside their room, everything seemed to be where they had left it. Katie moved their notes, files, and computers to one side of the table in order for them to sit down and eat their dinner.

As Katie ate the scrumptious stew, she looked through the photographs that John had taken of the crime scene—putting together in her mind the killer's mindset, preparation, and execution. She scrutinized the photos of the round holes in the ground they had discovered and marked for John to document.

"Alright, what's on your mind? I've known you long enough and we've worked more than our fair share of cases," said McGaven. He popped a piece of bread into his mouth.

"I'm not sure, but..." Katie got up from the table and walked over to the fireplace. She felt a distinct chill. On one side were the fire irons, stacked neatly together: poker, mini broom, and long tongs. Next to them were two long bamboo canes—walking sticks. She picked one up, examining the bottom. "Do you think something like this could have made those holes we saw in the ground along the roadside?" She showed her partner.

"Yeah, it's possible. Actually, it makes sense because if you were hiking or walking along the trails many people use these."

"I think we need to check out the area tomorrow morning —*early*."

"For?"

"I think it's possible that there might have been someone else there."

"It was a harsh storm last night. You really think someone could have been walking?"

"I want to rule it out. We've seen stranger things."

"Tomorrow is going to be a long day," said McGaven.

Katie nodded. "The medical examiner and tattoo artist should be interesting."

"Don't forget we need to check out some of the local hardware stores about the rope and who might know how to tie a bowline knot. Although, it's fairly common among anyone with a boat or outdoor enthusiasts."

Katie leaned back in her chair, sipping her sparkling water. "Have you talked with Denise today?"

"I was just going to do that after I finish this stew." He scraped the bowl with his spoon. "What about Chad?"

"I'm going to call him now," she said, walking to the bedroom area. She missed her home. She also knew that Cisco, her German shepherd and military K9, was waiting for her and would be missing her.

Katie kicked her shoes off and got comfortable in the overstuffed chair. She could hear McGaven already talking with Denise, but couldn't hear what was being said. It was difficult for both of them, being away from their homes and the department while plunged into a murder investigation like this. It was a very particular type of homesickness.

She pressed Chad on her contact list and listened to it ring.

"Hello, gorgeous," said Chad. His voice was upbeat. She could hear the background of the firehouse. Voices and dishes clattering.

"Hi. I miss you."

"How's it going there in Coldwater Creek?"

"It's going. Beginning of the homicide investigation, but it's never easy when the victim is a young girl."

Chad let out a breath. "So sorry, babe. How long do you think you'll be there?"

"Hard to say. I'll know more tomorrow." Katie had a feeling they were destined to be in Coldwater Creek for most of the week, but she didn't want to think about that now.

"I was thinking..." he said.

"About?" She couldn't help but smile. His voice inflection reminded her of when they were teenagers and he wanted to share some great news.

"After you're done with this, we need to get away. Go somewhere quiet without all the distractions of the jobs. A cabin in the woods, near a lake, no noise, no people, no demands —just us."

Katie closed her eyes. "That sounds heavenly." It had been too long since they had gone somewhere that didn't have to do with either a cold-case investigation or fire inquiry.

Suddenly she could hear the firehouse's alarms sounding.

"I hate to say this but I have to go," Chad said. "I thought I'd have more time."

"Be safe. I love you."

"Love you more."

The phone disconnected.

Katie remained in the chair a moment feeling her tired body nagging at her to go to bed. Her mind was still whirring with not only the crime scene, but also Ivy's room and the conversation with her friends. It was like an endless loop. She had the distinct impression that there was something obvious she was missing. For a police detective, it was one of the worst feelings to have.

Katie quickly got ready for bed. She waved a goodnight to McGaven as she walked from the bathroom back to her bedroom nook, before climbing into the big comfortable bed. Within minutes, she was sound asleep.

# FIFTEEN

Katie stood at the quiet roadway near the Bates campground and the entrance to the hiking areas surveying the surroundings with a new perspective. The cool morning air chilled her, so she zipped her jacket tighter around her neck.

The perfectly round holes were still visible. They appeared to be made by something manmade and not by animal or nature. It was probable that the holes came from a walking stick. It made sense. The area's terrain was uneven with hills and loose gravel.

*Was there someone else at the scene?*

*Were they with the killer, or were they a chance passerby?*

The morning was crisp and heavy clouds blocked out any sunshine, creating a dreary atmosphere. However, it made it easier for Katie to study the area. She could see the contrast easier without the blinding sun shining and casting shadows. Glancing up, looking toward the area where the body was found, she saw McGaven doing a detailed search, weaving back and forth, walking in straight lines, looking closely for anything that had been missed.

Katie slowed down her breathing. Her mind had been spinning ever since she woke up this morning. She had awakened in the quiet room of the inn to feel her heart beating fast. The stresses of the investigation, especially as it was a teenage girl, pushed her to her limit. All morning her senses felt heightened and skyrocketed her emotions. Her symptoms of PTSD weren't too far away; her inner fight was always near.

She closed her eyes, trying to encourage her heart rate to slow. She detected several new things immediately. The sound of the birds. The slight breeze coming from the north. The rustling of the wind through the pine needles. A car revving its engine in the distance.

*Smoke.*

"Anything?" said McGaven as he climbed up the hill to the road.

Katie was amazed that a man with his stature, six foot six and a half, could move almost silently in a forest. She was fortunate to have him as her partner—he always had her back. That thought made her smile.

"You have something you're contemplating. Let's have it," he said, trying not to smile.

"Do you smell that?"

He took a breath, looking around. "I smell pine. And... smoke. Like someone just stoked up a fire."

"Yeah, it's coming from that area. It wouldn't be a campfire at this time of morning and weather. Anyway, I don't think there are many campers, if any, out there now." She pointed across the street. "Are there any homes there? I don't recall after looking at the map of the town."

McGaven pulled his cell phone from his jacket pocket. "Let's see." He looked around to gain his bearings as he swiped the screen of his phone, searching for buildings and property lines.

Katie crossed the road, and shortly noticed a narrow path that looked to have been walked many times.

"Nothing is showing. There is a large building and maybe some outbuildings, but it's farther away. I can't get an address or even an owner's name."

"I want to take a look around," she said.

McGaven jogged across the two-lane street to join her.

"What's so important about this area?"

"Those holes look like they've come from someone's walking stick. And, I'm curious about why the killer chose this area."

"Probably because it's so isolated." McGaven's expression turned sour.

Katie didn't say anything as she walked up the manmade trail. Suddenly she spotted more holes—every couple of steps. There weren't any visible footprints. Everything had been mashed together by the rain.

McGaven noticed them too. "You think someone else was here?"

"In theory... I do think it's more than possible. But who and why is another thing."

Her partner took a few quicker steps and walked in front of her. The trail cut through several areas, zigzagging around the trees, but it was still clear that there was a path well-trodden, and not by animals.

Katie studied the area around them as they moved up the pathway. The terrain began to level out, making walking easier. There wasn't any area that was muddy, only packed moist soil. Then she began to notice areas that had been slightly cleared by gentle scraping. It was difficult to see at first, but there were subtle clues to support her conclusion.

Above them snippets of sunshine were finally breaking

through the heavy cloud cover, falling in between the trees and giving the area a more alive appearance. Colors were brighter. Forest greens more vibrant. And that's when she saw it—a reflection of something in the trees. For an instant the light bounced off some type of line.

Katie watched McGaven move faster, making his way toward an open area.

"Gav," she said.

He turned and slowed his pace with a questionable expression.

"Gav, wait."

Katie saw that the clear lines were crossing through the trees. She had seen things like this before—in Afghanistan. It was a trap.

"Gav!" Her heart skipped a beat.

Katie ran up to her partner, pushing him hard and causing him to tumble to the left side of the current path they were on.

"What the...?" McGaven tried to regain his balance to stand up. He looked around—back and forth across the path, seemingly expecting the worst.

"Don't move." She slowly moved her hand and pointed to the clear tripwires—two were inches from the ground barely two feet from them, and several were woven in different directions from the trees. It was clear that one set would snare you, and the others were cleverly connected to large branches—made to smash a body passing by, or possibly impale it.

McGaven let out a breath. "Who would... Why... Those are human snares and not animal traps... but... why...?" He couldn't finish his sentence, still stunned by the fact that he had almost walked right into one of them.

"I've seen things like this before. It's when you want to stop your enemy." Her words seemed stilted and hung strangely in the air.

"Anyone could have stumbled upon these—hikers, kids, anyone. It's only fifty yards from the road."

Katie slowly got to her feet, aware there could be any number more trips. She helped her partner up and then she slowly directed him to back up the way they came. "Stay right here."

"What are you going to do?"

Katie searched around and found what she was looking for —two decent-sized logs. She picked one up then, taking a breath, heaved it towards some of the wires. As soon as the log connected with a wire, there was a strange whizzing sound and a large branch crashed to the ground.

Katie then tossed the other log up into the trees where it set off a series of actions causing several branches and a tree trunk to slam down on the ground with a force that deeply rever-berated.

"What do you want to do? Call the chief?"

Katie shook her head. "Not yet."

"Are you really thinking that you want to hunt for whoever set these trespasser traps?"

Katie knew she was acting impulsively because she was still shaken by the snares. "You're right. Let's ask the chief and get some answers."

By the time they walked back onto the roadway, McGaven was on the phone calling the chief. But it seemed the chief wasn't giving any answers as to why there could be booby traps on that property—he said something about checking on something.

Katie stared back at the area that had held the cleverly set traps. She had hoped that the chief would have the answers they needed, but just as in their investigations yesterday, she had a hunch that things were not as they seemed.

# SIXTEEN

*Tuesday 0950 hours*

Katie and McGaven drove up to the address that Chief Baker had given them and turned into the parking lot, but it didn't seem to be the right place. The address was correct, he had said on the phone, but there wasn't any signage letting them know if they were where they were supposed to be. The morgue and medical examiner's office wasn't located at the hospital in town, but rather in an old city building that once had been the water treatment plant.

The two-story cement building only had letters from A through G spray-painted on different sections. The parking lot didn't offer any indication of where to park and who was authorized to park there.

Katie cruised around the area to see if they could ascertain where the entrance was located. There were a half-dozen cars parked, she assumed belonging to employees.

"I agree with you," said McGaven craning his neck to see if he could spot the entrance or the medical examiner's area.

"I didn't say anything."

"Not out loud, but you're sighing, your body language, and the fact you're staring daggers."

Katie couldn't help but chuckle. "I didn't know that I was so transparent."

"It's taken me a while to read you, but I think I'm getting pretty good at it."

Katie pulled into an available space and cut the engine. "Well, this is where I'm going to park."

"It's as good as any." McGaven pulled the handle to get out of the vehicle and it broke off in his hand. "Uh, Katie."

She turned and saw what had happened. "What do you want me to do?" She tried hard not to laugh.

"Another stupid trap. I can't open this door from the inside." He tried to move the remaining piece of lever inside the door, but had no luck.

"I'll get it." Katie quickly got out and rounded the front of the sedan to open the door for her partner.

"Why, thank you. Curbside service."

"Can't wait for our car to be fixed."

"Sal said by the end of the day."

"Fingers crossed," said Katie looking around. "Doesn't look like the chief is here yet."

The detectives walked to one of the entrances where the door was located under the stenciled "C" above.

Katie didn't notice the security cameras until they were closer to the building. In fact, there were many cameras, tucked up under the eaves and disguised as motion lights around every area of the building and parking lot. Some were small, barely detectable, others were more obvious with domes, and many seemed to be high-tech with infrared capability.

"Do we knock? I don't see an intercom," said McGaven.

"I'm sure they already know we're here," she said, waving her detective's badge at one of the cameras.

Just like clockwork, the lock disengaged and popped open

an inch. Katie pulled the door open and after they'd walked through it slowly shut behind them.

Inside, it was streamlined and as ambiguous as the outside. It had a vibe of a storm or disaster shelter. No names available. No main desk receptionist. The beige tile floor was spotless and the walls were painted a dull gray. There was no artwork on the walls. No plants. Nothing to indicate they were inside a working and habited building.

Katie glanced at McGaven.

"Let's just keep going until someone finds us," he said.

Katie looked at every door expecting to see someone or something indicating the medical examiner's office.

They kept walking until they came to an elevator with extra-wide doors. It opened as they approached.

"That's creepy," said McGaven more to himself.

Katie stepped inside, followed by her partner. They had had elevator troubles in a hotel a while back on one of their previous cases and the memories quickly came rushing back once they stood in the lift.

There were only two places to go—second floor or the basement. Katie pressed the button for the basement as the elevators doors slowly shut. There was no turning back now. Her heart rate increased, but she pushed through the discomfort, focusing intently on the case.

The elevator door opened and they were greeted by bright lights and a shiny floor. Finally, there were signs of life as a male morgue technician dressed in blue hospital scrubs pushed an empty gurney by them.

"Excuse me," said Katie stepping from the elevator. "Where would we find Dr. Sanders?"

"Down the end of the hall in the exam room," he said, pointing in the direction.

"Thank you."

Katie and McGaven followed instructions and headed down the hallway and turned the corner.

The familiar cleaning agents hit Katie's senses as she saw the examination room. She could hear the ventilation whirring above their head. It was larger than she had expected. There was one main room that could accommodate three bodies and there was a room for what appeared to be for evidence and assorted files. It all appeared appropriate and efficient. She wasn't exactly sure what she was expecting—but everything seemed as it should.

A tall woman in her forties with light brown shoulder-length hair and silver eyeglasses was leaning over a body looking closely at its organs inside the chest cavity. Her hands moved around with purpose—as if she had lost something and was trying to recover it.

Katie waited a moment before she said, "Dr. Sanders?"

"You must be the detectives on loan from Pine Valley," she said, never looking up from the chest opening.

Taking a step into the exam room, Katie said, "I'm Detective Katie Scott and this is my partner, Detective Sean McGaven."

"Nice to meet you both. Please call me Deborah. It's true I went to medical school, but I've never been comfortable with the formal address of 'Dr. Sanders.'" She finally stood up straight and smiled at them. Her face lit up—she appeared to be genuine.

"Nice maze you have here," said McGaven.

"I would have thought the chief would have briefed you on it."

"No, he failed to tell us a few things," said Katie.

"Well, you're here now." She pulled her blood-riddled gloves off and tossed them into the special can labeled "Medical Waste." "Come this way," she said.

Katie and McGaven trailed the doctor into a smaller room

where an autopsy table had a sheet over the body. Katie assumed it to be that of Ivy Miller. She slowed her pace. It struck her hard, having to discuss the autopsy findings of a fifteen-year-old girl. It was the worst part of being a detective.

Dr. Sanders picked up a file and flipped it open. "Okay," she said. "We've packed up the evidence and it's heading by special courier to John Blackburn, forensic supervisor at the Pine Valley Sheriff's Department. The contents: plastic bag, rope, fingernail and hair scrapings."

"When will it arrive?" said Katie.

"It looks like it will be there before the end of the day. My records say that either John Blackburn or Eva Crane will receive the evidence." The medical examiner closed the file and looked at the detectives. "Okay, cause and manner of death." She sounded like she was going to recite a grocery list.

Katie waited patiently even though she knew what they were going to be. She watched Dr. Sanders gently fold back the sheet covering Ivy's naked body. She glanced at McGaven, who had a stoic expression, and his body stiffened; he always had a difficult time during this part of the investigation, but managed to stay professional and keep his focus alert to what they would learn.

"As you already know, this is Ivy Amber Miller, fifteen years old. She was in good health. She had some issues with her wisdom teeth that needed to be extracted, but overall she was a healthy young woman." The medical examiner indicated the purplish areas around her neck. "Cause of death is strangulation; a crushed larynx, not suffocation. From everything I've seen, she was already dead when the bag was secured over her head. I put the time of death around 11 p.m. to 1 a.m. at the latest."

"Anything unusual?" Katie watched the doctor closely.

"At first, I would say no. But, I looked closer at the tattoo. It seems new, as the ink is so vibrant. I would say done within the last week or so." She positioned Ivy's arm so the detectives could see it closer. "What do you see besides the rose and vines?"

Katie leaned in and scrutinized the ink work. "It looks like there's... some kind of shadow."

McGaven nodded in agreement.

"Close. Check this out." Dr. Sanders opened a drawer and pulled out a black light source. She switched off the overhead lights and then directed the light source at the tattoo. It showed another image, which was a side profile view of a man. It wasn't enough for identification, but it was definitely a male.

"How did they do that?" said Katie.

"Inks made with ultraviolet colorants can be used to make a coating that is invisible to the naked human eye. It's like what they use when you go to a club where you can't see the symbol and then you put your hand under a light source—and there it is. Those are usually done by fluorescent ink pen."

"Law enforcement uses these types of fluorescent inks for sting operations like marking money, drugs, and car parts to identify later," said McGaven.

"Is it temporary or permanent?" said Katie.

"From what I see it's temporary and would have eventually worn off."

"The tattoo artist has some questions to answer," said McGaven.

"He may not have known about it because it might have been applied before or after the rose tattoo."

"What about the word 'More' carved in her back?" said Katie.

"There wasn't any evidence that I could lift, but the cut seems to be from a large sharp knife, like a hunting knife or possibly a utility knife, not a precision instrument like a scalpel."

"Something a camper or fisherman would have?"

"Yes, something like that."

A technician came in with a file and gave it to the medical examiner. She quickly scanned the paperwork.

"Here we go. The answer probably to your next question," said Dr. Sanders. "Her toxicology screen is clean. Nothing unusual. No drugs, legal or otherwise."

"I see," said Katie. She couldn't get rid of the image of the profile of the man on Ivy's arm.

*What did it mean? Was she looking at the face of her killer?*

"She has scratches on her body," said Dr. Sanders, indicating the areas. "Here on her arms and her chest. But what bothers me is that usually I see deeper wounds from a struggle. These seem to have been made after the fact, as if someone scratched her up when she was unable to defend herself. I would say they're superficial. There weren't any marks on her wrists or ankles indicating that she was bound. This is only a guess, but going by my experience, I would say she was strangled first and the rest was post-mortem." The medical examiner waited for the detectives to ask any other questions.

Katie thought that the killer seemed more interested in the posing of the body and the results of the murder than in the actual act of killing. "The manner of death?"

"Homicide."

"Thank you, Doctor... rather, Deborah, for conducting the autopsy so quickly. I'm sure that her grandmother appreciated it."

"Sydney actually demanded it the moment she knew that Ivy was dead."

Katie thought it was odd that the medical examiner called Ivy's grandmother by her first name. "You know Sydney?"

"Of course. She's quite popular around here. I mean, I know it's just a small town, but Sydney is it. She keeps so many charities going."

"I see. Did you know Ivy too?" said Katie. She was surprised that the medical examiner didn't mention this sooner.

"Yes, ever since she was a little girl."

"Would you know anything about any problems or trouble she might have been in?" Katie's stomach twisted. Once again, she felt like everyone around them knew something about this case that she and McGaven didn't.

"No. Just kid stuff. You know, boys, makeup, and clothes. Nothing nefarious, if that's what you mean."

"I see. Well, thank you for your time," said Katie.

McGaven nodded.

"If I can answer anything more for you, please don't hesitate to reach out," said the doctor.

Katie and McGaven left the room. Katie glanced back, to see the medical examiner was carefully covering Ivy up; as she did so, she whispered something in the ear of the dead girl.

The detectives made their way back to the elevator and stepped in. Katie had many thoughts and questions whirling around her mind about what she just had witnessed.

The elevator doors opened. All the effort Katie had put in to stay calm and controlled on the inside as well as on the outside were gone. Her mind flashed with visions of the crime scene, and she was rapidly processing the new information that Ivy had been murdered first and the setup and posing of her body had been introduced after the fact. She hurried to the main door and pushed it open. The cool air hitting her face made her body relax some.

"Was that weird, or is it just me?" said McGaven. He had kept quiet until they were outside and a little distance from the cameras.

"Weird doesn't even begin to describe it."

Chief Baker sped into the parking lot, pulling up next to Katie and McGaven. The window eased down and he leaned out toward them. "Your assistance is needed, ASAP. We've got another body," he said.

"Where?" said Katie. Her heart pounded.

"Oak Valley Creek."

# SEVENTEEN

*Tuesday 1130 hours*

Katie raced along the curving roads behind Chief Baker's patrol car, lights flashing as they headed toward Oak Valley Creek. Her mind rushed with thoughts of another homicide in a town that had only one homicide in its entire history. Now it was two in two days.

*Was it the same killer?*

*Was it one of Ivy's friends?*

She didn't want to admit to herself that she had already known that there would be another victim. The killer had already told them so—*MORE...*

"Try the number again," said Katie.

McGaven re-called the Pragers' residence, but there was no answer and no voicemail to leave a message. He shook his head.

"No!" She slammed her hands on the steering wheel. This couldn't be happening on their watch. Another victim.

"We don't know it's one of Ivy's friends yet." Her partner tried to calm her nerves. He knew they needed to keep steady heads.

Katie glanced at her partner. "The odds aren't good."

The chief's police sedan ahead of them took a sudden, sharp turn off the roadway and along a track that twisted down the hill. Dust plumed in the air, obscuring the car's bumper, and for a moment the police cruiser disappeared from view.

Katie's anxiety was perfectly matched by her need to know more. She noticed that they were just west of Bates Hiking and Camping, and the nearby traps. They continued to drive downhill through the trees until Katie could see the rushing creek that lay at the bottom of the small ravine.

Officer Lane's cruiser was parked just to the left, about twenty-five yards from the water. The trunk was open.

"Oh, great," said Katie.

"What?" said McGaven swiveling his head scrutinizing the area.

"Officer Lane is here and has his trunk open. He better not have interfered with the crime scene or covered up the body."

"Do you really think he would make that mistake again?"

"Normally, I would say no, but here and now... I'm not so sure."

Katie pulled in behind the chief's car and was out of her vehicle before the chief.

Katie and McGaven headed toward the creek to find Officer Lane. They didn't stop to confer with the chief, they were too desperate to see what they were going to be dealing with.

As Katie stepped onto a more sandy terrain that trailed along the side of the moving creek, she saw the body. Goosebumps scuttled up her arms and a deep heaviness settled in her body. She was suddenly cold, as if an icy wind had caught her off guard, slicing right through her soul. Working homicides would never get any easier—and some were worse than others.

Officer Lane spotted the detectives and immediately hurried to meet up with them. His face was pale and he stared at the ground as he approached.

"Who called it in?" said Katie.

"It was an anonymous call," he said, trying hard to keep eye contact.

"Man or woman?"

"Don't know."

"Did they call the station?"

"No, ma'am," he said as he reached into his pocket and retrieved his cell phone. He handed it to Katie. "I got a text."

Katie and McGaven read the message: *Never... Forever... Find me at the creek...*

"I didn't know what it meant, but under the circumstances I checked out the area." His voice wavered as he spoke as he was clearly shaken.

Katie knew the officer was stunned, so she spoke carefully. "You did the right thing. Anything else?"

"I started north about an hour ago and then worked my way down here until I found her..."

"Did you secure the area?"

"I was just about to when y'all arrived."

"Did you touch the body?"

"No, ma'am."

"Do you have any evidence containers or bags?"

"Your CSI team stocked us with everything that we might need before they left."

Katie made a quick three-hundred-sixty-degree turn, taking everything in. The chief was waiting about twenty feet away. "Okay, we're going to search and document the scene."

The officer nodded.

"Do you have a digital camera, by chance?" she asked.

"I do," said Chief Baker.

"We're going to need it." Katie turned back to the officer. "We're going to need you to secure the area and wait on standby. Make sure no one comes near the scene. I don't think anyone will be out here, but just in case."

"How far should I secure it?"

"Anywhere where the killer could have entered or exited, and stay alert to recent tire or foot impressions. Indicate the locations with those cone markers."

Officer Lane nodded and jogged up to his cruiser.

Chief Baker hurried back with a digital camera.

McGaven took it. "Thanks."

"Detective?" said the chief.

"Yes."

"I'll let you do your work. If you need anything... anything, let me know."

"Thank you, Chief."

Katie turned and headed toward the body. As usual, she didn't want to examine it until she was ready. She had to prepare herself mentally, and sometimes physically, to address the trauma and then face it head-on. Her anxiety and panic could rise up at the worst moments, dragging her back to her time in the military, so she had to use her breath and relax her muscles to stay in the present.

She walked with purpose, taking in and studying everything she could in the lead-up to the body as she pulled on her gloves. McGaven was lagging back, looking for anything that might prove to be evidence; Katie knew he would back her up if she missed anything crucial. They had worked many cases together; where one left off, the other picked up.

Katie recognized the girl lying on her back close to the creek's shore before she got close. The first thing she saw was the short blonde bangs fanning slightly in the wind. The pink highlights glistened in the sunshine. Her nude body was porcelain-like, a beautiful figurine with arms outstretched and legs together, her eyes fixed, and looking up to the trees. Her face, from her nose down to her neck, was covered with a pink bandana that had been secured behind her head.

Katie stopped a couple of feet away from the body and

stared down at it. It had been barely a day since she had spoken with this young girl in her own bedroom. She remembered the questions she had put to Nikki, how upset she had been about her best friend's death.

Katie couldn't slow her reactions now. Emotions swirled around her and urgently tried to take hold of her. The crime scene seemed to freeze in time. It tugged at her heart and hurt her soul to see another one of the town's girls lying dead next to the rushing creek only a couple of days after her best friend had suffered a similar fate. This second death was Katie's own fault, she told herself. She should have taken up part of the patrols to go by Nikki's house. She should have pushed harder on Chief Baker to have security for the girls stationed outside the house. Biting her lip, she fought back tears. This wasn't the way it was supposed to be—it never was. Gathering her wits and stuffing her feelings deep down inside her to the place she stored all the emotions she couldn't deal with, she moved forward into action.

"We need to find Dawn now," said Katie, directing her words to the chief. "Go by the Pragers' house and Dawn's home. Find her."

Chief Baker left and in less than a minute she heard the patrol car rev its engine and drive away.

Katie could see Officer Lane unrolling crime scene tape, securing it to trees near the parking lot. She was glad that he had taken her previous criticism to heart and was now doing a good job.

Katie bent down to have a closer look at the body.

"What do we have?" said McGaven.

"It's Nikki Prager. I can't see if she's been strangled like Ivy was." Katie carefully moved the bandana up and could immediately see the purplish marks around her neck made by a thin type of rope.

"No bag this time?"

"No, but the killer has used this bandana, perhaps to represent suffocation." She examined the body, and couldn't help but notice the tattoo. She wondered if there would be the shadowed profile of a man once the tattoo was put under a black light.

Nikki's rigor mortis hadn't set in long and Katie estimated that the girl had still been breathing barely a couple of hours ago. Her extremities were stiffened and, like Ivy, there was pooling of blood where her body made contact with the ground. It meant that she had been murdered where she lay. The medical examiner would have to determine the exact timeline.

"I wonder if the killer left his calling card?" she said.

McGaven assisted her to carefully roll the body slightly to the side.

Katie swallowed hard. On Nikki's back was a single carved word: *NEVER...*

"Another clue," said McGaven in barely a whisper. "Once I get to my laptop, I'm going to search these words to see if anything shakes out."

Katie turned her attention back to Nikki. The image of the young girl lying out in the open next to a rushing creek waiting for someone to find her was brutal. It took everything she had to push forward and not dwell on what had already happened.

*I'm so sorry, Nikki...*

There was nothing else she could do but find the killer now.

"Let's start documenting the body and the scene. I'll start a search with Nikki's body as the starting point," she said.

McGaven took several steps back and began photographing the entire area and gradually closing in on the body.

"Detectives! Detectives! Over here!" yelled Officer Lane. His voice was frantic and at a higher pitch.

Katie and McGaven stopped what they were doing and ran toward the officer.

Katie's heart pounded as she ran, following McGaven.

"What do you have?" said McGaven. His voice was even and calm.

"Over there." The officer pointed to an area in the trees. His eyes were wide and his complexion was pallid this time—he looked as if he might vomit.

"Wait," said Katie. "We need to approach with caution." She didn't need to remind her partner about the traps that had been set, or the need to protect the crime scene.

Katie and McGaven moved with great care. Katie took the lead and, as she rounded the corner, stopped. Horror gripped her, almost paralyzing her. She gasped as her stomach dropped with a sickening plunge.

"What?" said McGaven moving closer just as he saw the body.

"It's Dawn," she barely whispered.

# EIGHTEEN

*Tuesday 1250 hours*

Katie stood motionless, taking in the horrifying scene only six feet away from her. McGaven stood next to her and she could sense his shock too. Barely able to move, breath stilted in her lungs, Katie could only stare.

Dawn's beautiful long blonde hair, its tips tinged cotton-candy pink, just like Nikki's was, swirled around her face in a dramatic display. Katie felt as if the world had been slowed down to half speed.

Dawn had been secured to a pine tree by her wrists, pinned above her head with what appeared to be long construction nails. Blood oozed down her arms and onto the ground, making it likely that she had been nailed to the tree first, before her death.

Her naked body was covered in cuts and scratches—some deep. Her throat was sliced, leaving a hideous gaping wound—no plastic bag or bandana, just a knife to the throat. Dawn's beautiful face slumped forward, gazing at the ground. Her lips were slightly parted as though her last moments had been a pleading whisper. The word *FOREVER* was hacked into her bare chest.

Katie stepped back, taking a moment to view everything as part of the investigation, but also taking a breath at how horrible the two crime scenes were.

*MORE...*

*NEVER...*

*FOREVER...*

Three girls. Three messages.

Katie was glad that she didn't have to look into Dawn's eyes staring at her as she processed the scene. She wished that John and Eva were here to conduct the documenting and forensic process, but time was important and the brutal task was up to her and McGaven to complete. There was no one else. She felt the heavy weight on her shoulders to get it right—to bring the killer to justice.

*I'm so sorry...*

"We're going to need to secure this entire area," said McGaven, snapping Katie back into real time.

"Of course. We're going to need assistance with two bodies. I hope Officer Lane is up to it."

"I think he can handle it."

"It's going to be a crash course in CSI," she said. "But we need to get started and comb through everything right now." Katie was thankful it was still early, that the lighting was good and it wasn't raining. But it might not stay that way.

Katie jogged back to Officer Lane, who was completing his perimeter barrier.

"Officer Lane," she said.

"Detective, please call me Brett."

"Of course."

Katie didn't want to admit it, but she liked the young officer and could sense that he was of good character and integrity. "Okay, Brett, are you able to work with us again?"

"Yes, ma'am. Whatever you need."

"Okay. We need you to secure the second scene and conduct a careful search in the vicinity. Mark anything that looks suspicious or possibly left by the killer," she said. "Also, can you update the chief?"

He nodded. "Ma'am?"

"Please call me Katie." She hated being called ma'am even though she knew it was a mark of respect.

"Do you think we have a serial killer here in Coldwater Creek?"

"That is yet to be determined, but—between you and me—yes, I think so." Katie could tell that the young officer was distraught at the prospect of a serial killer roaming and preying upon teen girls in this small and until now peaceful town.

Brett went back to protect the first scene and ready himself to secure the second.

Katie and McGaven returned to the body of Nikki. After McGaven had taken all the photographs he needed, he took a few more, as backup. There wasn't going to be a second chance to record the crime scene properly.

"Okay," said Katie. She began to bag Nikki's hands and feet, to preserve any evidence. Hopefully they would be able to get some DNA of the killer.

For more than an hour Katie and McGaven worked silently and diligently to finish the documentation and collect the evidence.

"We're going to need to record the impression evidence," she said.

"I'll assist Brett," he said and left Katie.

Katie removed her small notebook and detailed what she had done. She also sketched the area to show where the killer and victims could have entered and exited. It would then be easier to gain a better perspective to recreate what happened in comparison with the local map.

Her cell phone rang.

"Detective Scott," she said.

"How are you holding up?" said Sheriff Scott.

Katie had never felt so relieved to hear her uncle's voice. "We're processing two crime scenes right now."

"What's the update?"

"Three bodies. One yesterday and two today. It's horrific." Katie walked carefully around the area as she bit her lip. The truth was she was already exhausted and deeply troubled by what had transpired.

"I've assured the chief that my two best detectives are on the job."

Katie let out a breath. "Uncle Wayne, I don't think we can do this." She thought about the girls, posed where anyone could have stumbled across their bodies.

"Nonsense. You've been in tougher places before. Take a moment, gain your bearings, and do what you do best. I expect no less from you."

"I know. It's this town... it's being away from the department..."

"Katie, stay on track and do your job."

"You're right, I know," she said, mad at herself for showing weakness. "We're going to need to transport the evidence back to Pine Valley and have John work on it."

"I'll have Chief Baker secure a place for you and McGaven, so you can have a headquarters to conduct the investigation properly. You need a better place to sleep too." His voice softened.

Katie knew that was the best idea, but she felt a pang of homesickness and wanted to be with Chad. She needed to have him by her side. She knew that part of her strength and resilience came from the security of being with him, of coming home to him at night, and so the thought of being marooned in

Coldwater Creek in the middle of a triple homicide, just when she needed him most, made her heart sink.

"Does that work for you?" said the sheriff.

"Yes. I think we'll be able to drive the patrol car back later today—it should be fixed. And we'll need some supplies and computers to help with our murder board."

"Good. Make sure the chain of custody is bulletproof."

"I'm requesting to bring Cisco back with us."

"What's your plan?"

"This town is very rural and we need to search a large area. We found traps set in the woods, so I wanted to make sure it's safe for all of us. Cisco has top-notch trailing and tracking skills for this type of thing."

"Request granted."

"And, there might be a witness from the first homicide. I think it could be a local or perhaps a transient. Cisco should be able to pick up on a scent to locate them."

"Katie, please be careful." The sheriff's voice was more like a concerned uncle and she could hear the unease in his voice. "We can't spare another detective right now, so keep me posted."

"We'll keep you updated as it progresses."

"You call me for anything. Understand?"

"Yes. Thank you." Katie felt an overwhelming sense of sorrow. She had been through so much and her uncle was her only living family. But he was also her boss and sometimes had to combine being tough on her with caring about her welfare. Sometimes she wanted to just close her eyes and wish for things to be less complicated.

The connection ended.

Katie stood for a moment feeling the breeze move softly over her and listening to the sound it made as it wove through the pines. It was calming and seemed in a strange way to be trying to convey a message to her from the dense woods. She would have to wait and see if she could decipher it through the story told by the crime scenes.

Katie and McGaven completed the delicate task of searching, documenting, and collecting evidence from Dawn's crime scene. Katie tried not to think about Nikki's body lying next to the creek alone as they waited for the morgue technicians to come and pick her up. She felt she had let the girls down and now they had paid the highest of prices. With every ounce of strength and perseverance she had, she pushed those negative thoughts from her mind. She would have to live with the outcome. And the best way to do that would be to catch the killer before he took another innocent life.

"Katie?" said McGaven. He looked at a text message.

Katie continued to organize the CSI evidence to get it ready for transport.

"Katie? You okay?" he said.

Katie finally looked at McGaven. "I'm fine. Just thinking about what we have to do."

"Looks like Sal came through," he said, referring to the text. "Our police sedan is ready. So we can pick it up anytime."

"Good news."

"Hey," he said, making Katie look at him. "It's not your fault."

"I know—no matter how much it *feels* like it's my fault. But we could have done more to keep those girls safe."

"These murders are unprecedented. Three victims in two days, in a quiet town like this. That's nuts. We alerted the chief of police and his officers to keep them under surveillance. What more could we have done? There was no way we could have known this was going to happen."

"What about others? Don't you think there could be more

to come?" Katie continued to look away from McGaven, writing on a chain of custody form.

McGaven didn't answer, watching her. It was clear that he was concerned about her, but there was nothing he could do for her at the moment. They just had to keep going at their jobs.

They heard vehicles approaching.

Katie and McGaven walked up to the parking area to find Chief Baker and the morgue van from the medical examiner's office had just arrived.

Officer Lane directed the technician to the creek to transport Nikki Prager and then Dawn Cromwell away.

The chief was carrying a manila envelope. He handed it to Katie. "I coordinated with Sheriff Scott to have you stay at the lake cottage. It's generally booked up almost year-round, but we made accommodations for you both—under the circumstances."

Katie took the envelope. "Thank you."

"I know staying at a bed and breakfast isn't the most fitting for a homicide detective office. The key and directions are inside."

"We're just about packed up and ready to transport the evidence back to our lab. We'll be back tomorrow, but first..." she said.

"I know you had a lot of questions for me. You seem a bit frustrated about that."

"Chief, you have to understand that time is extremely important in a homicide case," said McGaven. He kept his tone even but it was clear that he was getting impatient.

"I understand," the chief said.

"I'm not sure you do," said Katie, still feeling a tug that there wasn't something completely open about the investigation. "I don't mean any disrespect, but I need to be honest. We need to have complete transparency here. We can't conduct our jobs the way we need to if you hold out on information or decide to not tell us everything. We will keep to ourselves any, how do I say this, indiscretions or maybe things that would be embarrassing if let out. We don't care about things like that—anything you tell us is confidential. We need to get to the truth in order to find this killer."

"Detective Scott, there are some things you might not understand about a town like Coldwater Creek, but I assure you, I've given you everything I have."

Katie still didn't completely believe him, which meant to her that they would only have to work that much harder to find the killer. "We reserve the right to question anyone we see fit in this investigation."

"Of course," he said.

"What did the girls' parents say? Where were Nikki and Dawn last night?"

"They were at Nikki's house. Evidently they must have sneaked out sometime after midnight."

Katie sighed and watched the morgue technicians secure Nikki's body in a heavy bag.

"I had Maxwell Torrez check out where the traps were set across the way with a couple of his men—they didn't find anything. He owns the local fishing and hunting store—he would definitely know."

"We'll need to speak with him."

"Of course. His name and number are in the envelope."

"I appreciate that. My only other question at this point is... what are you going to do to protect the other teenage girls in this town?"

"Meaning?"

"Meaning, are you going to enforce a curfew, or give a talk at the school warning them about the potential threat? What?"

The chief took a moment before he replied. He seemed a bit uncomfortable. "We're doing everything we can to ensure the safety of our teenage girls, and for the entire town as well. You don't need to worry about that—just concentrate on what you do so well."

Katie was about to say more, but she decided against it. "Thank you for your generosity with the lake cottage. I'll be checking in with you when we get back tomorrow." She walked away.

"Thanks, Chief. We'll see you tomorrow," said McGaven.

The technicians had already put the body of Nikki Prager into the van. They were headed to where Dawn Cromwell was located.

"Brett," said Katie. "We're going to need your help. Do you have some tools in your trunk?"

He looked toward the wooded area where Dawn's body was still hanging from the tree trunk. His face went grim as his mouth turned down. It was clear that he knew what they had to do. "Yes. I'll get them." He jogged to his cruiser.

The two morgue technicians were young men who most likely were medical students. They looked at Katie and McGaven as they approached.

"We need to free the body from a tree trunk," said McGaven.

The men didn't seem to blink or show any emotion at the horrible task to come. They just nodded and patiently waited.

Brett returned with a duffel bag with various tools including a small saw, crowbar, and hammer. He looked at McGaven and waited for further instructions.

"We need to pry her loose. We can't just chop the tree down and take it with us." McGaven took a closer look, examining the nails and the thickness of the tree. "Maybe we can cut part of the tree trunk—like a divot so we don't disturb any evidence."

Katie's stomach churned. Her blood turned icy. She felt a bit weak thinking of how they were going to free Dawn's body.

*I'm so sorry...*

Katie ran to Brett's cruiser and grabbed a blanket. When

she returned, she tried to protect Dawn's face and body by tucking the blanket as a shield around her, allowing any evidence to adhere to it, hopefully keeping any of the particles from the tree contaminating the body. She couldn't stay and watch; instead, she concentrated on making sure all the evidence was accounted for, packed securely, and every form was completed and accurate.

McGaven, Brett, and the technicians worked diligently but carefully to free Dawn's body. After some time, they were able to pull the nails from the tree, leaving them still pierced through Dawn's wrists.

Katie watched as the morgue technicians pushed the gurney up the gravel terrain and then slid the body inside the van. Nikki and Dawn, best friends, would now ride to the medical examiner's office together and join Ivy. It was one of the most heart-wrenching spectacles that she had seen.

McGaven walked up to Katie. "We're done here. I'm having Brett finish up. He's a good guy."

"We need to get our car and then pack up," said Katie, not looking McGaven in the eye.

"It's okay," he said quietly. "I know we're going to get the guy who did this."

"How do you know?" said Katie. She searched for the right words, but nothing came to mind.

"How? It's what we do." McGaven smiled as he shut the trunk. "It's what you do—better than anyone I know."

# NINETEEN

It felt good to drive home in the police sedan. The car was as good as new and the steering wheel felt stable in her hands. Skidding off the road was a distant memory. As she drove back to Pine Valley, Katie had time to think about everything that had happened in less than two days.

McGaven rode beside her in silence since it seemed he, too, was thinking about the homicides and possibly of what the rest of the week would bring. There was a lot to accomplish, amid everyone's hopes that there wouldn't be any more deaths.

Katie drove into the Pine Valley Sheriff's Department to drop off the police vehicle and then she and McGaven parted ways. They would meet at her home in the morning to return to Coldwater Creek.

McGaven transported the forensic evidence from the Cold-water Creek crime scenes to the CSI lab and directly to John.

Katie drove to the sheriff's department K9 kennels. She had made arrangements to pick Cisco up there, as her uncle had had a series of important meetings today and wasn't able to keep the dog with him himself.

She drove into the K9 training facility and found a parking place in front of the kennels. As she got out of her Jeep, a tall, good-looking man dressed in SWAT fatigues and military boots approached her.

"Hi," she said, not sure of the officer's name. There were still a few officers at the department that she didn't know or hadn't met before.

"Detective Scott," he said cheerfully. "Nice to see you. I presume you're here for Cisco."

"Yes." Katie still wracked her memory for the officer's name.

"I'm SWAT Sergeant Ryan West."

"Nice to meet you. I thought Sergeant Hardy was going to be here."

"He left, but the sheriff asked me to open up the kennels so you could get Cisco."

"Oh, thank you. Much appreciated."

The sergeant unlocked the large metal doors to the barnlike building. There were several K9s barking. Katie stepped inside and immediately saw Cisco—he wasn't difficult to miss. His black sleek coat and amazing wolflike amber eyes were staring intensely. He gave a couple of barks and two spins in the kennel.

"Cisco," she said, approaching him. Her heart thumped as she saw her partner again and realized how much she had missed him. They had been through so much together—some things she had never told another soul. But she knew Cisco had been safe with her uncle and here at the kennels.

Sergeant West opened the kennel and Cisco burst out, circling around Katie with doggie snorts and whines. She snapped Cisco's lead onto his collar and leaned down to hug the dog, giving him a kiss.

"Thank you for meeting me here," she said to the sergeant.

"No problem. The sheriff said something about you investigating homicides over in Coldwater Creek?"

"Yes. McGaven and I are returning tomorrow and I'm bringing Cisco for some area sweeps," she said.

Ryan West studied her face. "You seem troubled."

Katie walked out of the kennel building toward her Jeep. "Well, a bit. It's just such a rural area and there have been some strange things happening over there."

He nodded. "Uh-huh? You know, we used to do some of our SWAT training there."

Katie stopped and turned to him. "Really? Where?"

"There's an old cement building just south of the Oak Valley Creek."

Katie's curiosity boiled over. That was in the vicinity of where they had found the traps. "What kind of cement building?"

"It was some old building, I think from the 1940s, where supplies and ammunitions were once kept."

"Really?" Katie's mind began cataloging the area. "You said you used to train there?"

"We used it to blow stuff up and run maneuvers. It held up great and took quite a few rounds—a real beating. It's actually quite large, with two stories and a basement, but when the new facility was built here a couple of years ago, we didn't need to travel there anymore. It's more stable here."

Katie remained quiet.

"That seems to interest you."

"Well, I've studied the map of the area, but I never saw anything referring to that building."

"I can't help you there. But I know at one point it was supposed to be demolished. Maybe it's gone now?"

"I guess Gav and I—and Cisco, of course—need to check things out."

Sergeant West pulled a card from his pocket and jotted

down some numbers. "Take my card, and if you need to know anything about that building when you get there—don't hesitate to call."

Katie took the card. "Thank you, Sergeant."

"My pleasure. I would feel better knowing that one of our heroes was safe."

Katie smiled. It always made her a bit uncomfortable being called a hero, because she felt she met and worked with a lot of real heroes who deserved thanks more than her.

"Be careful out there, okay?" he said.

"Be safe." Having a second thought, she turned and said, "Do you ever recall seeing any kind of traps set? Or, seen anyone living nearby?"

"Traps? No, never seen anything like that, but we mostly stayed within the vicinity of the building. Believe me, if there were any type of traps, we would have seen them." He thought a moment. "Never saw any cabins or tents, but did see some tracks, footprints, on several occasions. Didn't think much of it. People hike around there."

"Thank you again, Sergeant."

He smiled and walked away.

"We're going home," she said to Cisco as she opened the car door and he immediately jumped inside.

Katie drove out of the police K9 kennel area, her mind spinning with more questions than answers.

*Why wasn't that cement building on the map?*

*Why didn't Chief Baker mention it since he knew they were searching the area?*

Katie was almost home and she had tried to call Chad several times, but it went to voicemail every time. But as soon as she turned and drove up her driveway she saw Chad's large Jeep parked. Her pulse increased and skipped a beat. She was filled with relief and happiness, which was something she desperately needed right now.

She opened her car door and got out, followed closely by Cisco. She barely had time to get to the front door when it flew open. Chad stepped out and pulled Katie close. He whispered in her ear, "I've missed you." Then he kissed her right there on the front porch.

Katie could smell something absolutely wonderful coming from the kitchen. "Did you cook?"

"I'd like to take credit, but Jim at the firehouse made a big batch of his famous marinara sauce."

Katie walked inside, shutting the door. Her arms and legs were weak and she didn't realize how exhausted she was until she got home.

*Home.*

It was a comforting thought and it was where she felt safe— where she would recharge and get a fresh perspective. The three crime scenes really played a number on her mind and tested her abilities as a detective. With every case, she had some doubts and insecurities, but this town and the three murdered girls were definitely different in all aspects from anything she'd faced before.

"Go change and relax. I'll get things ready and feed Cisco," said Chad. He turned to head to the kitchen, not waiting for her to reply. Cisco, his ears at attention with the mention of food, tagged along behind him.

Katie went to her bedroom and sat down on the bed as she unzipped her boots and kicked them off. She quickly changed into sweatpants and T-shirt. She could hear dishes rattling and Chad's voice talking to Cisco. It made her smile. She fantasized about what it was going to be like when they were married.

Katie wanted to rest her eyes so she climbed on top of her bed to take a quiet moment.

"Dinner is served," said Chad ten minutes later, standing at the bedroom doorway with Cisco next to him. "Katie?" he said.

At first, he seemed disappointed but then he couldn't help but smile.

Katie had fallen asleep from sheer exhaustion, so Chad quietly covered her with a quilt and let his lips gently brush her cheek. He stayed a moment to watch her relaxed breaths. "Love you, sweet dreams," he whispered.

Chad quietly shut the door.

# TWENTY

*Wednesday 0700 hours*

Katie had just finished putting the last of her things in her Jeep when McGaven drove up the driveway. He jumped out of his truck. "Hey, you all packed?"

"Just about."

"Did you save some room for more stuff?"

"Of course... and for Cisco. How's Denise? Is she mad that you're going out of town again?"

"Not mad, but disappointed."

"Chad feels the same way. We're lucky they understand so well."

"It feels like we're going on vacation with all this planning," he said.

"I wish. What did you bring?"

"I swung by the office to get my laptop, files of everything we have, and checked in with John and Eva. He said he'll have some preliminary forensic results soon and will call us on the video conference when he does."

"Sounds good." Katie double-checked her stuff.

"You okay?"

"Of course. Why wouldn't I be?"

"This is a heavy case, we both know that. Plus, we have to stay in that town."

"I know."

McGaven started taking things from his truck and packing them into the back of Katie's Jeep. "I got your message about the mystery building."

"What do you think?"

"Don't know yet, but it does seem strange that no one has mentioned it."

"Speaking of strange, I asked John to see if he could clean up the images of the women on Ivy's flash drive. I'm hoping that we can identify whoever is on them."

"Great. I'm glad that John has a new forensic tech now."

"Yeah," she said.

"Hey," he laughed. "It's not competition, is it?"

"What? Of course not. We need good forensic personnel. I just hope she's as good as John thinks she is."

"Okay, just checking," he chuckled.

"Finish packing. I'm going to get Cisco and my last bag."

"Ten-four."

Katie went back inside her house.

Cisco was extremely happy, running from room to room emitting a low-pitch German shepherd whine. He knew that something was going on and he was getting to work. His posture was rigid and his senses were keen.

Standing in the middle of her living room, emotions caught her by surprise. They welled up inside of her. She had so many memories of growing up in this house, of her parents, and even thinking of the new memories she'd made living there with Chad made her breath catch suddenly in her throat. She missed Chad already as he'd had to leave for the firehouse early. She didn't know why everything seemed to be pressing down on her at this precise time. Maybe it was the three murders bringing back the pain and memory of what it had felt like when her own childhood best friend was killed. But there was no point in over-analyzing that now. She had a job to do.

Snapping back to reality, she gathered her last things, Cisco, and double-checked the alarm system before she left.


On the drive over to Coldwater, Katie and McGaven rehashed everything they knew so far about the murders. But several things were gnawing at her and they all circled around the town of Coldwater Creek itself. It still seemed that the locals were withholding information. How could they not see how much more difficult that would make it for the detectives to pursue the investigation? It wasn't as if they were lying to her—but they seemed to say just enough and not elaborate on anything. Her instinct told her that they would have to crack open some town secrets if they were going to solve these homicides.

McGaven used Katie's cell phone on the car's Bluetooth.

The number rang twice and was answered by Chief Baker. "Detective Scott. May I presume that you and Detective McGaven are on your way?"

"Yes, Chief. We should be there in about an hour."

"Great news. Your cottage is ready. Officer Lane brought over all the files from the three murders—interviews, backgrounds, and autopsy reports. Oh, and Mama made sure that you had some food and snacks from the inn stocked in your fridge and cupboards."

"That's very thoughtful, thank you." She looked at her partner as he raised his eyebrows and gave the thumbs-up sign.

"I'll see you when you get here," the chief said.

"We had a couple of questions for you, if that's okay," she said.

"Of course."

Katie thought she detected a different tone to his voice. "Is that cement building still standing near the area where McGaven and I found the traps?"

"Cement building?"

Katie thought he was stalling for some reason. "Yes, the one that Pine Valley Sheriff's Department's SWAT team used for training a few years ago."

"Oh yes, that's right. The city council has still not decided that building's fate. It's still standing."

"I see. Is there anything else you can tell us about it?" Katie made a sour face.

"It's just an old building that was used for storage during World War Two—at least, that's what I've been told."

"You've never had any calls to that location or heard about anything unusual going on there?" Katie glanced at the GPS, which was loaded with directions to the lake cottage. "I guess what I'm trying to say is... has there been anything happening near that building to bring it to your attention?"

"Not that I can recall," he said.

"Okay, we'll see you shortly."

"Drive safe. Bye." The connection ended.

Katie remained quiet for a couple of minutes after Chief Baker hung up.

"So what do you think?" said McGaven with a little sarcasm to his voice.

"I still think he's keeping something from us... and I think he's very careful what he says."

The GPS instructed Katie to make a left turn, which she followed.

Cisco let out a whine and his tail thumped against the back car door.

"Hang on, Cisco, we'll be there soon," she said.

"I don't remember taking this road," said McGaven as he

looked around at the forest becoming denser with each passing mile.

"I took the address the chief gave us and this is the most straightforward drive according to the map. It's actually on the other side of Oak Valley Creek."

"But I bet I know what you want to do first."

"What?"

"You want to find that building."

"Well, sure. We're going to have to wait for forensics and the autopsies for Nikki and Dawn. So it's a perfect place to start so we can deduce if it's a point of interest or not."

McGaven shifted in his seat to readjust his seatbelt. "When do you want to question friends and family?"

"The chief had his officers question them, but I'm sure we'll want to verify some things when we look at the files."

"I've been trying to search out those words written on the girls, and also to see if there's any significance to that saying of 'you can look but will not always find more.' I can't find anything yet. It's going to take some time and they may be nothing but ramblings after all."

The GPS beeped and instructed Katie to take Steam Springs Road.

"Looks like we're close," she said.

"Wow, look at these places. Large and no doubt pricey."

"You're right," she said. Katie imagined what a vacation would be like in a quiet place in one of those big homes. "Our place is going to be that little cabin at the end of the road." She giggled.

"Not necessarily. Bet you twenty bucks it's a nice house."

"You're on."

"Forty says that there's a private dock."

"Easy money," she said.

Cisco barked twice.

Within ten minutes, they were looking for 3475 Steam Springs Road.

"There it is," said McGaven.

There was a white fence with a mailbox with an easily visible number. Crowns of pine trees surrounded the property. There was a stepping stone path that led to the creek and there was a small dock located at the end.

"Well, I'll give you that dock," she said.

"I told you."

Katie turned the Jeep up a small gravel driveway. As she drove, she noticed that they were slightly moving up an incline. There was nothing to see yet, until they rounded the last corner where the driveway leveled. That's when the detectives saw the house. It was a pretty home painted a light gray with white trim and a line of windows that looked out over the creek. It wasn't the largest house on the street, but it was beautifully maintained with a small garden. A square deck of approximately fifteen feet by fifteen feet had two chairs and a small table set on it. Two tall plants in turquoise pots were placed at two corners of the deck.

"Okay, I'll take my forty bucks in cash please," said McGaven. He snapped his fingers.

"Wow, this is beautiful."

"Hope it won't be a distraction."

"No, but it will definitely be a great place to work," she said.

They got out of Katie's Jeep and walked up to the deck. The view was amazing and they cherished the moment and their surroundings.

"I think we can almost see the area of the crime scenes," said Katie.

"That's quite eerie."

"Everything about Coldwater Creek is eerie."

# TWENTY-ONE

*Wednesday 1145 hours*

Katie unlocked the door with the key Chief Baker had given her. Cisco raced in to check everything out. Once inside, she could immediately detect a slight scent of cleaning solution. Obviously someone had made sure everything was clean and tidy before they arrived.

Cisco kept his nose down and inspected everything. He trailed around, spending time checking out chairs, seat cushions, and kitchen appliances. The search would keep him busy for a few minutes.

The interior was nice but the furnishings were outdated. However, everything was pleasant and comfortable. Plumped-up cushions sat on furniture with oversized arms, making it appear something from the 1980s, most likely when the cottage was built.

There was a small table at the entry, which had a neat stack of files with a paperclipped piece of paper attached to the top. It read: *Detectives.* Moving farther into the cottage, the main area was open and airy with the living room, kitchen, and small dining area incorporated into one big living space. There were bedrooms off it, each with a double bed and a private bath. But the vista through the windows was definitely the million-dollar view—with the thick band of trees and the creek that was more like a small river. It was beautiful and serene. The cottage had that restful vibe and made you think of a place you would love to visit on a regular basis. Home—at least for now.

"Well, let's get the Jeep unpacked," said McGaven.

Katie began toting things inside as Cisco trailed along back and forth between the car and cottage. It took the detectives close to half an hour to empty the SUV and begin organizing everything in the cottage.

McGaven had a folding whiteboard with legs that he set up next to the dining table. It wasn't ideal having the murder investigation spread out in the main area but it was the best place for them to work.

Katie set up the computers and printer and sorted out the files. She would begin a killer profile on paper soon, but she had already started to compile it in her head. She took her personal bag as well as Cisco's stuff into one of the bedrooms. She wouldn't unpack until later. Right now, she was ready to check out the area where the cement building should be located.

McGaven set up the internet and Wi-Fi links and began typing out several search words for the cement building in Coldwater Creek. His searches were set up to go through several databases before rendering results.

"One down," he said.

"You ready?" Katie was becoming impatient.

"One more thing," he said as he pulled out three surveillance cameras. One was for the interior and looked like a nice small mantel clock. He placed it on a bookshelf so it had almost a one-hundred-eighty-degree perspective of the interior.

Both Katie and McGaven secured the other cameras, one in the backyard and one at the front door. They used a ladder they found in a garden shed to make sure the cameras had a decent view.

"Okay," said Katie. "Everything looks good. Are they set up on your phone?"

McGaven thumbed through some security applications on his cell and found what he was looking for. He showed her that he could see the three areas. "Everything looks good."

"Let's go," she said.

Katie drove to the Bates hiking and campgrounds. She did a quick drive around and saw that no one was parked. As a secondary precaution, Katie found a secluded place that would shelter the Jeep from anyone driving past the location.

Once out of the SUV, Katie secured her Glock in her hip holster, making sure it was ready in case it was needed. McGaven did the same. She quickly changed shoes to more appropriate hiking attire. The air was cool but there was no rain in sight. She fitted Cisco with his search harness, which consisted of a slightly padded non-tear material that protected his chest and allowed breathability. Katie snapped a long lead on him and they were ready to go.

"You ready?" said McGaven. He didn't need to ask, but it was a sort of code between them to say let's get moving.

"Yep," she said as she slipped her cell phone in her jeans pocket.

The detectives crossed the quiet road and began to walk up the narrow path, which they had done only two days ago, but this time, they proceeded with caution.

They didn't have to go very far before Katie noticed several sets of boot prints around the area. "I guess the owner of the hunting shop and his buddies did come out here to check out the traps."

"Looks like."

McGaven took lead, with Cisco in the middle and Katie taking up the rear position. The path was narrow and it was easier hiking in single-file formation.

Katie felt a prickling sensation on her arms and up the back of her neck. It was familiar to her, the anticipation of something, but it also acted as a reminder that they were looking for the unknown.

They reached the area where the traps had been rigged, but everything was now gone. The shoe prints were visible and appeared to have walked around to all the trees in a twelve-foot radius.

"It looks like the men were here checking the traps out," he said.

"Or removing the evidence." She walked around the trees and spotted the two logs she had thrown to deactivate the traps. "It still seems suspicious."

McGaven scrutinized the area as well, looking at the ground and up in the branches. He walked to the edge of the circle of trees. "Without a map or coordinates, which way do we go?"

"Sergeant West said that it wasn't far across the street from the Oak Valley Creek, so I say we go east until we see something that might lead to the building."

Cisco was in search mode and checked out the trees and footprints in the area.

"Can you get Cisco to pick up a lead?"

"If someone has been here and at the abandoned building recently, he should be able to track. But if no one has been here in a while, we might have to find it using our detective skills." Katie let out the lead to about ten feet in front of her. She gave the German command, "*Such.*"

The dog's demeanor changed at the training command, knowing it meant business. His body stiffened, his head held higher, pricked ears pointing forward listening intently, while his tail relaxed.

The detectives walked carefully with heightened senses, Katie and Cisco leading.

It was second nature to read her K9 partner and Katie knew Cisco's every twitch, head snap, and pace. She watched him carefully for any indication that there was a building close.

"There had to be a road or driveway where SWAT could bring their vehicles up," said McGaven.

"It's been a few years and several winter seasons since. Maybe it's washed away and more difficult to see?"

McGaven kept looking around to see any indication of a roadway.

They moved slowly and cautiously.

There was a hint of smoke again.

Katie stopped. "You smell that?"

"Yeah, I thought I caught a whiff earlier."

Katie continued to lead the way a little bit faster, going east round groups of trees and expecting to see a large cement building appear at any moment. The birds had been chirping when they had started the hike, but now it was quiet. She glanced up but the forest was still, no breeze, and if there were birds in the trees, they were silent.

"Wait," said McGaven. "I think I found something."

Katie turned to see her partner look at the ground several yards back. She and Cisco hurried to his side. There were chunks of cement in all shapes and sizes, which could have been caused by an explosion from SWAT training.

"Here's part of a rural road," he said, running his hand along the dirt where it looked as if there were old tire tracks from heavy trucks.

Katie stood up straight and looked southeast. "That would mean the building would be in that direction."

She and Cisco hurried. She now had the dog reeled in at

her side. There was a cluster of small oak trees and several more pines. The undergrowth was dense with dead branches and tall weeds. They forced their way through the foliage to find, just behind the thicket, the side of a cement structure.

"There it is," she said. They had found the building. For some reason even the sight of it made Katie edgy and uncomfortable.

"It really is here," said McGaven. He pushed some of the dead brambles out of the way.

"Yeah, but it looks more like an ancient building hidden in the forest than an old storage place." Katie moved in for a closer look.

The building was definitely as large as Sergeant West had described. The structure was two stories with very few windows, all of which were on one side. Weeds and ivy had grown up the sides and covered most of the roof. The color of the exterior wasn't the off-white that a cement building should be, but rather a yellowish green, from lichen and mold and old leaf-fall. The roof was of heavy composite, which had partially disintegrated with age. However, the edges and corners of the roofline were still sharp and intact.

Katie had never seen anything like it. It reminded her of a bomb shelter or special bunker. It seemed like a strange location for it, but maybe that was the point.

Looking around and walking back and forth, McGaven said, "How do we get in there?"

Katie followed Cisco who had found the faint, worn path that must have once been used to go into the building. "Over here, I think."

They walked through the trees following the faint line that was packed down from years of people moving back and forth.

Katie came to an area where there were rocks outlining an entrance to the cement building. There was an old heavy wooden door missing its doorknob, which had left behind it a round, empty hole. But that wasn't what made her gasp a breath in, causing Cisco to sense her distress and give a low growl. It was the black spray paint on the door at eye level and the four letters spelling out:

*MORE...*

.

# TWENTY-TWO

*Wednesday 1400 hours*

The word hung in the air as if the killer had just whispered it into Katie's ear. The atmosphere seemed to cool around her. As McGaven snapped photos of the door with his cell phone, Katie moved closer and touched the hole, which at one time had had a regular locking handle. She could feel even cooler air blowing from the inside. It intrigued her, but she realized that there were most likely cracks and holes in the building allowing for air to flow freely—especially if the SWAT team went through training exercises with flash bangs and bullets that put stress on the old structure, chipping away at its interior.

McGaven turned his phone toward Katie. "What do you think? I know it's not real science, but..."

Katie looked at two photos; one was from Ivy's back and the other from the cement building's doorway. The formation of the letters, especially the "m" and "e" with the added swooping flare, were similar. "You're right. It wouldn't hold up in court, but for our purposes it looks like these two inscriptions were made by the same person. Text the images to John to see if he agrees."

McGaven nodded in agreement. "What do you want to do?"

Katie was about to push the door open.

"Wait. Let me rephrase that. We should have a team search and investigate this building."

"By team, do you mean Chief Baker and Officer Lane? Or maybe the guys from the hunting store? Or wait, why not Officer Daniels, although who knows where he even is half the time." Katie stared hard at her partner. She hated sounding so sarcastic and implying that everyone in law enforcement in Coldwater Creek was unreliable, but they were flying blind in this investigation.

"Okay, okay. I see where you're going, but we need to stay alert and safe. Understand?"

"Fine. We'll stay together. Don't worry, Cisco will protect us."

He smiled. "I know that, but all I have is this mini flashlight," he said as he pulled it out of his pocket.

"I have a flashlight app on my phone, so we're good."

"Katie, you have to stop and think about this," he said, lowering his voice.

"Let me put your mind at ease. We don't know when this was spray-painted on the door—it could have been a couple of years ago. And I don't see any footprints or tracks around here that look recent." Katie still had reservations about the building, but it wasn't from anyone inside—killer or no killer—it was the condition of the building that bothered her the most. However, it was still standing so she was going to take her chances.

"Let's do a walk-through of the building and then we can reassess," he said.

"Okay, but we stick together."

"Absolutely."

Katie rewound Cisco's lead, making it slack and about five feet out from her. She glanced to her partner as a routine check before pushing the door. It was much heavier than it looked, and the hinges were old and rusted. The door wasn't hollow but solid and more than five inches thick. She used her weight and pushed harder. The frame was intact, but the hardware was worn, warped, and screeched a terrifying sound. Chills ran down Katie's spine as a wave of cold penetrated her body.

The door had opened a couple of feet, just enough for them to squeeze through.

McGaven flipped on his small flashlight and the beam lit up the area, casting eerie shadows.

The cement interior seemed empty, but they soon realized there was a never-ending maze of room after room, making the building resemble a disjointed jigsaw puzzle. There were pass-through window openings that made her glance at them twice, as if someone could be hiding behind one. It reminded Katie again of being in some kind of bomb shelter. The temperature was ten degrees cooler than the outdoors and most likely didn't deviate but a few degrees no matter what time of year. Strangely, there was no detectable smell. No mold. No musty odor. No remnant of what was once inside—and no leftover stink from SWAT drills.

Katie watched Cisco's demeanor as they moved forward through the maze of rooms. Sometimes he disappeared around a corner and it was difficult to see his black outline pausing every once in a while. There were scattered shell casings speckled throughout from the SWAT maneuvers.

"There's nothing here, just rooms," said McGaven. "And more rooms."

"Doesn't that seem odd?"

"Not really. It's a cement building, about seventy years old. Outdated for usefulness. There's no access. I can see why the city council wants to demolish it." McGaven swung the light from left to right, illuminating every corner. He maintained about a five-foot distance behind Katie.

It made perfect sense to Katie that this building would make a great hiding place, a secret meeting place, or even a place to keep someone against their will. Who would even know they were there? It was just far enough away from regular streets and homes to make it completely isolated. The hiking and camping areas were plentiful in other areas, and most wouldn't venture off the trails. There were no resting places, picnic areas, or campgrounds near that would help to attract locals or visitors.

"You're quiet. That's worrisome," said McGaven.

"Just thinking... I'm sorry, but this building gives me the creeps and seems more like the home for a sinister predator than a surplus warehouse."

"Noted."

"Why would this town need a structure like that? Out in the middle of nowhere? Actually... it's a perfect place for this town."

"Now, you're not getting jaded about Coldwater Creek, are you? You need to stay objective."

"Noted," she said. Katie had to admit to herself that she did have less than favorable feelings about this town. She needed to heed McGaven's suggestion to stay objective.

Cisco had been using his tracking senses, which kept him using his nose at half his own height above the floor. He was aware of everything around them, even things the detectives couldn't see and hear, but he didn't keep his nose to the ground. Suddenly he stopped and kept his body still and his eyes focused straight ahead.

Katie raised her right hand to indicate to McGaven that something was up.

All three of them stood still between two rooms. Listening. Watching. Waiting for something to show itself.

Cisco released a low guttural growl and his hackles rose from between his shoulder blades down to the top of his tail.

Katie strained to hear anything—but it was quiet with the occasional whoosh of a breeze filtering through.

McGaven swept his searchlight. The beam showed something in the next room on the floor. It looked large and dark. "Keep moving, slowly."

Katie followed the direction of Cisco's nose but was unable see precisely what the object was.

As they moved deeper into the room, she made out a wooden crate that had been turned on its side to make a makeshift table. The top had been slightly burned, blackened and waxy, from the use of candles.

"Is that what we saw in Ivy's photos?" she said, remembering the blurry images of a woman and a candle.

"It definitely looks like it."

Cisco curiously checked out the improvised table, sniffing the top and underneath before padding back next to Katie.

"There was something here, but it has been cleaned up," she said. There were traces of ash and it was difficult to tell if it was something like paper or an object that had been burned. "I wonder why they didn't take this?"

"Maybe the person was in a rush or they left it for others."

"Others?" said Katie. She had never thought about more than one person.

"This could just be a partying place for the local kids."

"But, there would be signs of kids. Garbage, beer bottles, and fast-food wrappers." She looked around the room. "Also, what's the one thing that you would expect to see in an abandoned building, either inside or out, that we don't see here?" She watched McGaven look around.

"Graffiti," he said.

"Doesn't that seem strange to you?"

He nodded.

Katie used her cell phone to take several shots of the room, trying to replicate the angle of the women in Ivy's photos. "We might have found the place where those photos were taken, but not who or why."

Photos done, Katie and McGaven, with Cisco in the lead, quickly went through the rest of the first floor of the cement building. The stairs leading to the second floor had been blocked with rubble—there wasn't an obvious way to enter the upstairs. It looked like there had been an explosion a while ago—that would line up with when SWAT ran maneuvers here.

"Let's go. We can come back with others to get access to the second floor," said Katie. "We can bring tools and better flashlights too." She thought about it. "Wait, let's look for another entrance."

Katie and Cisco hurried to the opposite side of the first floor and found a rickety wooden staircase. She began to climb carefully but soon realized that the stairs were solid under her weight. She reached the top where a large reinforced door with heavy locks stood. "Strange," she said, examining it.

"What do you see?" said McGaven from below.

"Looks like a new door, heavy, reinforced, and some serious locks. We definitely can't get in without proper tools." Katie was disappointed. A new door and heavy reinforced locks meant only one thing. There was something important on the other side. Something shiny caught her eye, so she bent down, retrieving a nine-millimeter bullet that had never been shot. She rolled it between her thumb and forefinger.

"What is it?"

"A nine-mill bullet."

"Strange."

"Maybe not," she said. "We'll have to come back prepared so that we can break down the door."

"Now's the time we could use SWAT's expertise," he said.

"That's for sure." She was disappointed at not knowing what was being hidden behind the door.

"We have a ton of work to do back at the office—the lake cottage."

Katie thought of the autopsy reports for Nikki and Dawn. A chill ran through her.

As they were heading back through the disjointed rooms, Katie stopped McGaven. "Does it seem like we're being played?"

"What do you mean?"

"Well, I still can't help but think that the chief and others are keeping information from us—but somehow in a way that will make it appear that they're doing everything they can. Almost like they want us to fail. I'm sorry, that sounds ridiculous, but my instincts keep telling me something's wrong and I'm not sure exactly how to process it. Maybe it's just my suspicious mind and being out of my own town."

"So what you're saying... you think that we've been invited here because of our track record, but they are going to make it almost impossible to solve these murders. Why? Why have detectives from another area to investigate? What would that prove?"

Katie nodded. "It's a theory."

"Almost impossible still isn't impossible," he said. "We'll have to show them that we can solve these cases and expose what's been happening in Coldwater Creek."

"That's exactly what we're going to do. The motive for killing three teenage girls is still muddled."

Katie and Cisco headed to the front door and found it shut. She knew they had left it open after they entered. She motioned to McGaven as she pulled her gun. They proceeded to move in formation on each side of the door, listening.

There was silence outside except for the breeze blowing through the small hole that had once housed the doorknob.

Katie couldn't figure out why they hadn't heard the sound of the door closing along with the terrible screeching of the hinges.

Katie nodded to her partner as she put her left hand on the door and began to pull. Just as the door opened about a foot and she peered out, there were two gunshots.

# TWENTY-THREE

*Wednesday 1530 hours*

Katie and McGaven took cover away from the wooden door, waiting for more gunshots. There were two distinct shots with a couple of seconds between each fire. The sound and the pause between firing indicated to Katie that it was from a large-caliber revolver about fifty yards away.

Katie crouched down next to the right side of the entrance as Cisco instinctively moved to protect the left side of her. She could feel his heat and his heart thumping, ready for anything. For an instant, her mind flung her back to being in one of the gun battles in Afghanistan with her army team. The sounds and scents accosted her, and even though she knew it was a memory, for that moment it suddenly felt as real as it had that day. Perspiration poured off her forehead and down her spine, despite the cool breeze. Concerned that they were pinned down by an unknown assailant, she looked to her partner. McGaven was also crouched down low on the other side of the heavy door. He didn't say a word, but motioned with his hand towards the exit.

Katie nodded. She knew that he meant that he was going to head out and she needed to cover him. They couldn't just wait and it would take too long once they called for the police chief or officers to reach them.

McGaven made eye contact again, to make sure she knew what he was going to do. She understood completely. They had been through many dangerous situations together and this circumstance was no different.

Katie unhooked Cisco from his tracking lead and coiled the leash attaching it to her jacket. Cisco was trained to stay with Katie as she moved through battle and gunfire. Inside the cement building, it was no different than being in a foreign country. She watched McGaven count down with his fingers from three to one...

He pulled the heavy creaky door open as Katie took up her cover position next to him directing her weapon in front of her. For such a tall man, McGaven showed how agile and stealthy he could be during stressful moments.

Katie watched him move out of the building and into a cluster of trees. There were no more shots. She watched every angle from her vantage point for any sign of movement. She kept the area in sight as her partner moved deeper into the trees and took cover again. Then it was her turn and he would cover her.

McGaven gave the thumbs-up and then sighted his weapon farther into the forest.

Katie reached down and patted Cisco's left side. She could feel his accelerated breathing, his body poised; he was ready to move in sync with her. There was a part of her that wished she hadn't brought him, but as she glanced downward and saw his expression—driven and eager—it made her realize how lucky she was to have him there.

She didn't need to give Cisco a command; he knew exactly what to do and would stay next to her until she commanded him otherwise. Katie inched forward and stood up, looking from left to right. She ran with speed and her footsteps made little noise on the forest floor. She had sighted her cover in the next group of overgrown pine trees. The large boughs bent down towards them, as if welcoming her and Cisco in their arms.

Katie made it to the largest tree and crouched down with one knee on the ground and the opposite foot planted firmly. Cisco huddled in beside her and waited. She scanned the area, listening for anything out of the ordinary around her, but there was nothing. From experience, though, she knew that there was someone waiting—unmoving.

Katie felt a hand on her left arm. McGaven had made his way to her. Both detectives searched the surrounding area, but still there was nothing.

"What do you want to do?" whispered McGaven.

"I know that the shots were from over there," she said softly, pointing straight ahead in the thickets.

Katie and McGaven moved in unison, each one responsible for checking beside and in front of them. The forest seemed to buffer them from anything else. The trees, overgrown grass, and tall dead weeds, protected them from the unknown.

*Thump...*

*Thump...*

*Thump...*

Katie mouthed the words, "What is that?"

McGaven shook his head.

Both were cautious as they moved forward.

Katie looked at everything as if it were a trap.

Without warning or a command, Cisco bolted ahead of them and disappeared in the trees.

Katie's fear had been realized. She called out, "Cisco, *platz*," which told the dog to stop and lie down in his tracks. "Cisco!"

Katie and McGaven ran after the dog. The K9 seemed to

know where he was going because every time they caught up, the dog bolted as if making them follow him.

Finally, Katie turned a corner and stumbled upon an old man sitting on a tree that had fallen in the forest.

She stopped.

Cisco sat next to the old man, who had a long gray beard and was wearing a long raincoat, old ratty boots, and holding a .45-caliber handgun in his right hand. The dog was relaxed and panted lightly, as if had known the man for years. It deeply troubled Katie. She felt her world begin to split and didn't want to think about the reality of losing Cisco.

Raising her Glock and aiming it directly at the man, Katie demanded, "Put the gun down."

McGaven followed suit, preparing his weapon as well. "Put it down now!"

Instead of lowering the gun, the old man leaned over to Cisco and said, "What do you think?"

Katie blinked in astonishment. Questions flitted through her mind. Who was the old man and what he was doing holding a gun? His weather-beaten face had miles of creases with a history to support them. She estimated that he had to be at least eighty years old.

"Cisco, *hier*," she said calling the dog to her.

Cisco stood and immediately trotted over to Katie and took his position.

Relief filled her but Katie didn't lower her weapon. She noticed a walking stick leaning next to the old man.

"Who are you?" said McGaven.

"I could ask you the same," the old man said. "You're not one of the local cops, so I'd venture a guess that you're outta-town cops."

"Detectives," she said. "Lower your weapon."

"Ah, detectives. That's what this town really needs. Did you know there's a killer on the loose?" He coughed and laughed under his breath. He put his revolver back inside his coat in its holster, but he stayed seated. He showed the detectives his hands in good faith.

Katie slowly lowered her gun, but didn't immediately holster it. "Let's start from the beginning."

"If you like," he said.

"Who are you?

"I was born Joshua David Kimball," he said.

"Mr. Kimball, why were you shooting out here?" said McGaven who had already holstered his gun.

"Shooting at the damn squirrels, but my eyesight has failed me. Afraid I'm not much of a shot with those furry little rats."

"Who else is out here with you?" said Katie. She noticed his eyes were pale blue, making it appear that he was blind, but she knew that he could see them.

"Just me."

"Where do you live?" she said.

"I have a cabin a quarter of a mile west."

"You live alone—out here?" said McGaven.

"Son, I told you it was just me. Shelby used to live with me but she died six months ago."

"Your wife?" said Katie as she finally holstered her weapon.

"No, lost the only woman I ever loved almost twenty years ago. Shelby was my dog, a German shepherd. Had her almost fifteen years."

Katie thought about the traps, but knew by the physical capability of Joshua he wasn't able to climb trees to set them. "I'm sorry to hear that." She eyed the walking stick and wanted to stay on track even though her heart ached for his losses. "Were you down on the road across from the Bates campgrounds on Sunday night?"

"I don't reckon."

Katie and McGaven moved closer to the old man.

"Well that's interesting because there are several walking

stick holes in a cluster around the area where possibly a killer stopped his car," said Katie watching the man closely.

"Don't know nothing about that. Holes are holes and can be made anytime by hundreds of things. But you as detectives should know that."

"Well, I bet if we compare your walking stick to the holes, they'll match. And since it was raining, we have a pretty good idea they were recently made."

"I see. You must be forensic detectives?"

"Cold-case homicide," said McGaven.

Katie could see that her partner liked the old man. He relaxed his posture and he seemed to be entertained.

"I bet she's solved a lot of those cold cases," said Joshua to McGaven.

McGaven laughed. "More than you know."

Katie glanced at her partner.

"She's solved every case that has come her way."

Joshua studied Katie. She knew that his sight was poor, but he still looked at her closely.

"I would have guessed that," said Joshua. "If I were a betting man."

"Mr. Kimball, we are here to investigate three murders. If you know anything, anything at all, we would appreciate your cooperation," she said.

"Well, you know my name. What's yours?"

Katie sighed. "I'm Detective Katie Scott and my partner, Detective Sean McGaven, from the Pine Valley Sheriff's Department."

"Nice to meet you and this is...?" he said, gesturing towards the dog.

"This is Cisco."

"Why do I get the feeling this isn't any regular dog?"

"He's a retired military K9."

"Hmm, how many tours did you do?"

"Two, but we're not here to talk about me. We're trying to solve a murder, actually three murders—teenage girls, to be exact. And time isn't really on our side."

"Well, I wouldn't know anything about that." He rubbed his hands and wrist.

Katie noticed a faded tattoo on the back of his right hand. "With all due respect, I don't believe you." She decided to tone down her approach. "We've been here since Sunday night. Our car broke down and we landed here just as there was a murder. Our boss talked to Chief Baker, and well, here we are."

"I see," he said.

"Your town seems nice, but I get the feeling that not everyone is telling us the complete truth. Even you," she said.

The old man stood up and wavered slightly before he grabbed his walking stick. "Very well. Lucky for you I trust Cisco. Follow me." He turned and began walking west, moving at a good pace for his age.

Katie looked at McGaven.

"You heard the man," he said.

Katie wasn't relieved. In fact, she worried that they might be walking right into a trap. There wasn't any indication of a house or cabin where they were going. She would have preferred to do a background check on Joshua Kimball first and speak to the chief before following him to his cabin in the dense forest. Alert, with her senses highly tuned to their surroundings, Katie made sure they were alone and no one was tracking them. She kept Cisco close to her side as they moved deeper into the forest.

# TWENTY-FOUR

*Wednesday 1645 hours*

Katie followed McGaven and Joshua deeper into the maze of trees. She and Cisco lagged behind so she could scan the area as they went to make sure they weren't being lured into an ambush or being watched. Now, more than ever, her gut instinct told her that nothing was as it seemed, so she had to stay on the offense. Her military training kicked into high mode.

It took less than fifteen minutes before Katie began to see signs of habitation. There was cut timber stacked neatly in a protected area for firewood, animal skins were drying on a wooden frame, and several long garden pots had plants growing in them. It appeared that Joshua was self-sustaining, and probably living off grid. That could account for why his house or cabin wasn't on the maps they previously studied.

Katie noticed that the forest was quiet, no sounds of animals or even the wind intermittently fanning through the trees. As they approached Joshua's home, she detected the distinct sound of running water. She knew that it wasn't Oak Valley Creek, but it could be a smaller creek running behind the cabin.

She glanced down at Cisco, who trotted along happily like they were on a hike. Katie knew to pay attention to Cisco's behavior; dogs could sense things long before most humans.

Katie heard McGaven talking to Joshua but didn't hear exactly what they were talking about. She hurried her pace, rounding the last tree. There was a good-sized cabin, but it wasn't like a typical hunting or fishing cabin, it was a custom home. Obviously well maintained, the residence was one story, taking up a fair share of the forest floor. Logs of light wood piled up made up the structure.

Beneath hanging planters that must've had blooming flowers in the springtime, there was a well-worn welcome mat with now-faded birds and flowers imprinted on it. Just left of the cabin was a black cast-iron pot hanging over an open fire, simmering with what seemed to be soup, which caught Katie's senses.

On the right side of the cabin was a large stainless tank. It looked to be about eight feet tall in a slender cylinder. Katie guessed that to be Joshua's water supply. There were several short tubes attached to the side, which indicated it had some type of purification system. Everything around the cabin seemed clean, organized, and highly efficient.

Katie watched McGaven follow Joshua into the cabin. She and Cisco stepped up onto the porch and then stood in the home's entryway. The walking stick leaned against the wall on the right side of the doorframe. The smell of coffee caught her nose and she immediately craved a cup of java. She moved farther into the home.

"Detective Scott," said Joshua. "Would you like a cup of coffee?"

"Yes, that would be nice, thank you," she said. The deep dense canopy of the forest made it difficult for sunlight to penetrate and Katie had become chilled.

Joshua handed her and McGaven each a large cup.

"Thank you," the detectives said.

The rich hot drink warmed Katie almost immediately.

"Now, what would you like?" said Joshua to Cisco. He went to the sink, where there was a unique faucet, and filled a bowl of water. Bending down carefully, he put the bowl on the floor as Cisco gratefully drank.

Katie couldn't bring herself to completely trust Joshua, but she would try to get some answers about the murders and the town.

Joshua took off his long jacket and hung it on a hook by the door. "Now, please sit down and we'll see what I can help you with." He took off his holster and hung it on another hook, which he had done many times before.

"Thank you," said McGaven.

Katie and McGaven moved into the living room. There was a couch and a chair, both well- worn and decades old. However, they were well cared for, as was the interior of the cabin. A colorful knitted afghan was folded over the back of the chair, which was clearly where Joshua spent his time. There was no television, but Katie saw in the corner on a small wooden table was a CB radio and a laptop computer. She wondered how they were powered. There were two lamps giving light to the interior, but they were dimmer than usual light bulbs.

As McGaven and Katie took a seat on the couch, Joshua sat in his comfortable chair that faced the fireplace. Cisco stretched out on a small woven rug in front of the fire. Katie realized the fireplace smoke they had detected earlier was likely coming from here.

"Now, this is better, right?" said Joshua.

"Mr. Kimball, how long have you lived here?" said Katie.

"I think, what we've been through, you can call now call me Joshua."

"Joshua then," she said.

"Let's see now, we bought fifty acres about fifty years ago. Long before the town was as populated as today."

"Fifty years?" said McGaven.

"Yes. We built this cabin piece by piece more than forty years ago. Been here ever since." He took a drink of coffee, savoring it.

Katie tried to imagine building a cabin in this location more than forty years ago, and he had been alone for twenty years. "Do you have family?"

"Afraid not." He looked to the wall where several framed photos were hanging. "My son was killed in Sacramento during a store robbery—it's been about thirty years now."

Katie felt her heart ache for what this man had been through only to be alone now. "I'm sorry, Joshua. As I said earlier, we were brought in to investigate the murders here."

"I understand."

"But you don't think we're going to be able to do that," said Katie slowly. Her intuition seemed to override what they've learned so far.

"Not my place to say."

"But you don't think so," said McGaven.

"I'd imagine that you two have hit some closed doors."

"Some."

"It's not my place to tell you what to do."

"But it is your place to tell us if you know something about the murders," said Katie. She kept his gaze because she recognized that he knew something.

Joshua laughed, revealing his sparse teeth. "I bet you don't make a lot of friends, Detective Scott."

"Tell us what you know."

"About?"

"About what you saw on Sunday night."

The old man sighed and leaned back to get more comfortable. "It was raining hard, so I didn't see much."

Katie smiled. "But you saw something."

"I see a lot of things that aren't my business. But on Sunday night, I did see a car driving up to the place you said."

"And?"

"The car almost ran me over, but they didn't see me."

Katie waited patiently.

"My eyesight isn't great, but I saw a blue, gray, maybe green, four-door car come to a skidding stop. A young woman got out of the passenger side and ran down the hill."

"Could you identify the woman?" said McGaven.

"I'm afraid not. Saw dark long hair, but her face was hidden by her hood and she ran off so fast."

"What about the driver?" said Katie.

"Same. I could tell it was a man with a hood pulled around his face, but I couldn't tell if he was old or young. If I had to guess, I'd say twenties-thirties. But again, I don't know. I swear that's all I know."

"Anything else you can remember would be helpful. Did he have a limp? Could you see anything about his hands? Was he carrying anything? Even if you think it's not important—it could prove to be."

"I'm sorry, but that's all I know."

"How did the woman seem? Scared? Mad?"

"I'd definitely say scared; she tripped once and then ran."

"You didn't recognize either one of them from town?"

"No."

"I get the feeling that there's something else," said Katie.

Joshua sat silent for a moment. "When the man left the car and went after the woman, I walked up to the car. I'm not sure why, curious, I guess."

"What did you see?" said McGaven. "What was inside?"

"It was empty. I couldn't read the odometer, but it was more than one hundred thousand miles, maybe two."

"What else?"

"There was some clothing rolled up in the back and a small towel on the passenger seat. I think there was blood on the interior's door, but again, it's difficult for me to tell colors sometimes, especially in poor lighting."

"Anything else?"

"That's all I know."

"Can you tell us anything about people here in Coldwater Creek?"

He laughed again. "That's quite a bagful."

"What do you mean?"

"This town isn't what it used to be. People keep secrets here now, and don't want anyone poking around."

"We're trying to solve a murder case. Three murders, to be exact—teenage girls. We need to know what those secrets are."

"What do you want to know?" he asked as he gazed out the window.

"Well, we've been working with Chief Baker. He's the one who got permission from our sheriff to work these cases, but he..."

"But he hasn't been forthcoming."

"Well yes."

"I knew his dad, Henry Baker, well. Good man. But he passed away about ten years ago. Many good people either passed or moved away. Then..." He stopped mid-sentence.

"What happened here?" said Katie.

"I can't say precisely, but things began to change. People were different. Secrets. Secret meetings of sorts."

"But there haven't been any homicides here," said McGaven. "Just a few accidents."

"Accidents. Yes, I suppose that's what they would say."

"They weren't accidents?" said Katie.

"I'm not an investigator, but things seemed fishy." He glanced at his wall of photos again. "There was a drowning about two years ago. They said it was an accident, but I think they may be wrong."

"What makes you think it wasn't an accident?"

"Well, a few things. Richard Winters was an expert outdoorsman—he was in his early forties. He would take tourists on adventures like whitewater rafting, mountain climbing... you name it. So when I heard he drowned by accident and it wasn't because of a harsh winter storm, I didn't buy it. The cause of death was drowning—not a stroke or heart attack that caused the drowning."

"What do you think?"

"I think someone killed him. Why, I couldn't tell you... but he obviously knew something he wasn't supposed to..."

His comments spurred Katie's imagination and curiosity. She wondered if there were more of these unusual accidents.

Katie looked at the wall of photos and saw two diplomas from Southern California for engineering. That made sense to her. Retire and build your log cabin in the woods to enjoy the rest of your life away from the hustle and bustle of the city. "Did you know any of the recent victims? Ivy Miller. Nikki Prager. Dawn Cromwell?"

"The names don't ring a bell. Who have you met since you've been here?" He eyed the detectives curiously.

"Chief Baker, Officer Lane, Officer Daniels, Dr. Deborah Sanders," said McGaven.

"Mama from the Wild Iris Inn, her son Lenny, Mrs. Prager, morgue technicians, Sal from the garage," said Katie. "We're going to be interviewing the owner of the hunting and fishing store and a tattoo artist."

"I see."

"What can you tell us about them?" she said.

"Not much, I'm afraid, but my advice is to watch your backs and pay attention. Don't take anything at face value. Look deeper."

"Like?" said Katie.

Joshua remained quiet.

"Anything else?" said McGaven.

"You're the detectives. Detect. Dig. Don't give up until you find your answers."

"Thank you for your time and for the great coffee," said Katie. She pulled out a business card and put it on one of the lamp tables. She wasn't sure if Joshua had a cell phone, but she figured he'd have a way to contact them. She jotted down her address at the lake cottage.

Joshua rose with the detectives and took the opportunity to pet Cisco, who leaned in close to him. "You take care of them." He turned to Katie. "There's a faster trail. Just go out the front door and take a left to follow the path."

Katie and McGaven stopped at the front door waiting for Cisco to join them.

"Oh, just one more thing," said Katie. "What do you know about the cement building we just came from?"

It was the first time that Joshua showed any emotion. "Not a good place."

"What was it used for?"

"This and that. Even a SWAT team used to run their drills, I guess you would call them. Quite the noisy group."

"Does the word 'more' mean anything to you? It was spray-painted on the front door of the building.

He shrugged.

"Joshua, please, what are you not telling us? We know that some kind of meetings took place there. What were they doing?" Katie wouldn't let Joshua look away. "Tell us. Teenage girls are being killed in your town, and we need all the help we can get to stop any more innocent lives being taken."

"I don't know, but what I do know... they were getting stronger."

"Stronger?"

"That's all I'm going to say. I'm not going to speak out of line on things I don't have the facts on." He paused. "If I were to give you any advice... start with this town... at the very beginning."

Katie, McGaven, and Cisco walked out the door as it shut quietly behind them.

"Guess that's it?" said McGaven.

"For now."

The detectives started down the trail.

"Meaning?"

"It's a place to dig for more information."

*Don't take things at face value...*

"I'm on it," he said.

As they headed down the trail, Katie kept running through the entire conversation between them and Joshua. There was more behind the new information and answers the old man had told them.

"What do you think?" said McGaven finally.

"I think... I still think that we've got to get to the bottom of what's going on here and the killer will eventually surface. It's like doing the perimeter of the puzzle first and then it begins to fill in the rest."

McGaven's cell phone alerted to a text message. "Okay. Looks like we're on."

"For?"

"Medical examiner Deborah has some things ready for us and wants us there ASAP. And she has requested that we come in the service entrance around back," he said.

"Sounds like we're moving up in the food chain..."

"Looks like."

"I think it's about time to rattle the cages and see what shakes out."

# TWENTY-FIVE

*Wednesday 1805 hours*

Katie and McGaven drove into the parking lot for the medical examiner's office. They had made great time taking the trail that Joshua suggested—it cut their hike in less than half the time. The talk with the old man and the visit to the elusive cement building still lingered in Katie's mind. She was anxious to get back to the cottage and get started on the murder board and dig for more information on some of the townspeople as well as background on the area. It was like hunting for treasure because they didn't know what was waiting to be found.

Now looking at the cement building they were about to enter, it reminded Katie of the same type of architecture, if that's what it could be called, as the two-story cement structure in the woods. Were they built by the same people? By the same corporation?

Katie found an empty space to park next to the back entrance. The weather was cool and it was shady at this time of day. Cisco would be fine waiting in the Jeep—it wasn't appropriate or within agency policies to bring him inside. McGaven set up a security camera on the dashboard, just for added measure, in case anyone or anything wanted to mess with the car or Cisco.

Cisco whined but took a couple of turns in the back seat and settled down for a nap.

Katie and McGaven walked up to the back entrance, where there were two large elevator doors used for the morgue entrance. It was the second floor and they needed to drop to the basement.

Katie searched for a buzzer or an intercom but couldn't find any.

"How do we get in?" said McGaven.

"I'm not sure. Maybe you can text Dr. Sanders?"

McGaven punched in the request, responding to her last text.

Within two minutes, there was a loud mechanical noise that moved huge pulleys, and the elevator doors finally opened wide. It was large enough to drive an entire vehicle into it.

The detectives stepped inside.

Katie couldn't help but be anxious. Once again, without an obvious cue, the elevator began to lower.

Katie tapped her fingers on her leg just as her cell phone alerted. It was Chad. She couldn't speak to him now and made a mental note to call him back. What she wouldn't give to be home having dinner with him instead of going to the morgue.

The large elevator door opened like a well-oiled machine.

Katie immediately recognized the interior. It was vacant—with an almost abandoned feeling. Glancing at her watch, she saw it was after 6 p.m. Most of the staff would be gone.

The detectives stepped out and oriented themselves in the hallway, heading straight to the large exam rooms. The main room, which had a small auditorium with seating, most likely for training and educational purposes, was lit up.

Katie stopped, looking for Dr. Sanders, but there was no

one around. Inside the exam room, there were two gurneys. Both were covered. The only indication that there were young female bodies lying underneath were the feet with pink painted toenails sticking out.

"Where is she?" he said.

"She knows we're here—or somebody does." Katie didn't want to enter the room yet. She would be seeing the girls' bodies soon enough.

Suddenly there was the sound of someone walking down the hallway, heels clicking with every stride. Dr. Sanders rounded the corner.

"Hello, Detectives. Thank you for coming on such short notice. I know you must be terribly busy." She smiled, showing off her perfect teeth and fire-engine-red lipstick. The medical examiner was dressed in a fitted dark navy cocktail dress with matching high heels. She must have noticed the expressions of surprise on the detectives' faces. "Oh, you must be wondering why I'm dressed like this. I'm on my way to a dinner for a friend's birthday party."

Dr. Sanders went to one of the tables and pulled on a pair of gloves as well as slipped on a white lab coat. "Okay, let's get started." There were two file folders waiting and she opened the first one.

Katie, with McGaven slightly behind her, moved farther into the area.

The medical examiner approached the first gurney and pulled back the sheet, revealing the body of Nikki Prager.

The morgue always made Katie flinch, even though the bodies were cleaned up and had been examined fully. There was an element to that process that made victims seem even more vulnerable than they were at their crime scene.

Katie vividly remembered chatting with the girls and the unimaginable heaviness that had been plaguing her came over her again as she looked down at Nikki's body. As with Ivy's death, it was clear her friend had been strangled.

"We have a sixteen-year-old female, Nikki Prager, who was in excellent health. There were no signs of any disease in the body," said Dr. Sanders. She tilted her head, looking closer at the girl's neck. "Cause of death was asphyxia due to strangulation. Manner of death I'm ruling a homicide."

"What type of rope would cause that type of mark?"

"It's consistent with Ivy Miller's neck wounds. I would say a twine rope. You know, like the ones you can find in a hardware store."

Katie nodded. She knew full well that those sorts of ropes were extremely common and would be difficult to run down and individualize. It would be a dead end.

"I'm sorry that I can't be more precise, but rope is rope."

That was a strange description to use for an examination of a homicide victim's wound. "Can you send photos to our CSI supervisor? He may be able to zero in on what made that wound."

"Already done," she said and smiled again.

Katie thought that the red lipstick made the medical examiner look almost ghoulish in the sterile environment with the sharp fluorescent lighting. "Great."

"We did a fingernail scraping as well as combed her body and hair for any foreign particles. And yes," she said, "everything is heading to your forensic supervisor at Pine Valley Sheriff's Department by special courier."

"What was her approximate time of death?" she said.

"I would say between 1 a.m. and 4 a.m. It was cold that night, so the decomposition would be slowed down slightly—making it one hour either way."

That hit Katie hard because it told her they had spoken to the girls only hours before their deaths. Which asked the question… were they meeting someone they knew or were they lured to the location?

"Anything unusual we should know about?"

"Toxicology screen was clean. Neither one of the girls had been drinking or doing any kind of drugs—illegal or prescription."

Dr. Sanders ran her hand along Nikki's arm, turning it slightly to reveal the tattoo.

"Did the same dark profile show under the black light?" asked McGaven as he leaned forward to examine it.

"I thought it might, but unfortunately it didn't."

Katie was disappointed, wanting a specific and unique signature of the killer to link all the victims.

"Her body was relatively clean. She didn't have many defensive wounds. And by my calculations, she was killed after Dawn Cromwell."

Katie looked at Nikki's hair, which had been cleaned and was now lying gracefully on the steel metal table like a crown. The pink tips highlighted on the ends looked more like an adornment. Katie became overwhelmed for a moment and felt as though she wanted to break down. She knew that there might have been a way to save these girls, even if they had kept them under twenty-four-hour surveillance. Anything. She clenched her fist and tightened the muscles in both her arms to push the emotions away so she could concentrate on what they needed to know.

Dr. Sanders left the sheet drawn back from Nikki's body and walked over to the other body. "Brace yourselves, this one isn't pleasant."

The sheet was ripped back, like taking a Band-Aid from a wound. Dawn's body was riddled with scrapes and scratches, both defensive and offensive wounds. It appeared that she had fought with everything she had, but it also looked as if she had been tortured as well. The deep gash across her throat looked to be a savage signature of the killer. Dawn's injuries were evident at the crime scene, but now cleaned up and lying on the table they seemed more extensive. The word "FOREVER" carved into her chest ratcheted up the horror.

Katie tried to piece together the killer's possible motive for the level of violence inflicted. Why Dawn and not the other two girls?

"Dawn Cromwell, fifteen years old, was in good health. She had had an abortion recently—maybe six to eight months ago."

That surprised Katie. She recalled the quiet girl sitting on the bed flipping through magazines. *Fifteen was very young. Who had she been involved with?*

"There were also traces of alcohol in her system and an antianxiety drug—clonazepam," said the medical examiner. She looked at the detectives, pausing and waiting for questions.

Katie was still trying to connect the dots. "Anything more? Any sexual assault?"

"No, no signs of sexual assault or having sex—same as with the other girls. I examined her tattoo as well, but there was no man's profile hidden beneath." Dr. Sanders picked up Dawn's right arm. "There were, however, deep incisions on her tattoo, almost as if the killer, or someone, tried to cross them out. The holes through her wrists and arms were done with construction nails. Pretty gruesome stuff."

"Why do you think she was killed before Nikki?" said Katie.

"If you look closely at some of her cuts, including the word 'forever,' they were inflicted at various times. Some were newer than others." She pointed to various wounds on the body and limbs. "But there weren't any wounds on her face. Her lividity was less than Nikki Prager's."

"She was tortured and killed after Nikki?"

"It appears, but then she received the final slash across her throat. It was a newer incision. Cause of death was hypovolemic shock, caused by hemorrhaging, loss of blood, which led to stopping her heart. I'm also ruling this death as a homicide."

"Do you believe from your examinations the same person committed all three murders?" said Katie.

"If Dawn Cromwell's injuries were consistent with the others, I would say yes. But she wasn't strangled. The only thing I can tell you is that the amount of pressure used to crush the larynxes of the other two girls was the same. It seems consistent. However, there was great force used to torture and slash the throat of the third victim." She watched the detectives' reactions. "All three girls were murdered and excessive force was used."

Katie and McGaven drove back to the cottage and neither said much along the ride. The medical examiner had sent photos and reports directly to McGaven, and said she would be available if they needed her.

"You're not going to say anything?" said McGaven watching his partner closely. "I'm betting Dawn Cromwell's condition at the crime scene as well as her abortion has you thinking."

Katie smiled. "I hate it when you can read me. It's eerie."

"As eerie as this town?"

She turned slowly up the road that paralleled the creek. "First impression of the girls yesterday was that Nikki was more of the alpha girl, but now I'm thinking it might have been the other way around. Dawn fooled us into thinking she was the shy girl and let Nikki do all the talking. She was sexually active to the degree that she'd had to have a fairly recent abortion. It makes me wonder..."

"What about the excessive force used on her?"

"That tells me that the killer must have had some type of interaction with Dawn. A friend, boyfriend, someone new she had met. It was definitely overkill—and that usually means it's personal."

McGaven remained quiet.

Katie turned up the driveway. "We need to find out more about the girls and who they were chummy with in town. But one thing is definite—there's someone in this town, besides the killer, who knows who killed them."

# TWENTY-SIX

*Wednesday 2030 hours*

When Katie and McGaven got back to the cottage, they hit the ground running. Katie immediately set up the murder board to record everything they had uncovered so far, which would help them to decide their next move. It was too late to speak with the tattoo artist and the owner of the hunting and fishing store, but that was first on the list for the following day.

The files Chief Baker left were open and spread out on the table. Katie had notated the names and what the interviews uncovered—if anything. McGaven had printed hardcopies of the pictures of the bodies showing the tattoos and the injuries.

Katie hovered by the kitchen table. There was an abundance of information, but nothing seemed to help or point to her next move. Unfortunately, it felt as if they were getting inundated with information, but nothing was exactly what they needed. She had to figure out the best way to classify what they had so far and, because of time, pick the right evidence to follow.

"Huh," she said.

"Huh what?" McGaven had set up computers on the coffee table and was in the process of initializing searches and sending emails.

"I just realized that we've acquired a ton of information about the town, but very little about the girls. In fact, their autopsies weren't as helpful as I'd hoped."

"I'd say there's a whole host of information from the crime scenes."

"That's not what I mean. Things like the rope, plastic bag, bandana, they are manufactured by the millions and are probably in every type of store. For the most part, those will most likely be dead ends."

"Way to go, partner, let's give up before we start," said McGaven trying to hide his smile.

"I want to look at the behavioral evidence of the three crime scenes. What do we have?" She looked around, trying to figure out where she could put a list for the killer. Katie wanted to keep the boards for crime scenes, forensic evidence, persons of interest, and any miscellaneous information. Grabbing one of the colored pads of sticky notes, she began writing.

"What are you doing?"

"Killer stuff," she said.

"That's nice."

"I'm going to use this large pantry door to stick killer behavior notes to keep them separated from everything else." She began sticking them in neat rows as a starting point that they could elaborate later. "What we know so far..."

KILLER:

*Organized/Disorganized*—specific locations, planned/not planned, time enough to pose bodies, not leaving victim evidence behind: clothing, personal belongings. Trophies? Getting rid of evidence? Were the girls lured or brought? Ivy had been chased by killer after escaping car. Was her crime scene just a matter of convenience and then a starting point that leads to the other crime scenes?

*Strangulation*—posing with suffocation implication (Ivy, Nikki). Choosing to imply suffocation death with the bandana and bag. Why? What's the significance? Convenience? Drama? Fantasy?

*Throat cutting and impalement*—(Dawn) What is the significance? *Why* Dawn and not Ivy or Nikki?

*Carved words on backs*—Ivy (MORE) and Nikki (NEVER), but Dawn's chest (FOREVER). Significance? Sequence?

*Shows signs of passive/aggressive behavior*—organized/disorganized, thought out plans but did they go wrong with Ivy, then torture and overkill force.

*Works in comfort zone*—local? Statistically, criminals usually work within a comfort zone—approximate five-mile radius of where they live.

*Outdoorsman (hunting/fishing)*—bowline knot. Comfortable outdoors.

*Killing for purpose or cause?*

*No signs of sexual assault.*

*Not about power/assertive? Purpose?*

*Knowledgeable about outdoors, knives, ropes, and rural landscapes. Booby traps?*

*Cement building*—connection? "MORE"

"I like it," said McGaven reading over her shoulder.

"It's a start. I feel we're just scratching the surface."

"Is it possible that the killer knew we were investigating and decided to raise the stakes by killing Nikki and Dawn the next day?"

"Good point. It's likely, but that would mean we might have a long wait before he strikes again." Katie bit her lip as she contemplated several things at once. "I was thinking.

Remember when we drove into town and that car raced right at us?"

"Yeah, right before we crashed."

"We didn't crash. We were diverted."

"Splitting hairs," he said.

"Do you remember what color that car was?"

McGaven paused, thinking back. "I think it was dark blue. An older-model four-door. I couldn't be sure what make it was. It could have been domestic or foreign. The weather was brutal and it was next to impossible to see details."

"Right. Joshua said that he saw a car matching that description, but wasn't sure if it was blue or green."

"You think the killer passed us that night?"

"Possibly."

"Let me check on older blue four-door cars registered in Coldwater Creek," he said going back to his computer. "I should be able to search DMV records."

"Joshua also said that it seemed to be a young man, twenties-thirties."

"But he never saw his face."

"You can tell a lot by the way someone moves. I think that's what he was basing his opinion on," she said.

"What's your take on Mr. Kimball?"

Katie paused, thinking about their conversation and how they'd met. "Tough. Been through too many losses. He's reclusive. I think he wants to help us, but there's something stopping him. Not wanting to get involved because it might interrupt his way of life. His conscience says otherwise."

"You think he's telling the truth?"

"If it wasn't for Cisco, I would say I wasn't sure. But Cisco has never steered me wrong about someone's character yet."

There was a sleepy moan from the dog lying on the other end of the couch.

"There are four possible cars, but I just got a hit on a 2009

Chevy Malibu registered to Travis Leonard Ramos," he said. "And, the mailing address is 1227 Main Street."

Katie looked over at her partner. "Isn't that the Wild Iris Inn?"

"Of course," he said. "Mama's name is Sadie *Ramos*. Remember?"

"I do, but there wasn't a Mr. Ramos."

"Lenny, maybe?" said McGaven. "It's an older model car that would fit into a young man's budget."

"Speaking from experience?"

"Something like that." He keyed several coordinates on the laptop. "I'm going to send Denise a few things to check out: Travis Ramos, the Wild Iris Inn, anything newsworthy for Coldwater Creek, anything about the elusive building."

"Great idea."

Denise was the supervisor in the records division and was great at searching for information.

Katie continued sorting through reports and interviews. "We need John's report on the forensics ASAP." She made a list on the board. "I've noted the people we've spoken to in person."

Suddenly there was a loud bang against the side of the cottage, rattling some of the framed prints. Instantly, Cisco stood up on the couch and barked three times.

Katie immediately dropped to her knees and crouched toward the entryway. She grabbed her gun and a flashlight from the side table. McGaven wasn't far behind her. This time he had a large flashlight and his Glock ready.

"It came from the back," she said. "Cisco, *hier*."

The dog was at her side in seconds, waiting for commands. She rushed him into her bedroom and quietly shut the door. Cisco's snorts and low whines pierced the door.

"It wasn't a gunshot," said McGaven.

"It didn't sound like it." She reached the side glass door leading out to the deck area. Turning to McGaven, she said,

"Let's sweep the area. I'll go left and you right? We'll meet around back?"

He nodded.

Two more bangs hit the other side of the house.

Katie's heart raced as she stood up, instantly turning off the interior and exterior lights. There was no use making them a bright target. She had to pause a moment to let her eyes adjust to the darkness.

She touched the door handle, slowly turning it and pulling it open. It moved with ease and perfect silence, like a well-oiled machine. She turned back, looking at McGaven, and he nodded. Twice in one day, she thought, what were the odds? Somebody didn't want them here and they were trying some scare tactics, but what more were they prepared to do? How far would they go?

Katie moved outside quietly, pushing her gun forward along her path. The ground was soft and when she stepped on the wooden deck, it seemed to bow under her feet. She quietly moved around the side of the house not wanting to turn on her flashlight yet. The moon, as well as some of the floodlights from nearby neighbors, illuminated the area enough to see if anyone was hiding.

Making her way to the corner, she used the reflection in the windows in addition to her own view in front of her. She didn't see any movement or indications of someone being on the property. When she rounded the first corner, she saw several dark objects on the ground. They looked like small cylindrical bags, and she didn't want to touch them until she knew exactly what they were.

Moving closer, she recognized them instantly. Beanbag rounds—officially called flexible baton rounds—invented in the 1970s. They were used as a less lethal means within law enforcement in place of shotgun shells. Not all police agencies used them, but many did. Each bag consists of a small fabric "pillow" filled with #9 lead shot weighing less than a pound. The bag is fired from a normal 12-gauge shotgun. When fired, the bag is expelled at around two hundred to three hundred feet per second.

She waited a moment for McGaven, but he still hadn't reached their meeting point. Katie saw a flash of light coming from the creek. When she scanned the area again, there was nothing to see but the many scrubby bushes along the edge that led down to the water's edge. They must've been planted as a way to keep the erosion to a minimum.

Katie looked around again, but didn't see McGaven. She wanted to get to the shoreline and have a look around, wanting to make sure it wasn't just some kids out to get into trouble.

She could see a faint trail leading straight down that was obviously once used as a shortcut to the creek. The sound of water flowing became louder—even though it was called a creek it was more like a mid-grade river. She paused to listen for any voices. Nothing. There was just the sound of the water.

As she inched her way farther, the unstable terrain forced her to holster her weapon. The sandy clay ground became slippery.

Dropping to her butt in a sitting position, Katie had to slide the rest of the way; otherwise, she was afraid she would fall and tumble down the hill. Once she had reached the bottom, the ground was stable but rocky, making her sway as she stood up. She strained to see if there was any movement in the creek. It appeared dark and absent of anyone in a boat or canoe. Where did the beanbag shots come from?

Just as she was about to turn around, Katie was shoved forward with force. Her body hit the creek hard, face down. It felt as if she had dived into stone. Stunned, and finding it difficult to take a breath, she realized that the wind had been knocked out of her. She thrashed in the water to keep her head above the surface. Her vision was obscured by the water in her face but she caught a glimpse of a thin, dark figure dressed in dark clothing with a hood obscuring his face. By the way the person stood, Katie knew it was a man staring at her, curious, studying her. The details of his face or his age weren't discernible from her vantage.

"Hey! Who are you?" she yelled, coughing out water. Her thoughts were jumbled as she fought disorientation, but if the unknown figure was going to kill her, he would have already succeeded.

Finally catching her breath and gaining some strength in her arms and legs, Katie swam against the moving icy water, pushing back toward the water's edge. When she looked at the shoreline again, the man was gone.

Katie dragged herself to the rocky shore, crawling on her hands and knees, and then sat down trying to catch her breath. Her heart rate was high and a pulse in her head pounded in unison. Her first thought as she stared out at the creek and looked up and down the rocky shoreline was that it would have been a perfect place to commit a murder.

*Was that the killer?*

"Katie! Katie!" yelled McGaven. His voice became louder the closer he came.

Katie could hear him above the rushing water, but she was too exhausted to get up. "I'm here," she said, amazed by how weak her voice sounded. "I'm here," she repeated. It took all her strength to raise her right arm.

She began to shiver through her water-soaked clothing and heavy boots. Her teeth chattered. Her wet hair was plastered against the side of her face.

McGaven ran to her and dropped to his knees. "Are you okay? What are you doing down here?" Katie could see his eyes, wide and filled with deep concern.

"I'm okay... I saw a flash... and... I thought someone might have been in a small boat or canoe..."

"You don't ever venture away and not tell me. Especially after today. You got that?"

She nodded.

"Did you see anyone?"

She nodded again.

"Who?"

"I don't know... He pushed me into the water... It almost knocked me out..." Katie could feel her pulse begin to settle down.

"Can you get up?"

"I think so," she said.

McGaven helped her up and put his arm around her waist to help her walk. Her legs felt rubbery beneath her.

"You think you can make it up the hill?"

Katie looked at the hillside she had slid down and wasn't sure if she could make it. "I'll try."

McGaven pulled his cell phone from his pocket and dialed a number. "Yes, this is Detective Sean McGaven. I'm at 3475 Steam Creek Road. A detective has been attacked. Please send Chief Baker immediately." He hung up and helped Katie to climb the hill back to the cottage.

# TWENTY-SEVEN

*Wednesday 2335 hours*

Katie had changed into dry clothes, wrapped herself in a warm blanket, and was on the couch in front of the fire when Chief Baker and Officer Lane showed up a half hour later. Cisco was at her side, never moving an inch away from her. The dog remained quiet but kept a watchful eye on everyone.

"Detective Scott, are you sure what you saw?" said the chief as he made notes.

"Yes, I'm sure."

"You've been through a traumatic experience. Maybe some of the details might be hazy?"

Katie kept her frustration under control. "I've given you my report. Nothing is going to change."

McGaven entered the room. "Looks like the only thing we have on camera are the beanbag rounds hitting the cottage." He looked at Katie. "I'm sorry."

Officer Lane came inside the house carrying a leather satchel. He sat down next to Katie and opened the bag, revealing a medical kit.

"What's this?" said Katie.

"Officer Lane is an EMT. I want to make sure that you're okay; otherwise, I'd have to insist that you go get checked out at the hospital, which is forty miles away."

"I don't think—" began Katie. She just wanted to put the incident behind her and move forward on the investigation.

"I agree," said McGaven, interrupting her. "You should be checked out."

Katie sighed but agreed under protest. The sooner she was checked out, the sooner they would leave.

Officer Lane took Katie's blood pressure. "It's a little elevated, but that's normal after a stressful incident." He checked her pulse, looked into her eyes to see if there were any signs of a concussion, and checked out her wrist. "Everything seems fine, but your wrist might be sprained. Put a cold compress on it and take some aspirin tonight before you go to bed."

"Thank you. I'm exhausted." Katie couldn't help but notice that Officer Lane's boots had mud and fine gravel caked on them. It was recent and consistent to the shoreline. "Were you out for a walk?" she asked, watching the young officer.

"Yeah, I always take an evening walk. It helps me unwind from the day."

"Did you see anything interesting?" she said.

"No. I usually see deer but tonight it was quiet." He didn't look Katie in the eye as he busied himself putting things away in the medical kit. "You should make an appointment with your general practitioner when you get back to Pine Valley—just to be on the safe side."

"Well now, I think we have everything we need for now," said Chief Baker rereading his notebook.

"Aren't you going to take the beanbag rounds as evidence?" she said.

"Of course. Officer Lane here will attend to that."

"Do you use these types of rounds?" said Katie.

"No, we haven't ever had the need to—we're not a big city."

"I see."

"Will you be okay?" the chief said.

"Of course," said McGaven.

"Give me a call if there's any other problem. Most likely it was probably kids or a prank. We've been getting a couple of calls about vandalism at some of the nearby homes." The chief walked through the dining area and spotted the notes about the killer's profile on the cupboard door. He paused to read them, but didn't say anything. "Good night." He moved on.

"Good night, Chief," said McGaven.

"I'll be a minute gathering those shotgun beanbags," said Officer Lane. "And then I'll be out of your hair. Good night."

They left.

McGaven locked the doors and made sure that the cameras were all working properly. He came back to the couch and sat down. "You okay?" There was worry in his eyes as his frown lines were more pronounced.

"Yeah, I'm fine."

"Ever since we've been here, things haven't been normal. I think maybe the secrets Joshua referred to could be what's holding this town on a lockdown."

"I can see your point."

"I'm going to run a few more searches before I turn in—I'm amped from everything and there's no way I could go to sleep right away."

"I'm going to sit here enjoying the fire and gathering my wits," she said.

Cisco grumbled and made himself more comfortable.

"I'm surprised you didn't mention anything about the cement building and Joshua to the chief."

"I'm sure he knows about it, so I didn't feel I needed to

remind him. There will be a more opportune moment." Katie was becoming sleepier by the minute. She shut her eyes, listening to the sound of the crackling fire. McGaven was still talking about the searches when Katie drifted off to the sleep.

# TWENTY-EIGHT

*Thursday 0730 hours*

Katie woke with a gasp and sat up—she had wrestled with bad dreams most of the night, seeing images of the dead girls trying to reach out to her. The fire had burned down and there were only a few embers left behind. She looked around and everything seemed to be as it should. Cisco wasn't on the couch anymore and she could see that McGaven's bedroom door was open. The house was quiet.

Katie stood up and stretched. Her back and wrist were sore and her neck felt like there was gravel in it when she turned side to side. The sun shone in through the windows across the side of the cottage, the rays falling across the floor. It appeared to be a beautiful day, sunny with a few clouds. It was early, which meant it would still be cool outside.

She rummaged around in the kitchen to look for coffee and something to make for breakfast. From under the counter, she found the coffee maker and Mama had supplied the coffee—along with many other things.

A cold wet nose bumped her hand. "Hey, Cisco. Bet you're hungry."

Katie prepared the dog's food and then poured herself a cup of steaming coffee. She scrutinized what to have for breakfast. There were eggs, bacon, and toast available. That was as good as any home breakfast. She left everything on the counter and ready to go, then grabbed her cup of java and went outside with Cisco.

She stood on the deck, sipping her coffee and looking out at the creek. It seemed less gloomy and foreboding in the daytime, observing the rushing water. The image of the person standing at the shoreline, watching, waiting, and studying her made her shiver. It was the killer—her instinct confirmed it, even without any proof. This type of personality profile hinted at the fact the killer felt in control in his hunting and killing grounds, but the appearance of the two detectives showing up made him curious or angry—or maybe both.

She watched Cisco smell every bush and plant around the area. He too stopped and watched the water below, moving his head up and down, catching all the scents.

"Morning." McGaven appeared. He was still dressed in an oversized T-shirt and sweats with his hair not as groomed as usual.

"Morning. There's coffee."

"I know, the smell woke me. It's nice here," he said, standing next to Katie. "Feel better this morning?"

"Yes, but my back and wrist are a little sore. Not moving as fast as I usually do."

"I'm starved," said McGaven.

"Well, there's eggs and bacon for breakfast."

"You had me at coffee."

Katie laughed. They went inside to make breakfast with Cisco following closely behind.

. . .

After breakfast and showers, Katie and McGaven were ready to head out to interview some of the persons of interest in town.

The sound of a loud beeping interrupted their departure.

*Beep... beep beep... beep...*

"Oh, that's a video call," said McGaven hurrying to the computer on the coffee table. "Hey, it's John."

Katie joined her partner and sat down on the couch. She saw John's smiling face and could see the lab behind him. There was also a glimpse of Eva moving about.

"How you guys doing?" said John.

"We're hanging in there. Some strange things are going on and I don't think we're very popular here," said McGaven.

Katie saw John's smile turn into a frown. "Are you getting any help from local police?"

"Some," said Katie. "We're drowning in too much information."

"I assume you read the autopsy reports?"

"Yes. We've met with the medical examiner twice."

"The information we received was good and the evidence was properly packaged. There's some interesting things and I hope what I've found will help you." John shuffled papers around as he moved the laptop to another table. "Okay, I've linked my computer to yours so that you can see what I'm explaining. Eva will be emailing you photos and information so you'll have it."

"Great," said McGaven.

Katie was eager to see what John had found out. And if there was anything that would help them narrow down suspects and assist in what direction to take the investigation.

"Okay, let's start with Ivy Miller."

Katie and McGaven nodded and waited with extreme curiosity.

"First I want to tell you that there weren't any foreign particles that had been scraped from the body, no stray hairs or fibers. But, the rope used to tie around her neck isn't just an ordinary twine rope. It's a nylon rope, not polypropylene. It's consistent with rope used for boating and in marinas."

"Why do you think marine and not construction or something else?" said Katie.

"That's what I was going to tell you. When I examined the rope and carefully deconstructed the bowline knot, I noticed some distinct characteristics. There were areas of the rope that were lighter and darker. Check out the magnification."

Katie saw where the rope was definitely lighter in pigment. "Is that caused by weather? Or manufacturing?"

"Good questions. The lighter areas are caused by extreme exposure to sunshine. So what many marine enthusiasts do is move the rope and retie it differently because of exposure. It allows for more use and avoids wearing out a portion of the rope."

"So it wears evenly, especially if the boat sits for an extended length of time without moving," said McGaven. "What would this rope be used for specifically? Docking? Anchor?"

"Generally this type of nylon rope is used for dock line and towing lighter loads like a dingy, waterboarding, or waterskiing. It takes a while for the UV rays to get to nylon rope, but it eventually happens. I would say this rope was taken from somebody's own stash and not straight off the store shelves. It would most likely be in use now and we could compare them."

"We just need to find the source," said McGaven.

"It could still narrow down the suspect pool with anyone who would have this type of rope for a boat or water activities." Katie thought about who they had met already. Then she conjured the image of the man on shore. Was he the marine enthusiast and outdoorsman?

"We traced the plastic bag and found that it's from a company called ReadyBags and they are extremely common.

You can buy these bags anywhere. I bet you have a box of them in your kitchen right now. I don't think this will help your investigation. Again, it was probably something the killer already had."

"It seems that the killer is using old or used items so there's no way to track him at the local hardware store buying these things," said Katie. "But he doesn't seem concerned about anyone tracking him down by what he already has in his possession." It confirmed her theory of an organized offender who knew the area well—and felt comfortable.

John's face came into view. "Ivy's bracelets were interesting. They aren't just cheap silver bangles you can buy anywhere. They are antique and made from European silver with hallmarks designating where and when they were made. Eva looked up the symbol and it's 1887. This isn't the silver bullet to solve your case, but it will help to tell you something about the victim. I would venture a guess they were probably a gift or passed down from a relative. Might be something worth investigating further?"

"And they were something she seemed to wear all the time," she said, remembering the photograph of Ivy, Nikki, and Dawn.

"Now, the tattoo I can't really help with, but I would say more than likely it was done locally. It would be doubtful she would travel a distance to have it done."

"She and her friends didn't have a car or driver's licenses. We're going to talk with the tattoo guy in town since all the girls had the same rose theme done by the same artist," said Katie.

"The image underneath was done after the tattoo."

"Are you sure?"

"It was showing signs of disappearing—and it's comprised of a mixture of thymolphthalein indicator, ethyl alcohol, sodium hydroxide solution, and water. If it was applied first, then the process of tattooing would have worn most of it off—this type of image generally lasts about three days.

"Also, I had Eva work with some new photographic software and she was able to clean up two of the photos off Ivy's flash drive."

Katie was excited that they might be able to identify two of the women. They would have something to show people they were going to talk to—including the chief and his two officers.

"Give me a second," said John.

Katie could hear the keyboard and mouse clicking. Within seconds, there were the photos of the two women from Ivy's collection. They looked to be somewhere between thirty-five and forty-five. They didn't look familiar, but there was a reason that Ivy had these saved on her flash drive and hidden it in the teddy bear. It meant something to her. But what?

John toggled back and forth between the two photos and then he did a split screen. Both women were around the same age and had dark hair. One had long, wavy hair and a rounder face with large dark eyes. The other woman had thinner shoulder-length hair and bangs and her eyes were more almond-shaped in appearance. "Do they look familiar?"

Both Katie and McGaven shook their heads.

"No, but we're going to find out who they are if we have to knock on every door in Coldwater Creek," said Katie. "Wait. The one with longer hair seems familiar, but I'm not sure. What do you think, Gav?"

The photos stayed frozen on the screen.

McGaven leaned closer, "I don't know. But look at the clothes. Do they seem dated? I'm not a fashion expert, but the sweater with that thick rolled neckline..."

"I don't know. There's so much of all kinds of fashion. Retro. Chic. Modern."

"Don't forget disco and my favorite—the eighties," said a voice in the background. It was Eva.

When the screen popped back to video time, Katie could

see Eva leaning over John and they both were smiling like they were sharing an inside joke.

"Hi, Eva, nice to see you," said Katie. "Great work."

"Thank you. Just sent the photos to Gav's email."

Katie noticed how comfortable Eva was already and that she already called her partner by his nickname. "Great."

"We'll be able to show people," said McGaven.

"Let me also send them in a text. It'll be easier to have with you." Eva disappeared from view.

"What about the word 'MORE'?" said Katie.

"We've been talking about that," said John. "The letters and how they are carved seem to be consistent with the other girls—but that's difficult to determine when something is carved into the skin, which isn't stable and tears easily."

"What do you think the type of knife or cutting device was that made the incision?" said Katie.

"The cut isn't deep—it must have been barely a quarter of centimeter—and extremely thin and sharp. The cut didn't have the usual tearing and stretching that many incisions with knives do."

"I see. Would it be a knife used by a hunter, camper, or even a boatman?"

"Sure. Almost anyone could have a blade like that. But it was clear that the person who cut the word 'more' took time to do it and was fairly precise."

Katie sighed. "That's not a lot to go on."

"The killer was careful. We didn't find anything in her scrapings and combings." John's expression was solemn. "I'm sorry, but that's it for now. We're still running some tests on the other girls."

"Thanks, John. Everything helps. We appreciate your speedy work," she said.

"It helps having a technician again," he said with a smile. "I'll have more information maybe tomorrow." He leaned in toward the computer camera. "Both of you watch each other's backs. I can see by the looks on your faces that there's something weighing heavy on you. And Coldwater Creek seems to be a strange town. Be safe. More later." The conference call went to a blank screen.

Katie let out a breath and leaned back against the comfortable couch. "Where are we now?"

"We have people to talk to," he said.

"C'mon, Cisco."

The dog jumped to attention and beat the detectives to the front door.

There was a lingering thought Katie had as they double-checked the security cameras and climbed into the Jeep. She couldn't get the images of those women out of her mind. And the killer's messages on all three girls made her feel like she just felt a cold draft flutter through her body.

*MORE...*
*NEVER...*
*FOREVER...*

# TWENTY-NINE

*Thursday 1000 hours*

Katie drove to the Tattoo Lounge and pulled into a space before shutting the engine off. It was in an older area of town and the parking lot was partially filled with cars. The paving was old and there were cracks and raised areas where tree roots had pushed to the surface. The parking lines were faded, so the areas were haphazard. It was clear that maintenance wasn't enforced. Perhaps there was no budget for it.

"This is it," said McGaven unbuckling his seatbelt.

Cisco stood up, wagging his tail furiously.

"Sorry, Cisco, just us." Katie cracked all the windows. Instantly, she could feel the cool breeze blow through. She knew he would be comfortable and she wouldn't have to leave the engine running to keep the air conditioning on.

The dog grumbled and stared out the back window.

Katie and McGaven walked up to the door displaying a bright neon open sign. A little bell rang when they entered.

It was a small space and Katie inhaled the distinct smells of incense and essential oils covering the odor of disinfecting agents. There were two bays with comfortable reclining chairs similar to those found in a dentist's office.

"Can I help you?" said a young man in his twenties, emerging from a back room. He stared at the detectives suspiciously, noticing their badges. His lean body and average height caught Katie's attention.

"Hi," she said, trying to sound casual. She knew that at times in her career she had been too intense on first meeting people, mostly because she so badly wanted the information that would help solve her case. "Are you the owner?" She couldn't help but notice the amazing artwork of brightly colored images of nature and birds that covered his arms and chest. The long, bushy brown hair that partially covered one eye and his numerous face piercings made him seem a little unapproachable.

"Yes?"

"Tyler?"

"I'm Tyler Rey. I guess you're not looking for a tattoo today?" He never changed his deadpan expression and clearly didn't trust the cops. He kept his eye on McGaven.

"I'm Detective Katie Scott and this is my partner, Detective Sean McGaven."

"Aren't you a bit out of your jurisdiction?"

"Actually, we're with the Pine Valley Sheriff's Department."

"A little far from home."

Katie smiled tightly. She knew that the tattoo artist wasn't going to be easy to talk to. "Your work is quite impressive." She studied the photos on the wall of past clients.

"Thanks," he said as he grabbed a small towel and absently started to wipe down the chairs. "What can I help you with?"

Katie pulled out her cell phone and quickly searched for the images of Ivy's tattoos. She showed Mr. Rey. "Is this your work?"

He looked at them. "Yes, but the client brought in rough sketches."

"Ivy Miller?"

The artist hesitated, but it was clear that he knew Ivy. "Yeah, that was her name."

"You did these rose variations for Ivy Miller, Nikki Prager, and Dawn Cromwell?"

"Yes. Last I checked it wasn't against the law." He brushed his hair from his face. "It's kinda what I do."

"Well, they're underage. You have to be eighteen years old to get a tattoo in California."

"You going to arrest me?" He took a step toward Katie as if it were a challenge.

McGaven stepped forward and Katie raised her hand to let him know it was okay. She felt that the artist was just scared and trying to seem like he was tougher than them.

"Mr. Rey, we're not here to jam you up."

"Then what are you here for?"

"We've been called in to investigate the murders of those three young women."

He looked down. "I know. I heard about it." He clearly was saddened by the news.

"We are just trying to get some information and trace their movements in their last days. Will you help us?" she asked, hoping to appeal to his conscience.

"What do you want to know?"

"First we need to clear you as a suspect."

"A suspect? I'm no killer."

"It's only a formality. We ask this of everyone we speak to that could fit the killer's description." It didn't matter in this instance, but Katie wanted to see how cooperative he was.

"Okay," he said slowly.

"Where were you on Sunday and Monday night between midnight and four a.m.?"

"Sleeping."

"Can anyone corroborate that?" said McGaven.

"No. But," he said digging into his jeans pocket and pulling out a prescription bottle, "I take these for sleep. I have insomnia—ever since I was sixteen. When I take them I'm dead to the world. I don't wake up until seven or eight in the morning."

Katie saw the label which identified the drug as doxepin. It was a drug that helped people with insomnia to stay asleep. She also noticed that the prescribing physician was Dr. Deborah Sanders—the medical examiner—which seemed unexpected. "Thank you," she said. It didn't prove that he wasn't potentially the killer, but it did give them some possible information about his whereabouts and his condition.

He sat down on one of the leather lounges. "Ask me," he said.

"What?"

"Ask me if I knew them?"

"Did you?"

He sighed and turned his attention to one of the tables, which was set out with his tattoo tools. "Yeah, I knew Ivy. I knew it was wrong, but I loved her. We had things in common. We just clicked, you know? It just happened. She had a way about her—ask anyone."

"How long had you been seeing her?" Katie estimated Tyler to be twenty-two or twenty-three and Ivy was fifteen. The age difference concerned her.

"About six months."

"Did anyone know about your relationship?"

"No, at least I don't think so. Not even her friends."

"What do you mean?" she said.

"Ivy was a very private person when it came to relationships. Basically, she didn't want her friends to know about us."

"Why?"

"She didn't think that they would understand. The age difference. What I do for a living. I'm not completely sure."

Katie studied him for a moment. "We may need to come back for a few more questions."

"Anytime, Detective. But why would anyone do that to her? Kill her and leave her there... like that?"

Katie paused and glanced at her partner, who was looking at things in the studio more closely. "What do you know about her murder?"

"People talk. Everyone in town is buzzing about how she was left in the woods."

"Was she having any problems at home, or at school?"

Tyler nodded. "The usual." He could barely speak now, and was trying to hide his tears under his mop of hair.

"What do you mean?"

"She... she was unsure about herself even though she was positive and bubbly. She never got on with her mom and grandmother, that's for sure."

"Where is her mother?"

"Don't know. Ivy didn't know either. She just walked out one day about two years ago, and left Ivy to live with her grandmother—the witch. That's what Ivy called her anyway. I never met her, but I've heard from others around town. She's not a nice person if she doesn't like you—which includes a lot of people."

"Was Ivy afraid of something or was anyone threatening her?" Katie watched Tyler as he wrestled with his answer.

"About a week before... she was upset about something and said she didn't want to tell me about it until she knew more."

"More?" said Katie and the word hit her in the gut as she remembered the word carved into Ivy's back.

"That's what she said. I didn't want to push it at the time, so I don't know what it was about."

"If you had to take a guess, what do you think?" said McGaven.

"I don't know... but all her problems revolved around her family. If I had to guess, it had to do with them."

Katie took note. She felt the young man was telling the truth. "Did you know much about Nikki and Dawn?"

"Not really. Ivy was tight with them—they'd been friends forever."

"Did she ever mention either one of them having problems? With a boyfriend maybe?"

"I'm sorry... I never really paid much attention to stuff about them. They seemed nice, but I don't know... I think Dawn had met some guy... but again, I don't know."

"Was it someone from town?"

"I don't know... maybe..."

Katie took her cell phone and scrolled to the photos of the unknown women that were on the flash drive. "Do you recognize either one of these women?" She pushed the phone toward him.

"No... The woman with wavy hair looks familiar, but I couldn't tell you from where. Maybe I saw her around town."

"Are you sure?" she said.

"Yeah, don't know who she is," he said wiping his eyes.

"One more thing. With Ivy's tattoo, there was one of those fluorescent images like you would get at a concert or nightclub. You can't see it until you shine a UV light onto it."

"Oh man, was that still there?"

"What do you know about it?"

"We were just goofing around and I drew a shadow outline. I thought it would be gone by now. It was supposed to be me, to say that I would always be with her." He looked away.

"Thank you, Mr. Rey, for speaking with us."

He stood up. "Detective? Please tell me you're going to find whoever did this."

Katie felt his pain. "That's why we're here—and we're going to find the killer." She put her card down on the counter. "Please call us if you think of anything that might help us—anything at all. Anything you might remember, okay?"

He nodded. "Of course." It was clear that he was genuinely upset. Katie and McGaven left the studio and was heading back to the Jeep when they were stopped by a middle-aged couple.

"Excuse me," said the man.

"What can we do for you?" said McGaven.

"Are you the detectives from out of town?"

"Yes."

"Why haven't you caught the killer yet?" The man tried hard to maintain his emotions.

"We're conducting the investigation," said Katie.

"There was one murder and then two more after you got to town. How's that working with your investigation?"

McGaven stepped forward. "Look—"

Katie stepped in. "We understand how upset the town is... but we are following every lead as fast as we can."

"Oh really? Are you going to wait for another one of our teenagers to be brutally murdered before you take it seriously?"

The man's wife put her hand on his arm to steady him and calm his anger.

Katie could see their frustration and anger. "We're taking these cases very seriously. We're working around the clock and doing everything we can. Chief Baker is also implementing security as well until we have a suspect in custody."

"You're not doing enough. We want our children to be safe."

"Of course. And..." Before Katie could finish her sentence the couple walked away.

"Abrupt," said McGaven.

"Can you blame them? It's true, we were here and could've helped stop the murders of Nikki and Dawn."

"Hey," he said. "It's not your fault. We *are* doing everything we can. You're not going to carry that burden of what-ifs..."

Katie nodded but she still wasn't feeling that the investigation was going as it should.

They got to the Jeep.

Cisco's nose was pushed through the opening of the window, clearly wanting to get out and do some work.

"So are you going to get a tattoo before we leave?" she said, raising her brow.

"Nope. End of discussion."

"Really?"

"I saw the look on your face when you read the prescription bottle." McGaven abruptly changed the subject.

"The physician who prescribed it was Dr. Deborah Sanders."

"The medical examiner with scary red lipstick?"

"Yep. There's some strange overlapping here—it's going to make it more difficult to figure things out—to separate weird town coincidences from real clues."

# THIRTY

Katie and McGaven sat in the Jeep for ten minutes before deciding to get out. They were across the street from Torrez Fishing and Hunting. The old wooden sign was well worn and some of the letters' paint was almost completely missing. The place of business was inside of what used to be a small house turned into commercial property. Katie guessed that Maxwell Torrez lived in the back.

The detectives watched the store, but there was no activity. The sign said open but it looked to have been in that same position for years.

"Maxwell Alvin Torrez, age fifty-one," McGaven began, reading from an iPad. "Denise sent over all the info she could find on him this morning. I sent her a text when I knew we were going to have a chat with this guy."

Katie peered through her small binoculars. "It reminds me of a front business for something else. It could be anything. Drugs. Money laundering. Or worse."

"Torrez has been in trouble a few times. Trespassing, harassment, a bar fight, attempted assault."

"What a sweetheart." Katie already didn't like the man, but she had to be as unbiased as possible. Her emotions sometimes made her weak in questioning suspects or witnesses but she had to play things as impartially as she could. Sometimes it was one of the most difficult things to do on an investigation this raw.

"He's divorced since about ten years ago. No children. Up until ten years ago, he worked as a deck hand for a commercial fishing boat up north in the Washington State area. Then it looks like he got a business license for his store—and he's been here ever since."

"He would definitely know how to tie that bowline knot and use a hunting knife with some expertise," she said.

"Look at this," said McGaven as he turned the iPad toward Katie. It showed the driver's license photo of a heavyset man stating he was five foot nine inches tall and weighed two hundred forty pounds.

"Not the thin guy I saw on the shoreline of Oak Valley Creek—unless he lost a lot of weight."

Cisco pushed his nose to Katie, indicating that he wanted to do something.

"Soon, Cisco," she said.

"I saw a park near a sandwich shop. Maybe we can take a lunch break there and Cisco can do his business and stretch his legs."

"Sounds good." Katie thought about the killer. "He may not be the killer, but he could have some connection to him—or at least lead us to him."

"Well it's now or later," he said. "I think I saw movement inside."

"Let's go."

The detectives got out of the Jeep.

Katie noticed that the other houses and places of business

were either closed or empty. Behind her she saw heavy areas of trees, which meant there were plenty of hiding places. Her first thought, for some reason, was that there were security cameras watching the area. She casually turned her head as if she was glancing around, and spotted two cameras about twenty feet apart. They were directed partially at the store, each camera slightly turned in opposite directions. They looked sophisticated and might be from another source, like the town law enforcement, rather than a store owner.

They walked across the street and headed toward the door of the shop.

Katie whispered under her breath, "There are cameras watching us."

"Don't do anything stupid," said McGaven as he smiled.

Katie loved it when her partner could make funny remarks, but she could always read between the lines. His comment actually meant pretend you never saw them and they would figure out the details later.

McGaven tried to open the door of the hunting and fishing shop, but it was locked. He knocked. "Hello?" He tapped on the glass several times. In a few moments, there was movement from inside. "Your sign says you're open."

Katie waited patiently, realizing that McGaven was better suited to this interview. She looked into the main window, where she could see a clutter of jumbled items and stacked boxes. It looked more like someone's messy living room than a store.

There was a muffled voice from inside, but it wasn't clear what was said.

McGaven tapped the glass again. "Open up."

A bear of a man approached the door and looked out at the detectives. It was clear by his reaction, scrunched frown and tight lips, that he wasn't happy about the visit.

"Hi," said McGaven with a smile on his face. "We need to talk," he said and tapped his badge against the glass.

Mr. Torrez unlocked the door and opened it barely enough for his face to squeeze through. "What's this about?" He looked disheveled and sleepy, like he just woke up. He was shoeless with stained athletic socks through which his big toes poked.

"Mr. Maxwell Torrez?"

"Yeah."

"Chief Baker told us you checked out the area where we discovered the traps. Near where Ivy Miller's body was found," said McGaven.

Katie thought that mentioning the chief was a great way in. It sounded harmless enough.

The man turned his attention to Katie and gave her a once-over. He pulled the door open wider. "By all means, come in." There was a distinct hint of sarcasm in his voice.

Katie followed McGaven inside. When she stepped in, the strong smell of garbage accosted her. She frowned and tried to ignore it. In the corner there was an overflowing trash can that desperately needed to be taken out. She saw shipping boxes with brand names for various types of fishing and hunting gear: knives, fishing reels, reel lines, ropes, pulleys, clothing, and tackle boxes.

Mr. Torrez must've realized the stench. He grabbed the garbage bag and headed to the back door. "My maid is off today," he grumbled. When he returned he said, "What do you want to know? I told Baker that we didn't find anything and I assume he relayed that to you two."

"Yes, Chief Baker told us, but we want to hear from you," said McGaven. "I'm Detective McGaven and this is my partner, Detective Scott."

"Typical cops. Always wanting a different answer to the same question if they don't like it."

"Did you see any indication of these traps?"

"Nah."

"Footprints?"

"Could've been footprints once, but the dirt was all kicked around." He went over to the counter to light up a cigarette.

McGaven quickly searched for a photo from his phone. "I was wondering if you've ever seen a knot like this?" He pushed his phone toward the man.

"Yeah, any Boy Scout would know what that is... a bowline." He took a puff of smoke, held it, and blew it out. "You look like you were a Boy Scout."

"Nope."

Katie held her smile and remained stoic.

"What? Doesn't your partner talk?" said Mr. Torrez. "Or is she just pretty and not real smart?" He chuckled to himself.

Katie wanted to take him down to the floor in a headlock and see how much smack talk he would do then.

"First, Mr. Torrez," began McGaven, "I would suggest that you give Detective Scott some respect."

"Fine. My bad," he said, raising his hands in the air. "What else do you want?"

"We've been invited to Coldwater Creek to investigate three homicides."

"Three? I thought there was only one?" The heavyset man didn't seem really surprised at the news.

"Did you know the victims? Ivy Miller? Nikki Prager? Or Dawn Cromwell?" said Katie.

McGaven showed him some photos.

"Maybe that one," he said pointed to Ivy Miller. "I've seen her. Isn't that Ivy something?"

"Ivy Miller," said Katie keeping eye contact with the man. "How would you know a fifteen-year-old girl?"

"Whoa, wait a minute. You think I had something to do with her murder? You're way off base here." He grabbed a cup of old coffee that had been on the counter next to piles of paper-

THE ROSE GIRLS   203

work and old mail. "I know her grandmother and I've seen the girl around at the Burger Shack."

"What about her friends?"

"I don't know. Maybe? I didn't kill anyone."

McGaven took a step closer to him. "We can clear this right up by asking where you were on Sunday and Monday nights from midnight to four a.m."

"Here. Sunday night it was raining like hell and I was doing some inventory. And... Monday night... wait a minute... I was with the Dannys."

"What's the Dannys?"

"My friends. Danny Parker and Danny Perez."

"I see, and what were you doing?"

"We had too many beers so we all crashed at Danny's house. Check it out for yourself."

"We will. Just one more question—since the traps had been set in that area. What do you know about the cement building not far from there?" said Katie.

Mr. Torrez shrugged. "Not much. It's been around forever. I thought they would have bulldozed it by now, but I guess politics was involved, you know."

"Who goes there?" said McGaven.

"How should I know?"

"You hunting and fishing types, I'm guessing, should be all over that place."

"Not my thing. In fact, it's creepy. Been a lot of stories."

"What kind of stories?" said Katie.

"I don't know... ghost stories. They say that when people go in there they disappear... some crap like that." He looked at the detectives. "I'm telling you the truth. Why would I lie? I've heard stuff like that for years. Nobody really knows—at least not around town."

"Anything else strange about that area?" Katie watched his demeanor change. There was a whiff of fear or uncertainty. He knew something, but was too afraid to tell. She thought it was odd that he didn't mention the reclusive old man in the cabin.

He shrugged. Mr. Torrez seemed be different from when he had answered the door when he thought the questions were about the traps and not the murdered teens. "I don't know anything else, I swear."

"Thanks for your cooperation," said McGaven with a touch of sarcasm.

The detectives left the shop and walked to the Jeep, but didn't say anything until they were inside the vehicle.

"That was fun," said Katie.

"I should have just let you kick his ass."

"That would have been more fun," she said turning the ignition and slowly pulling away from the curb.

"I guess that was pretty much a bust."

"Don't write it off too soon. I saw boxes for nylon ropes and utility knives, which could have been supplies that the killer used."

"He's not the killer... he's too sloppy and lazy," he said. "But killers sometimes surprise us."

"True, but maybe the killer bought the supplies from him?" She looked at her partner.

"Good point. But that guy isn't going to let us look at his invoices. He probably doesn't keep records, not to mention customer names."

"There are ways to find out."

McGaven smiled. "I get it, some surveillance."

Katie matched his smile.

"I'm hungry."

Cisco barked from the back seat.

# THIRTY-ONE

*Thursday 1345 hours*

Katie and McGaven were seated at a patio table at the Burger Pit in downtown Coldwater Creek. Katie watched the Jeep, which was parked close by. People walked by and kids swarmed in and out of the restaurant. No one seemed to notice a black German shepherd observing their every move from the back seat.

"Sean! Your order is up!"

"That's us. I got it," said McGaven as he got up and went to the counter to retrieve their lunch. All eyes inside the restaurant seemed to be on him. No doubt the word went around about the two detectives from out of town coming in to investigate the murders of their girls. Heads swiveled as he walked by and went back outside. Some patrons stared longer and seemed to have scowls on their faces—either they were annoyed by their presence or upset that they hadn't caught the killer yet.

Katie noticed fliers with the faces of Ivy, Nikki, and Dawn tacked up on the bulletin board next to the patio. There were announcements of the murders as well as a vigil scheduled for the girls. It hit her hard seeing their faces.

Katie eyed the plates with big burgers and fries. "That looks great, but I think I'm going to have to go for a run later." She laughed.

"Worried about your figure?" he said.

"Not really, but I should burn off some of these calories and carbs! But actually, running helps me think and things seem to fall into place." She took a big bite of her burger and casually glanced around. "Are all eyes on us?"

"Yep. Well, maybe on you because you're a beautiful woman sitting here."

"More like because we're cops with guns and badges." Katie knew that McGaven was trying to make her feel better—easing the burden of the investigation, even if only for a moment.

"Okay, a beautiful woman with a gun and badge."

There were two young male teens sitting at a table across the patio who were staring at them, whispering back and forth, and then looking at Katie and McGaven again. They sent texts on their phones and tried to get a selfie photo with the detectives in the background.

"You see those two staring at us?" said McGaven. "They seem to have a lot to say."

"Maybe we should have a chat with them? What better way to learn about the teen circles around here?" She dipped a fry into a pool of ketchup and gave her partner that inquisitive look.

McGaven took her lead. "Hey," he said and pointed to the young teens. They sat up straight then acted nonchalant like they were minding their own business. "C'mon, I know you're curious. Come here."

The two teenagers slowly pushed back their chairs and stood up.

"C'mon," said McGaven as he munched his lunch. "We don't have all day."

Katie tried not to laugh. "You're going to be a great dad. You seem to have a way with kids."

The first teen stood at their table. "Yeah?" He was tall, lanky, and kept his hands shoved in his pockets.

"What's your name?"

"Brian."

"Brian what?"

"Brian James. This is Eddie Jenkins."

"Nice to meet you," said McGaven. "You know who we are?"

"Yeah, murder detectives."

"We're homicide detectives. I'm Detective McGaven and this is my partner, Detective Scott."

The boys nodded at them, clearly nervous. They glanced at the detectives' holstered guns.

"You aren't in trouble, so relax. Why aren't you in school?"

"They've made it half days this week—calling it teacher conferences and stuff. But we know why."

"Why?"

"Because of the murders. They're trying to keep us safe—security guards at school and stuff. Do you know who did it?"

"We're working on it."

"Chief Baker couldn't solve any case," said Brian. The two teens laughed, clearly making fun of local law enforcement.

"Did you know Ivy Miller?" said Katie.

"Yeah, she was in two of my classes."

"What can you tell us about her?"

They both shrugged. "I dunno. Like what?"

"Like was she nice? Mean? Have a boyfriend? Just stuff like that," she said.

"Why do you want to know? Don't you just find the killer?"

"Of course. But it helps us if we know more about the victim." She pulled some cash out of her pocket. "What's your favorite drink?"

"Chocolate milkshake with a crumbled candy bar."

"Wow, that sounds great. Have Eddie get both of you one," she said handing the money to Brian's friend. Eddie happily left to go order their milkshakes. Turning to Brian, she said, "What about Ivy?" Katie thought that separating the boys was a better tactic and one might tell more alone.

"I knew her through school—since the second grade—but she hung out in different circles. You know?" He fidgeted with his hands as he talked and kept transferring his weight back and forth.

"But you heard things, right?" said McGaven finishing up his burger.

"Some."

"Like?" she said.

"I don't know. Her mom left to go to a cult. Her grandmother is really strict, so Ivy had to sneak out a lot. Just stuff like that."

"What do you mean, a cult?" said McGaven.

"Like a group that did weird things like séances and stuff. I really don't know. That's just what some of the older kids were saying. They'd hang out at night in the woods."

"They were trying to contact the dead?" she said.

"I guess so."

"Would Ivy do that?"

"I dunno."

"What about Nikki Prager and Dawn Cromwell?"

"I really didn't know them. They seemed okay enough. I saw the three of them hanging out all the time."

Katie wanted to get more specific, or at least get something they could use. "Did Ivy have a boyfriend?"

"Not at school, but I saw a guy come and pick her up."

"What did he look like?"

"Older. He had tattoos. Curly brown hair."

That sounded like Tyler Rey from the tattoo studio. "Did he drive a blue car, four-door?"

"I don't remember, but I don't think so."

Katie knew it had been a long shot, based on the car of Joshua's eyewitness account. She retrieved a business card from her pocket. "Take our card, and if you see anything or hear anything that might help us find the killer, will you let us know?"

Brian took the card just as Eddie returned with the chocolate shakes. He nodded to them. Taking his shake, he said, "Thanks, Detectives."

Katie and McGaven watched the boys go back to their table.

"Think they know more?" said McGaven.

"I think everyone we've talked to knows more."

"Agree."

"But, Sydney Barrett-Miller needs to be interviewed again. At the very least, we need to get into Ivy's first bedroom, according to the girls."

"And we're not going to announce our visit in advance or let Chief Baker know."

# THIRTY-TWO

*Thursday 1530 hours*

Katie and McGaven sat in the Jeep looking at Ivy Miller's house. It was quiet in the neighborhood. Again, Katie thought it was unusual: no cars, no people out walking, no dogs barking, just silence. Most of the houses in the neighborhood were upscale, but this residence was clearly the most exclusive.

"Think she's home?" said McGaven.

"There's one way to find out," she said.

McGaven looked in the back seat, where Cisco was snoozing quietly. "Think you tired him out enough?"

"I would say so. He ran after the ball at the park—that always makes him tired for about ten minutes." She laughed.

"Then we better get to work," he said, opening the door.

Katie stepped out and looked at the houses up and down the street. The lot across from Ivy's house was small and wooded. The thought occurred to her that there might be surveillance cameras there too—just like across from Torrez's hunting and fishing store. She tried to act calmly as if looking for something else and then casually glanced up to where cameras would be most effectively located. There they were. The high-tech surveillance cameras were placed in the trees with the perfect bird's-eye view of the street.

McGaven waited on the sidewalk in front of Sydney's home.

Katie walked to meet up with him as they headed to the front door.

"Two more cameras?" said McGaven barely above a whisper.

"You bet."

"Interesting."

"I'd say." Katie pressed the doorbell button, which immediately made a lovely chime accompaniment. "I think we've underestimated this town for technology."

The door opened wide and Sydney Barrett-Miller stood there, expressionless. "Yes? What can I do for you, Detectives?" She obviously remembered them, but there was hint of annoyance in her voice.

"Hello, Sydney. I hope we didn't come at a bad time," said Katie.

"Any word on my granddaughter's killer?" Her tone was flat and emotionless.

"It's still an ongoing investigation. More complicated now with the murders of her two best friends."

"I heard about that. Just tragic. Nothing like this ever happens in Coldwater Creek."

"We had just spoken to Nikki and Dawn the night before their deaths. They mentioned that Ivy had had another bedroom when she first moved in."

"Yes, that's right."

"Would it be possible if we could take a look at it?"

"What are you looking for?"

"We wanted to see if we could find out more about where she was the week before her death, or maybe find her cell phone. We like to be thorough." Katie watched the woman closely. Sydney seemed very controlled and as though she could adapt well to different situations—careful not to show her hand. It was difficult to tell if she was grieving or just irritated by their unannounced visit.

"Of course. But I'm going to be going out later." She opened the door wider for the detectives to enter.

"Thank you," said Katie. The large grand entrance was now filled with moving boxes—some open and others sealed up with packaging tape. "Are you moving?"

Sydney closed the front door. "I'm packing up some old things. I'm not sure if I want to stay in this town anymore. I'm thinking of moving to the city. My lawyer and broker have some housing prospects for me."

"Oh," said Katie looking up the staircase.

"Ivy's old room is upstairs down the second hall to the left." She turned and walked back to the kitchen. Within seconds, Katie could hear the sound of ice cubes tumbling into a glass.

McGaven led the way up the decorative staircase. Katie followed, paused a moment to look down at the first floor—something seemed out of place. It took her a moment, but the two lamps were missing from the wood tables. It didn't mean anything, but she did wonder if they were packed or had been broken.

Katie caught up with McGaven just as he approached the closed bedroom door. It was located on the north end of the house, which was cooler. The sunshine wouldn't shine through the windows much here.

McGaven slipped plastic gloves on and then opened the door. It was dark and much smaller than the other room. There were two windows with shut white blinds, a small twin bed with a pink and purple comforter, two white nightstands, a small corner desk, a tall dresser, and a half-size bookcase, partially filled. The bedroom was about ten by fourteen feet.

Katie slipped on her gloves and then flipped the light switch next to the doorway as a single ceiling bulb lit up the room with a harsh yellowish hue.

McGaven moved to the desk and began looking through drawers and moving paperwork on top.

Katie spotted a framed photo on the nightstand. As she neared the photograph of a woman and Ivy when she was about ten years old, she gasped. "Gav, look at this," she said, holding the delicate silver frame.

"Is that..."

"I think so."

McGaven scrolled through photos on his phone until he stopped on one of the women in the cement building with a candle burning. There was no doubt that the woman in the photo was Ivy's mother.

"So Ivy had a weird photo of her mom that she had kept hidden? Where did she get it? Did she find it from her mom?"

"No one seems to know where her mom is—Sydney said that she just left."

"I think the secrets are starting to unravel," he said. "We need to find her."

Katie turned the photo over and opened the back. She took off the cardboard piece and there was a folded piece of paper hidden. "Here we go." She unfolded the paper and there was a handwritten note with a freehand sketch of a rose at the bottom:

*Ivy baby, I have to go away for a while. Stay strong. Be good. I will come back for you soon. Love you more than you know, Mom*

"It's dated a little over two years ago," said Katie. "I wonder if Ivy told anyone?"

"I don't know."

"Maybe we're looking at Ivy's murder all wrong." Katie

paced in the small room, rehashing everything they knew about the case.

"Go on."

"We've been investigating under the assumption that Ivy was murdered by a possible boyfriend, a jealousy situation, hate, revenge, or even by a serial killer, but what if she was killed because she found something out about her mother?"

"And Nikki and Dawn were collateral damage, or just in case they knew same thing Ivy did?"

"This town no doubt has secrets that are being closely guarded. The surveillance cameras around everywhere make me think that someone wants to make sure that no one uncovers them—even to the point of murder."

"There are so many ways to go."

"I think that's by design," she said.

McGaven let out a sigh. "We're being led around on a wild goose chase—not knowing what is part of the real homicide investigation and what's fabrication or distraction."

"Of course," she said. "How could I've not seen this earlier?"

"Hey, there were so many weird things going on the moment we tried to drive through this town. Everyone who we talk to seems to be hiding something or just doesn't want us to know certain things. But why?" He looked in the drawers next to the bed. "So Ivy's mom leaves one day and everyone says she's disappeared. But no one ever hears from her again—and there's been no missing person's report. It's just left as is..."

"Swept under the rug... no one questions it."

The detectives searched the rest of the room, including the closet and under the mattress. No journal, cell phone, or electronic device of any kind.

"Think we should jam Sydney up about the photo and note?" said McGaven.

"No, but I do think we need to strategize."

"I agree. Starting with Ivy's murder. Looking at everything leading up to and after."

"Exactly. There has been too much interference to throw us off the trail. With everything we know now, real evidence and red herrings, let's go back to the beginning."

"The scene of Ivy's crime?"

"That's right."

# THIRTY-THREE

*Thursday 1930 hours*

Dark clouds rolled across the sky, making it seem later in the evening than it actually was. A light mist blanketed the countryside, reducing visibility and giving the trees and landscape an almost sparkling appearance from the millions of tiny water droplets that had fallen on them. The roads were mostly deserted, and when Katie drove down the now-familiar single-lane country road heading to the Bates Hiking and Camping area—where Ivy Miller's body had been found—she could feel a shiver slide down her spine. Right now, in the dark light with the wreaths of mist, the area held an unnatural appearance, the immense trees casting shadows all around.

Katie turned the Jeep onto the narrow gravel pathway that descended a hill to the rural parking area and found a spot tucked away at the far end—again, if someone were to drive by, they wouldn't immediately see her car.

For some reason, she thought about Chad. She hadn't called or sent a text today. She was looking forward for this case to be over.

"I can tell by the faraway look on your face, you must be thinking about Chad," said McGaven.

"You know me too well. I just realized that I haven't talked or sent a text to him today. What about Denise? Have you talked to her?"

"She sends cute text messages."

"That sounds like her."

"Anyway, why are we looking at the first crime scene at nighttime?"

"Because everything seems to be happening at night. We have to start thinking like the people from around here—namely, like the killer."

"Not all of the people here are involved, I hope."

Katie hoped not either. She leaned over her partner, opening the glove box to retrieve her utility flashlight. She then reached back past Cisco to grab her warmer jacket.

The dog whined and became antsy. He wriggled on the back seat, not able to sit still.

"He's ready to play ball again."

"I want to check things out and then have Cisco run a track. The breeze usually ceases at night so any scents would stay stationary," she said. "It's a long shot but I think we need to begin looking at these cases from all sides."

At the word "track" Cisco had sat up at attention with his intense stare, looking from window to window.

"I've been thinking about those words that Ivy wrote on the magazine page and the killer's hand-carved words: *More*, *Never*, and *Forever*." McGaven paused. "And that text message to Officer Lane: 'Never... Forever... Find me... at the creek.' How did he know which creek or area?"

Katie shrugged, thinking about the messages. "He said that he thought of Oak Valley Creek and started searching at one end. Seems plausible. You think he's lying?"

"Not entirely. But there's something missing," he said.

"Now you sound like me—but I agree with you."

"And those words on the girls' backs. Does it seem random or does it all gel into something more meaningful to the killer? Is he trying to give us clues or mix random things up?"

Katie changed her jacket and zipped up the warmer one. She leaned back. "Thinking too hard on these words can make you crazy."

"Maybe that's the point?"

"One thing is clear. How many times have you seen the word 'More'?"

McGaven thought about it. "Well, on Ivy's back," he said, raising his index finger to keep count, "the handwritten message on the magazine page, and the cement building's door. Oh, and in the note written by Ivy's mom. Four times."

Katie nodded. "And if we look closer, I think there's even more. It's a clue, but I don't know what it pertains to yet. More we should be looking for... more time... more victims... more information? It will drive you crazy thinking about it."

"You still want to have a look around?" he said.

"Of course."

"Just ramping up your courage," he said with a smile.

"You have my back, remember? I'm never scared." She opened the door and felt a rush of cool misty air enter the vehicle. Katie stepped out and quickly shut the door, while McGaven set up the video camera and locked the Jeep.

Katie looked into the woods and wondered what Ivy thought as she ran into the darkness. Did she know her killer? Did she know that what she was doing could possibly get her killed?

"I want to check a few things," she said. "There seems to be a theme in Coldwater Creek."

"Besides the murders?"

"The cameras. These aren't personal or property cameras.

They appear to have been purposely set up as a way to keep tabs—either on certain people or just on the town as a whole."

"So you're thinking that there might be cameras near the crime scenes?"

Katie nodded. She loved being in sync with her partner—they ended up thinking the same way. "And at night, it'll be easier to see them if we shine the flashlights in the trees—there should be some kind of flash from the lens."

"Let's go check it out," he said.

"Then I'll put Cisco on a track."

The detectives began walking down the narrow gravel path just as they did when Chief Baker brought them here on Monday morning. After all the incidents, Katie thought that morning seemed a long time ago. The forest and surrounding areas were still visible, so they didn't use their flashlights—yet.

Instinctively, both detectives kept quiet and walked quickly, as if something was pulling them toward Ivy's crime scene.

Katie's nerves were rattled and she shivered, not knowing if it was the cold or from the unknown.

As they neared the tree where Ivy's body was posed facing the trail, there was a silhouette, dark, resembling a thin person with his back to the detectives. He wore a dark hoodie, which was pulled up over his head. He stood at the tree where Ivy had been, looking down.

Katie stopped and put her hand on McGaven's arm. She didn't want to spook whoever it was—but just to study him first before they confronted him. There was no doubt that the figure in the early darkness was similar to the person who stood on the shoreline at Oak Valley Creek.

There were some items piled up on the ground against the tree. There were flowers, cute stuffed animals, photos, and some other small things.

Katie sucked in a breath and began to slowly approach the

unknown person ahead of McGaven. She wanted to see his face. Who was he? Was he the killer? Keeping her steady pace, she got to within twenty feet of the man. He must've heard their approach, or just had the feeling that someone was near, because he suddenly bolted and ran deeper into the forest.

Katie took off after the man with pure instinct and adrenalin. She didn't wait to contemplate what they should do—she sprinted into the forest. Turning on the flashlight, keeping it downward so her eyes could stay accustomed to the light, she ran with every ounce of energy. She could see his agility and quickness, he was taking the corners fast, not slowing down.

The trees were thicker here, clustered together and extinguishing any evening light left. She rounded a corner and lost the man—yet he wasn't that far ahead. Then a familiar tug at her gut reminded her that someone, maybe the killer, knew how to set traps. She slowed her advance. The forest responded by silencing any noise, no matter how slight. Her mind, full of everything they had seen and investigated, made her realize that someone could be watching her—in person or from one of the many surveillance cameras planted around town.

She stopped then turned around in a full circle, trying to catch her breath.

There were no sounds of footsteps hitting the forest floor.

No movement in the brush. No gentle sway of branches caught her attention.

*Where did he go?*

Katie swept the flashlight beam from side to side and then turned around the way she had come, repeating the same sequence.

The fleeing shadow man seemed to have disappeared into the forest's layers without a sound or the use of a flashlight, as if he were only an apparition. A ghost. Another diversion of sorts. She and McGaven had already experienced more than their fair share of distractions that only seemed to complicate the investigation.

Trying to calm her pulse, she remained still where she stood.

She targeted the light toward the direction where the man had disappeared—the escape route was off the regular trail—so she slowly moved forward, fixated on where he could be until... her footing slipped on a combination of loose gravel and wet terrain. She skidded and slid before catching her balance.

Mad at herself for not paying close attention to her surroundings, she was about to turn around to retrace her steps when she was ambushed. A shadowy figure with considerable strength slammed into her, causing her to lose her balance. There was a moment she was catapulted into the air giving her the strangeness of freedom, until she hit the ground hard, sliding down the hillside. Trying to grab anything to stop her descent, she dropped her flashlight, causing it to erratically spin in the opposite direction, flashing around the forest. She pumped her legs trying desperately to slow down or stop, but it seemed as if she would fall into a deep abyss. Her sense of direction turned upside-down and she didn't know what direction she headed.

What seemed like minutes was only seconds before she landed in a soft area of overgrown foliage. Sitting up, she took a moment to take inventory of her body. All hope had dwindled of finding the identity of the shadow figure—at least for now. But she guessed he would show up again.

Katie stood up with only slight pain in her back and shoulders from the riverbank incident. The forest was dark, and she could only make out basic shapes of trees and large boulders around her. There was no way of knowing if there was another way to get back to the crime scene and the parking area, so she began to climb back up the hill a foot at a time by grabbing vegetation and secure rocks wherever she could.

"Katie!"

Relief filled her. "Down here!" She grimaced as she pulled herself up farther.

"Katie, you okay?"

She used all the remaining strength she had to keep going until she was near the top. She could see McGaven's flashlight beam sweep erratically across the forest, coming closer. "I'm down here," she managed to say. Now she could hear McGaven's running footsteps and heavy breathing approaching.

Katie was about five feet from the top when she had to rest to catch her breath. Her arms were trembling through pushing her strength to the limit. A bright light lit up her view.

"You okay?" he said as he got to his knees, extending his right arm.

Katie inched up a little bit more until she touched McGaven's hand, grasping it firmly. With a final pull, she landed on top.

"What happened?" he said.

"He ambushed me again and shoved me down the hill. He's fast and agile. We'll get him next time."

"Did you manage to see anything identifying about him?"

"Nothing." Katie was frustrated at herself because she should've anticipated the surprise attack move. She felt her pulse begin to return to normal and her dizziness subsided.

McGaven helped her up. "Let's call it a day."

"No way."

"What else can we do right now?"

"I came here to run an article track for anything that might have belonged to Ivy—and I'm not going back to the cottage until I do that."

"Yes, ma'am."

"We still have more information to go through, but we need to make sure that the crime scenes are cleared."

McGaven didn't say anything.

"What's wrong?"

"I'll look for the cameras."

"If possible, we need to find out the company's name with the make, model, and possible ID number. I want to know who bought them—and why."

They reached the parking area where Cisco and the Jeep waited. There was no indication of any disturbance in the vicinity while they were gone, and Cisco was calm.

Katie opened the hatch and pulled out a duffel bag. She prepared Cisco for the article search by putting on his tracking vest and long lead.

"You sure you're okay?" he said.

"I'm fine. Nothing that a hot bath and a good night sleep won't cure." She grabbed another flashlight and a couple of evidence bags, slipping them into her coat pocket. Checking two walkie-talkies, she double-checked they were charged and ready. "Here," she said, handing one to McGaven. "I want to make sure we have contact if we get separated again." She clipped one to her belt.

Katie had Cisco jump out. He was happy and took two circle turns with low whines—it was time to work.

McGaven secured the Jeep and took a bottle of water to Katie.

"Thank you," she said, opening it immediately to take a gulp.

"You sure you want to do a search with the daylight gone?"

"It doesn't matter to Cisco. His nose doesn't know the difference between day and night. Besides, it gives us cover. Let's make it work to our advantage."

The detectives walked to the crime-scene site where Ivy's body had been posed.

McGaven kept his eyes upward to the trees, searching for

cameras. It was difficult to see in the darkness, so he systematically searched all the trees with a lower flashlight beam.

Katie directed Cisco to the tree where Ivy was found. She wanted to begin an article search. The dog would begin an exploration of the area and stop at anything unusual with traces of human scent. She commanded, "*Such verloren,*" then let out the leash to give the dog some moving room and watched him sniff around the tree.

In search mode Cisco's body language changed from relaxed and calm to focused, his body tense. His steps were well placed, his nose moving in various levels to catch a scent, his tail down and his ears perked forward; all directing him to find the trace of odor.

Cisco was on the move.

Katie glanced behind her where McGaven kept a distance in order not to interfere with any scent. He kept Katie in his view and she knew that he wasn't going to let her out of his sight this time.

Cisco paused, pushing his muzzle in the air and moving his head from side to side. Then he settled back into the track with his nose to the ground, trotting at a moderate pace. They searched for almost fifteen minutes.

Katie watched the dog's demeanor, looking for any type of hesitation, pause, or head snap to indicate something of interest was worth checking out. She knew him well and even when she thought it was impossible—Cisco knew—and that's all that counted.

The dog continued to the left of the point of origin, making his way down a path then veering to the left. He spent a fair amount of time in a thicket area. There were pieces of escaped trash lying around, but there was something more. Reflecting in the light beam, Katie saw a piece of plastic. Bending over, she realized it was part of a cell phone cover. She placed it in an evidence bag.

After watching Cisco for a solid five minutes, the dog stepped back and barked then lunged forward again.

"What is it?" she said and searched the area. Cisco kept up his ramped-up state and whined as he gave two barks. Katie knew that McGaven must've heard the barking and would be there shortly.

Katie continued to search through the prickly brush hoping that there wasn't poison oak anywhere near. Just when she was about to give up, she touched something cold and metallike. Directing the flashlight, it reflected on a rectangular shape—it was a cell phone with a pink case.

"Got it," she said. It had been discarded, most likely, and it looked to be in rough condition, but there was no doubt it had belonged to Ivy. "Good boy, Cisco, good boy." She slipped the phone into another evidence bag.

Katie and Cisco were heading back toward the car when she saw McGaven. There were flashes of light from his cell phone camera. She waited until he was done. Looking up, she saw the distinct outline of a surveillance camera.

McGaven walked up to meet her. "Got it. My hand was a bit shaky but cell phones can take pretty sharp photos."

"What is it?"

"It's PikeRock Industries and the identification number #PRI329400."

"Fantastic. Now we can trace who bought it, right?"

"I think so. I'm not going to stop until I get either a name or address—or both. How'd you guys do?" He was still smiling because he had got some real information at last.

"Pretty good," she said, holding up the bag with the pink cell phone.

"You got Ivy's phone?"

"I believe so. It was discarded and hidden well."

"That's great." He gave his partner a high-five.

"The extra search was worth it." Katie's mind was already

three steps ahead of what they needed to do with their new information. "But it might be a bust if the SIM card is destroyed."

"Let's get to work."

# THIRTY-FOUR

*Thursday 2115 hours*

The evening was ticking on but Katie and McGaven were hard at work. Katie had taken a quick shower and dabbed antiseptic to the scratches and minor cuts on her arms, hands, and the side of her face.

Katie watched the rain shower outside through the picture windows and thought about the town. The more she thought about its people and happenings, the more she realized that the town could be being run by someone, or maybe a group. She had taken Joshua's advice and started to search from the beginning. When she had searched the history of the town, one aspect captured her attention. The current population was 2,173, but five years ago it had been 2,675. How could a town population dwindle by about five hundred residents so quickly? Was it people who wanted to get away from here? But why? It couldn't only be due to new jobs or retirement. She thought about Sydney and her packing boxes. Was she skipping out of this town too?

"Bad news about Ivy's cell phone," said McGaven.

"What?"

"The SIM card is damaged. We won't be able to get anything from it."

Katie sighed. "Bad break."

"We've had a few."

They both turned back to their work.

"Got it," said McGaven suddenly.

Cisco made a grumbling noise from his place by the fireplace.

Katie walked back to the living room. "What do you have?"

"PRI, or PikeRock Industries, is a company out of New York. They are known for their surveillance equipment but, get this, they only sell to city, state, and federal agencies. Like city hall, US government, and any agency you can think of."

"Including law enforcement." Katie's mind filtered through all their interactions with the chief.

"Most definitely law enforcement. But don't forget if any police agency needed cameras, say, downtown and at road or freeway areas, this would be the place to buy it."

Katie sighed. "You know what this means? Whatever this town is hiding, it has *something* to do with its law enforcement. But we can't jump the gun here—we have to watch our next steps."

"This has been the most unnerving and aggravating case. I want to find the killer of those girls. How are they connected to the other happenings and those surveillance cameras?"

"My first instinct is that Chief Baker is playing us," she said. "I don't want to accuse any law enforcement officer of anything criminal, but at this point we need to stay alert and manage our suspicions." Katie paced, feeling the warmth from the fire. "He came to us. Why?"

"We were an opportunity because we got stuck here. It was perfect."

"I suppose, but he didn't know we'd be here. And the girls were going to be murdered."

"Think about it—we fell into his lap. If he had known that there were going to be these murders, they couldn't be investigated and then left as unsolved—he had to make it appear that they were doing everything humanly possible to find the killer—then eventually the cases would turn cold."

"So what better way than to bring in detectives from the county to do this." Katie took into consideration all the interactions they'd had with Chief Baker from the moment he knocked on the door at the inn. "Has the chief answered our questions? I mean really answered our questions? Dug in and helped us with leads?"

"You mean, besides taking us to the crime scenes and Sydney's house?"

"My point."

There was a ping and McGaven looked at his computer screen. "Yes!" he said with enthusiasm.

"What is it?"

"I sent a message to the tech support regarding that camera in the woods—I said that it was having a glitch. And I just received a message back with some troubleshooting suggestions. Since I gave them the identification number and location, they sent me back a message with the client ID, name, and address."

"Who is it?" she said.

"Brookings International, LLC."

"That sounds phony."

McGaven laughed. "It sure does, but the mailing address is 3222 Main Street, Coldwater Creek." He began a property search. He hesitated. Then searched again. "Well that's interesting. There's no such address as 3222. None of the addresses go anywhere near that high."

"What about 322 or 222?" she said.

"I'm ahead of you." McGaven's fingers expertly moved across the keyboard. "Nope."

Katie felt discouraged all over again. But still, they had learned some important information.

McGaven turned to his partner. "How do you want to handle this?"

"If we confront the chief or anyone associated with him, they'll get spooked and begin covering their trail. If they know we know... There will be a time when we do need to confront them—but not now. We need to watch."

"Like surveillance?"

Katie nodded. Her cell phone rang. "It's Uncle Wayne." She pressed the button to receive the call. "Hello."

"Nice to hear your voice," said the sheriff.

"We were just discussing the cases. You're on speaker, Gav is here too."

"I read your last report and I thought I'd better call you."

"Everything okay?" she said.

"I think that's a better question for you. Anything you'd like to share that wasn't in your brief report?" His voice was direct.

"You mean about an assailant and the beanbag bullets?"

"No."

"Then what?" She looked at McGaven.

"You're forgetting that I've been around law enforcement for a long time. I can tell when there's things going on, like strange circumstances, and being at a disadvantage in another town."

"Yes, you're right. In some ways no one will talk to us and in others we've been bombarded with information. There have definitely been some weird things here."

"I've been contemplating pulling you two out of there."

"No, don't do that. Not now. Those girls deserve justice and whatever is going on needs to be brought out in the open." Katie was adamant she wanted to stay. But whatever her boss decided, she would have to obey it and move on.

There was silence on the phone. "I'm going to allow you to stay for now, but if anything more happens like what's been happening, I'm pulling you out of there immediately. Got it?"

"Yes, sir," they said in unison.

"I have one more question," Katie said. "There's a large two-story cement building here—it's out in a rural location in the woods."

"The one that used to be for SWAT training. Yes, I'm aware of it. I've never been there."

"What do you know about it?"

"Not much. I believe it's owned by the city or county and set for demo."

"Anything more? Or any stories about it?"

"I don't even know who owned it then or if anyone owns it now. What's on your mind?" the sheriff asked.

"I think some terrible things might have happened there and it's somehow tied to this town."

"I'm not sure that I like where you're going with this."

"I, rather we, are trying to get as much information as we can about this town," she said, hoping that her uncle wasn't changing his mind now about yanking them out.

"I see."

"And, this is a bit unorthodox, especially for a homicide, but I wanted to get your permission to put Chief Baker on surveillance just until we know more about what we're dealing with here."

Again, there was a stilted silence on the other end of the phone.

Katie bit her lip, waiting for his response. Cisco must've sensed her hesitation and tension, so he came over and sat next to her, rubbing his head against her knee.

"I'm granting your request, but only at a distance to observe, not a full-blown surveillance. You report everything back to me and I'll re-evaluate the situation. You're there to investigate three homicides and this is becoming extenuating circumstances."

"Yes, sir."

"I'm going on record saying that if what you suspect is true, then you both are walking a very thin and dangerous line."

"Understood," she said.

"I hope you do. McGaven, you make double sure that Katie stays in line."

"I understand. Yes, sir."

"Katie, take care of yourself and don't be impetuous."

"I will." She knew that when he called her Katie, his role was more uncle than sheriff. "Please don't worry. We'll be fine," she said.

"Good night."

"Good night."

The line disconnected.

Katie leaned back against the couch and let out an exhale. She glanced at the small dining table, where there were piles of papers, photographs, notes, and Ivy's smashed cell phone. There was so much to do that needed a staff of people to sift through all of the notes and evidence. That meant they had to be selective and smart about what to spend their energies on.

"Don't look at that," said McGaven.

"What?"

"Don't worry about all that stuff on the table."

"I can't help it—it feels like we're drowning and there's no lifeline."

"Nope, we are gathering information." He turned to his partner. "You look exhausted."

"I am. Aren't you?"

"Yes, but I didn't take a ride down a hill in the forest this evening."

"That's a lovely way of putting it." Katie could feel her muscles tightening up in her back. Sleep sounded fantastic right now.

"I'm going to search a bit more then go to bed. You should too."

Katie got up. "I can't fight it anymore. I'll see you in the morning." She walked toward her bedroom with Cisco tailing behind.

"Oh, by the way, can we get through a day without you being attacked and falling down somewhere and bullets flying at us?" He ducked the cushion thrown at him and smiled as he continued his data search.

# THIRTY-FIVE

*Friday 0735 hours*

Katie's cell phone rang on the nightstand. She was in a deep sound sleep and didn't want to move from her comfortable place, but the ringing wouldn't stop. Finally, she clumsily reached for her phone and answered it, still with her eyes closed not knowing who was on the other end.

"Hello?" she said croakily.

"Good morning, gorgeous," said Chad on the end. He had a sexy voice that she had always loved.

Katie smiled and opened her eyes. Hearing his voice was the best way to start a day. She tried not to think about him too much when she was working because her heart ached with not being with him. "Hi," she said.

"I knew that I was going to wake you, but it was important."

She sat up. "What's wrong?"

He softly laughed. "Nothing's wrong. But right about now you should be smelling pancakes and bacon."

It was true. Katie could smell bacon and pancakes aroma wafting into her bedroom. "How did you know that?"

"And you call yourself a detective. I sent Gav an email last night that he should surprise you, from me, with breakfast. I really miss you, babe."

"I know. I thought that by today we'd be coming back to Pine Valley, but these cases have taken some strange turns."

"Good thing I'm so understanding," he said.

Katie smiled. "What have I done to deserve you?"

"I'm a free gift."

"You really are. Wish you were here right now." She closed her eyes, imagining his handsome face and strong, sensual kisses.

"Me too."

"Wake up. Breakfast is ready!" called McGaven from the kitchen.

"Right on time," said Chad. "Go enjoy your breakfast."

"I love you," she said.

"Love you more."


Katie finished her breakfast with McGaven and felt better. Her sore muscles were easing and she felt a burst of energy to take on the day and the investigation. Neither she nor McGaven said much while they ate; it was clear that they had many things weighing heavy on their minds.

A familiar ring tone came from McGaven's laptop. It was another video conference call from John.

Katie and McGaven went to the living room and sat down on the couch. They could see John's smiling face as he sat in his lab with computers around him.

"Hi," said John. "How are you two hanging in there?"

"We're doing fine," said Katie. She didn't want to burden him with the details of the case—at least not until they had solid evidence.

"Good," said John. "I have some news. I don't know if it's good or not, but it's more information."

Katie's hopes for something substantial in the forensic evidence began to dwindle as she let her pessimistic side surface. She tried to focus on a positive attitude, but realized that these cases were weighing heavy and beginning to take a personal toll.

"Give us what you have," said McGaven.

"First, I know that we are trained to stay objective, but I have to say these cases are such tragedies." His face was strained and tense, making it clear that working these cases was difficult for him.

Katie felt exactly the same way. She found it interesting that John made mention of this—he'd worked so many cases like it, including the murder of his previous forensic tech. Maybe that was why he was taking these cases so hard now. Or maybe it was just the toll of seeing three young lives cut off in an instant.

"Nikki Prager, whose body was found at the creek area, had no trace evidence on her. Nothing at all. It appears to me that she might have been bathed or at the very least wiped clean."

"Wiped clean?" said Katie. She had not expected to hear that. The medical examiner hadn't given any indication of this.

"It appears from the evidence that the body might have been washed, maybe in the creek? But I would give a solid eighty percent probability that the killer took extra care not to leave any evidence behind on her. Like Ivy Miller, her clothes were missing and there weren't any hairs or fibers on her. The only evidence left behind was the pink bandana tied around her nose and mouth. It was also clean—too clean, as if it had just been taken out the package. There were still creases and the starching was evident enough to indicate that."

"I'm betting it's from a company that has millions of bandanas in thousands of stores," she said.

"Correct. If that bandana had a print, picture, or something that would narrow down the market and who would carry it, I might have been able to pick up a trail." He moved his chair, taking the laptop with him. "Now, the strangulation marks are consistent to Ivy Miller's—same pressure, size, and placement from the same type of rope. Even though we don't have any rope—I would say they are consistent between the two bodies."

Katie thought it was good and bad news.

"What about the word 'Never' written on her?" said McGaven.

"The placement and type of cutting instrument used are also consistent with Ivy." He pulled up magnified images of both victims' necks side-by-side. "In my opinion, the same type of knife was most likely used to carve the words, but since I don't have the knife I can't say for certain. The incisions are extremely thin, so a hunting knife probably wouldn't be the weapon. I would say more of a specialty knife."

"Could it be something from a fishing tackle box?" said Katie. Her mind went through the inventory of Torrez's storefront.

"It's possible. It would have a straight edge, not serrated. There would be more damage to the skin if it was serrated and the wording would be muddled. I would say something like a filleting knife, but not the entire blade. It would be just the tip, where it's thin to make it easier for the killer to carve out words."

"Good info," said Katie.

"I'm sorry that I don't have more solid evidence."

"John, anything you find for us is always helpful," said Katie.

McGaven nodded. "Absolutely."

"Dawn Cromwell's injuries are completely different," John continued. "There are knife injuries, deep scratches, and bruising. The ME did swab some of the deep scratches, but there was no DNA or trace evidence of any kind. It doesn't make sense to me that the MO is so different here. I'm not an investigator or profiler of behavioral evidence, but Dawn's wounds are savage and erratic. I don't believe that only one person inflicted those injuries—unless they had several personalities."

He paused, and Katie and McGaven waited patiently for him to continue.

"Some of the incisions were barely below the surface while others were deep, nicking organs and tendons. Her throat being slit from ear to ear was an absolutely brutal action. There wasn't just one slice, but two. One was more superficial while the other was as if someone were gutting an animal—deep and direct." John rolled his chair back slightly and looked at the detectives. It was obvious that the examination of the photographs of Dawn's body, and the testing of the samples sent to him, had made him deeply troubled.

*Was it possible there had been more than one person?* The thought of more than one person killing Dawn, taking turns, perhaps, disturbed Katie. She was basing her preliminary profile on one killer.

*Was Ivy murdered for something she found out?*

*Something she saw?*

*Something she heard?*

"Was the carving of the word 'Forever' consistent with the others even though it was on her chest?" said McGaven.

"It was. I also wanted to mention that the nails used to fasten her to the tree were large-diameter construction nails. Again, they are common and can be found at any hardware or superstore."

"Thank you, John, for getting this examination back to us so quickly," she said.

"All in a day's work. I've sent you everything including photos and some diagrams of the injuries." He forced a smile. "I can imagine that it's stressful on your end. Let me know if I can do anything else. Be safe, you two."

"We will."

"Thanks," said McGaven.

The video connection ended.

Katie stayed seated, thinking about the savage murder of Dawn. The evidence of the bodies told them more about the behavioral patterns of the killer or killers they were searching for.

"Let me in on your thoughts," said McGaven.

"This actually tells us a lot."

"That there might be more than one killer?"

"Yes. And also that extreme anger was directly at Dawn specifically. It means that the killer made it personal and let his savagery be unleashed as if she was being punished. We could deduce that from the bodies, but now it's verified from John's perspective, it's something we need to concentrate on." Katie got up and went to her preliminary overview of the killer's profile and behavioral evidence written on sticky notes. She felt they were getting closer to his motive.

McGaven watched his partner.

"Usually a brutal crime such as this with a propensity for overkill means it's more personal. And this killer could have more of a connection to Dawn. A personal friend? New boyfriend?" she said, still reading over her initial list.

"How would a fifteen-year-old girl be associated with someone who would do this?"

"Gav, there are many documented cases where teenage girls themselves have been involved in killings. From killing a class-mate out of jealousy to killing their family members because they didn't get what they want. We don't like to think that a fifteen- or sixteen-year-old girl would participate in these heinous crimes, but it does happen."

"There's some information that I wish I didn't know."

"I think that Ivy was the initial target and that her death can perhaps explain why the other girls were murdered. These girls weren't killers. But whatever transpired with Dawn was different.

"It also comes back to Ivy and what she discovered. That's what started this entire crime spree," said McGaven.

"We need to find out who the hooded man is and what he knows."

"You don't think he's the killer?"

Katie glanced at the boards, running the information and John's assessment through her mind. "We can't be sure, but it's where we need to focus. We have to put these things into two columns for now—working and nonworking evidence."

McGaven downed the last of the coffee. "Where to?"

"Let's have a chat with Lenny at the Wild Iris Inn."

# THIRTY-SIX

*Friday 1005 hours*

Katie and McGaven sat in front of the Wild Iris Inn waiting and watching. Cisco was amped and edgy in the back seat, clearly wanting to go wherever the detectives were going.

Some guests came out and headed to their cars, obviously planning on seeing the town. They were smiling and laughing with one another, oblivious that someone was watching them.

"Obviously they enjoyed Mama's breakfast," said McGaven.

"Her food is amazing."

A few more guests filtered out.

Cisco pushed his gorgeous black head in between the seats and demanded to be petted and scratched behind his ears. Of course, both Katie and McGaven obliged.

"Look," said Katie.

Lenny came out dressed in dark jeans and a gray hoodie and carrying a towel. He was tall and lean, and easily resembled the unknown man Katie had had contact with twice. She wondered if she would recognize anything about his build or demeanor that would trigger a memory of her assailant. Lenny pushed up his sleeves as if he had something important to do and hurried around the back of the building, not noticing the detectives.

"Go around back," said McGaven.

"What do you say to turning up the heat a bit?"

"Sounds like fun."

"You're going to have to do it—you're definitely scarier than me," she said smiling.

"I'm not so sure—you can be plenty scary in the interrogation room. Feel free to jump in anytime."

Katie started the Jeep and slowly drove out of the guest parking area and around the building. There were parking spaces for Mama and her son, and any workers. Two of the spots had a carport area, which gave cover during the rainfall.

Lenny was working on a car, hood up. He was bent over the engine, diligently working on something.

Katie parked at the end of the building and they walked to where Lenny was working.

"Hi, Lenny," said Katie eying the tools and sparkplugs.

Instantly, Lenny stood up, smacking his head on the side of the hood. "Oh," he said, obviously surprised to see them. Rubbing the side of his head, he said, "Hi, Detectives." There was no smile or seemingly helpful attitude today, a distinct contrast from when he had offered to have the old patrol car washed and cleaned up for them when they first landed in town.

"You okay?" said Katie as she watched him closely.

"Yeah, I'll live."

McGaven had already taken notice of the car license plate and knew it was registered to Travis Ramos. "Travis?" said McGaven.

Lenny just stared at McGaven. "No one ever calls me that. How'd you know?" He looked at the detective suspiciously.

"We were tracking down the car that was near Ivy Miller's crime scene. A witness said it was an older model, four-door, green/blue vehicle. We searched registrations for this area and your name came up—Travis Leonard Ramos."

"Am I a suspect?"

"What makes you say that?" said McGaven.

"Green older car. I'm young, so you figure that I'm suspicious."

"We follow every lead, no matter how small, especially when it comes to a homicide investigation, so here we are. Where were you again on Sunday and Monday nights—midnight to four a.m.?" McGaven took a couple of steps closer to him.

"Sleeping. Alone. Unfortunately." He crossed his arms, trying not to fidget with his hands.

"Did you know Ivy Miller?" said McGaven.

"I already told you. I know who she is—or was. We didn't travel in the same circles. Besides, she was too young."

"Did you give her a ride between midnight and four a.m. Sunday night?" McGaven was intentionally working the young man with repeat questions, so that he might slip up or be caught out in a lie.

"No. Why would I?"

"You tell me."

"Oh, I see what you're doing. Trying to trap me into saying something that will incriminate me." He absently wiped his hands on the towel.

Katie watched the young man as McGaven questioned him. There were signs of deceit, with the averting of his eyes, his constant movement and wringing of his hands. When he answered something he didn't want to his voice was raised in a slightly higher pitch. She studied his body language, trying to work out if he could have been the dark figure that shoved her twice. It was a maybe. There wasn't anything physical that would connect him to the unknown figure, he just resembled it by strength and build.

"Look, man, I don't want to talk to you anymore."

"Lenny, do you know Tyler Rey?" said Katie.

He seemed to think a moment. "The tattoo guy?"

"Yes. What can you tell me about him?" said Katie. She tried to change the mood of the questioning, because he was about to close down the conversation and walk away.

"I dunno. He does cool work. I've seen him around."

"Why don't you have tattoos?"

"I just don't."

"Did you know that Tyler Rey would pick up Ivy Miller from school?"

"What?" he said with some emotion and then composed himself.

*Gotcha...*

"Did you ever see the two of them around together?"

He shrugged, looking more at the ground than the detectives. "I dunno."

"I bet you would have liked a girlfriend like Ivy. How about Nikki or maybe Dawn?" said McGaven. He took the opportunity to casually walk around the car, looking inside.

"Maybe."

"Lenny, do you know Maxwell Torrez?" said Katie, trying to keep Lenny engaged in conversation.

"Max? Yeah."

"How do you know him?"

"I've bought stuff from him. You know, like fishing stuff."

"Ever bought a knife?"

"A couple of times for fishing and camping stuff."

"What about nylon rope?" said McGaven.

"I dunno. I don't think so. What's up with the twenty questions?" He tilted his head, trying to figure them out.

"We're just trying to get a handle on some of the people in town."

"Are they suspects?" He smiled a juvenile toothy grin.

"Not really, but you never know. That's why we talk to people," said McGaven. "So why did you want to clean the old patrol car for us?"

"For twenty bucks. Why do you think? Kinda low on funds."

Katie had a sudden inspiration. "What were you looking for?"

"Nuthin."

"Did you find it?"

"What do you mean?"

"C'mon, Lenny. You saw an opportunity and you took it. You didn't want us to find whatever you hid in the car so you came up with the car wash idea." She watched him closely. "I'm going to ask you again. What were you looking for?"

"And I'm telling you—*nothing*..."

Katie shook his denials off. She had seen it many times when criminals were cornered. They lied—only until they were caught—then the excuses start pouring in. "Did you hide it in the trunk? Glove box? Or... did you hide it under the seat?"

Lenny reacted when she said under the seat. "I'm telling you I didn't kill Ivy, I didn't hide anything in the old cop car, and I'm not talking to you anymore."

"Okay," said Katie. "That's fine. We'll see you around town." She smiled.

"See you around, Lenny," said McGaven.

The detectives walked back to the Jeep where Cisco had his nose pressed out the window crack.

Before Katie got in, Officer Lane rolled up in his cruiser. "Hi, Detectives," he said.

"Hi, Brett," said Katie.

The officer rolled down the window all the way. "How are things going?"

"Could be better," she said.

He seemed to be nervous, checking the mirrors. "Did your forensic unit find anything to help you?"

"Some. Mostly behavioral evidence type of things."

"Oh," he said, not knowing how to respond to that.

"We want to thank you for helping us. You really were a big help."

"I'm sorry about the blanket thing."

"Everyone makes mistakes when they're starting out."

"Were you talking to Lenny?" He gestured toward the back of the inn.

"Yeah, just some standard questions. We're at a disadvantage here so we're talking to people who had a connection to the victims," she said.

Brett strummed his fingers on the steering wheel.

"Are you late for something?" she said.

"No, just doing my usual rounds and getting hungry."

"I wanted to ask you. On Monday night, did you drive by the Pragers' residence?"

"Sure did. About every half hour or so."

"And you didn't see anything? Anybody driving by or out walking near the home?" Katie had a difficult time watching his expression with his dark sunglasses.

"Nope. It was quiet. I wish I had seen something that might've stopped them from sneaking out. Then maybe..." He stopped talking.

"You can't change the past. Sometimes you have to forgive yourself and move forward."

Officer Lane looked at Katie and then McGaven. "You're right. Move forward."

"If anything comes up that we might need to know about— you let us know, okay?" she said.

He nodded. Without a word, he rolled up his window and drove away.

"That was interesting," said McGaven as he got into the Jeep.

"You can say it."

"What?"

"That was weird. Do you suppose he was keeping tabs on us?"

"It's a possibility."

"I think it's a high probability."

"Meaning?" said McGaven.

"Meaning we're starting to rattle enough cages to move this investigation forward."

# THIRTY-SEVEN

*Friday 1215 hours*

Katie and McGaven sat in the parking lot at the entrance for Bates Hiking and Camping. Katie couldn't get Ivy's face out of her mind. She tried hard to work these cases at arm's length, but she simply couldn't anymore. The photo of Ivy and her mother with the note made her heart ache. The idea that the killer might not be done yet kept Katie driving forward.

"Are you sure you want to hike up there again?" said McGaven.

"We're rattling cages, remember? I want some straight answers from Joshua. He knows more than he's saying." She thought about his history and that he was now a complete recluse in the woods.

"Do you think he told us the truth?"

"I do. He just didn't tell us everything," she said. "There's more to this town's story and I believe Joshua knows it. If we can't get him to open up, maybe Cisco can?" A smile washed across her face.

Cisco stood up in the back with his tail thumping against the seat.

"Shouldn't we crunch more information? Denise sent some background stuff and I still have some more searches. You need to work on the killer's profile and linkage."

"I do. And yes, we need to do that."

"Okay."

"I'm concerned, deeply concerned, that the killer is still out hunting. We can't let him kill another victim." Katie looked outside where the overcast sky seemed to put a gloom over the small town. It made her homesick and she wanted to be back in Pine Valley. She had never felt this way before except in the army, but she appreciated her own town so much more as she sat looking out at the trees and cloudy day. "We must press people in this town if it means we can save another life."

"You're right, but I'm going on record saying that I really hate going up in those woods."

Katie got out of the Jeep and readied herself, bringing an extra magazine—just in case. She fitted Cisco with his tracking harness but only took a six-foot leash as backup. McGaven again set up a camera at the car and secured everything.

Katie, McGaven, and Cisco set off to climb up the path that Joshua had shown them from his house. It was a quicker route, taking only twenty minutes or so, and they most likely wouldn't run into anyone. The entrance to the hike was behind a cluster of trees not readily seen by most. They took it slower than a casual walk, making sure that there weren't any traps or ambushes. Such a possibility was always in the back of their minds.

They trekked in silence and it was obvious that they were both extra vigilant to their environment. What should have been a pleasant walk was now scrutinized at every step as potentially treacherous. The gray overcast day added a gloomy factor to the uneasiness of their surroundings. Birds continued to chirp and perch in the thick trees. Where some areas seemed impenetrable it made Katie anxious to the point of paranoid. She snapped her eyes into focus when she saw shadows moving about in her peripheral vision—her mind playing tricks on her. It was like being in a war zone, a fact that made her more alert than ever, to the point of hypersensitivity and readiness for battle. She couldn't take anything for granted, and everything seemed like potential danger.

Cisco sensed Katie's adrenalin and he kept close to her left side.

As they reached the higher areas, the familiar smell of fireplace smoke wafted around the trees. They were close.

Katie was just thinking she couldn't take the stress anymore when she saw familiar things near Joshua's cabin with its neatly stacked firewood and long planting troughs for vegetables. There was a wind chime hanging from a macramé tether. It swung easily, making a pleasant chiming noise as the breeze pushed up from behind them.

As they rounded a corner, there was Joshua dressed in overalls and a navy blue knitted sweater, which was still fitted with a holster and revolver. He was bending over a large cast-iron pot above an outdoor stove, tasting the wonderful-smelling contents. Never turning in their direction, he said, "Thought you'd be back sooner."

It was now clear. Katie realized that the old man had originally given them just enough information to send them on their way. Giving them a chance to check things out for themselves—then they would eventually come back to get more answers.

Cisco trotted up to Joshua with his usual doggie greeting.

"Hey, boy, nice to see you again," he said patting the dog.

Katie watched and realized that Cisco had a definite fondness for the old man. That was a good thing for a dog, any dog, to really like a person. Cisco had been trained for tracking, trailing, and searching out bombs. For him to enjoy being around a man that they didn't really know, put Katie's mind at ease. She felt her intense sense of danger as well as her pulse rate subsiding, meaning she could concentrate fully on what they needed to accomplish.

"Just in time," said Joshua. "This beef and vegetable stew is about ready. I woke up this morning thinking that I would have visitors today."

"Did you know it would be us?" said McGaven. He seemed to like the old man as well as Cisco.

"Nothing's ever for sure—not even if we're going to wake up in the morning. But, it's a good probability. And look, here you are." He smiled, making his long gray beard move and showing his sparse teeth.

"We have some more questions for you," she said.

"I figured you might." He stood up straight and turned to the detectives. "Come inside while this stew simmers some more. The herbs need to infuse a bit longer. Besides, it's going to pour in a little bit and you need to get inside out of the rain."

He headed into the cabin as Katie, McGaven, and Cisco followed, entering in a straight line. Inside, Katie noticed that it was warmer than before as the fire was stoked up with a pleasant flame.

"Please make yourself comfortable." Joshua headed into the kitchen and began rattling some pots. "I have some fresh coffee. Would you like a cup?"

"Yes please," said McGaven. He sat down on the couch and rubbed his hands together as if warming them in the cozy environment.

"And what about you?" he said.

"That would be nice. Thank you."

Joshua turned to McGaven. "Is she always this talkative? All about business?"

"No, not always. Sometimes she can really get chatty."

*Chatty?*

Katie remained quiet. She wanted to take in the décor and the personal items in the cabin. She felt that she might've missed something on their last visit. The photographs were still in the same places. There were many with a younger version of Joshua and a pretty woman with her hair loosely pinned up. It was quite clear that they were in love. She thought of Chad. She wondered if they would be together taking care of each other until they were old.

*Nothing's ever for sure—not even if we're going to wake up in the morning.*

Joshua emerged from the kitchen with two mugs of coffee for the detectives, Cisco following closely. He handed one cup to Katie and smiled. She knew he seemed to make jokes about her, but there was a respectful quality in him that he managed to convey to her.

"Thank you," said Katie.

McGaven received his steaming cup.

Joshua sat down in his comfortable chair and Cisco downed near him, but in a place where he could see Katie.

Katie thought she would jump right in and get to the point. "You knew on our last visit that you were telling us only partial bits of information."

Joshua nodded. "Of course. You hadn't earned it."

"You are aware that we are investigating three homicides," she said. "Three teenage girls."

"I may be old, but I can remember previous conversations."

"Why do I get the feeling that you're toying with us?" Katie watched the old man, who seemed to be lost in thought staring at the flickering flames.

"What I'm going to tell you today wouldn't have made as much sense as it will now if I had told you on your first visit. You've been working, investigating, and talking to people. And

I'm fairly sure that you even have a few suspects in mind but can't make the evidence work. Am I correct?"

It unnerved Katie to hear Joshua talk like he had been listening to all their conversations. His intuition was spot on, but for a second Katie wondered if he was working for the group that seemed to be running them around the town.

"It's on the right track," said McGaven. His face was somber and he was serious. It was clear that he had the same thoughts as Katie—not knowing who to trust.

Joshua smiled. "Who have you spoken to?"

"That's not how this works," said Katie. "We are the detectives and we ask the questions." She knew her voice was a bit harsh, but this week had made her patience grow thin.

"All business."

"I don't mean any disrespect, so let me be blunt."

"Please go ahead."

She glanced to McGaven, making sure he was on the same page. His subtle nod gave her the green light. "You said that you knew Chief Roy Baker's dad. Correct?"

"Yes. We had been friends for a long time—we spent a good portion of our lives fishing and hunting together. Good man. I miss him, like so many others..." He looked to the photographs.

"What about Chief Baker? What can you tell me about him? I guess what I'm saying is... is he someone to be trusted?"

"Now you're finally asking the right questions, Detective." He paused and gazed into the fire. "He was a good kid, but there was always something missing in him."

"What do you mean?" Katie had an idea but she wanted to hear it from him. "Specifically."

"Let's just say there were always incidents, usually bad ones, that surrounded him."

Thunder rolled overhead, deep and rattling, as the soft sound of rain commenced.

It struck Katie that this man was able to predict when a brief rain shower would begin. He didn't have an application on his phone for the local Doppler radar, but rather, he knew the climate and had experienced it firsthand for decades. He was in tune with his environment and it was maybe also that way with the town. He knew the ins and outs of Coldwater Creek and Katie was going to ask him to uncover everything.

"Give us examples of these incidents," she said.

Cisco got up from his position and jumped on the couch, positioning himself between Katie and McGaven, listening to the conversation. The dog lightly panted and was keenly alert as his amber wolf eyes fixed on Joshua.

"There are so many to relate, and they seem to continue to this day. For example, his predecessor, Carl Langston, suddenly resigned and was never seen again. He gave no letter, no conversation with anyone, even his ex-wife hasn't seen him since that day. He vanished. It was perfect timing for Roy Baker. He was appointed, partly due to his father's influence, and has been chief ever since."

"That's interesting, but it isn't proof of any impropriety. There are many possible reasons and just because we don't know what they are—it doesn't mean that one of those things didn't happen."

"Sitting where you are and knowing what you know—I can see your point," the old man said. "But many people over the years seemed to go missing. And one of the connections has always been Chief Roy Baker."

Katie thought about the population drop of nearly five hundred in the past five to ten years.

"What do you think? Is the chief dirty or running some sort of criminal enterprise? What?" Katie thought about Maxwell Torrez and his two buddies.

"Perhaps. But Coldwater Creek hasn't been the same."

"He told us that there had been no homicides here, only a few accidents over the years," said McGaven.

"I can't give you firsthand accounts of being there and actually seeing it, but there's something wrong. My opinion, Ivy Miller was a planned murder and for everyone to see. Almost like a warning. The chief had to bring in outsiders—detectives to work the case to prove he was doing everything he could."

"But to kill Ivy's friends as well? Seems a bit excessive and the entire town knows it."

"That's the point. What better way to ensure people to keep their mouths shut—about anything?"

Katie thought about Sydney and the moving boxes. "What about Sydney Barrett-Miller?"

"Sydney has always been embroiled in some type of drama for as long as I can remember."

"We saw moving boxes at her house when we went to search Ivy's old bedroom," said McGaven.

"I'm sure she wasn't exactly forthcoming with you. And I don't blame her for leaving."

Katie got up from the couch and stood in front of the fire. She knew the room was warm, but she had chills and her blood seemed to turn cold. It was the first time that she thought they might not be able to solve this intricate and convoluted investigation. How could she let these three homicides turn to cold cases? They would end up in dusty files that no one would work again. Remembering the faces of the three girls and their crime scenes would haunt her forever—they deserved justice no matter what.

"You seem troubled," said Joshua.

"That might be an understatement." She turned to face Joshua. "Where is Ivy's mother?"

"Rebecca?" he stated carefully as if just mentioning her name could bring down a wrath of bad things. "I don't know.

She was another one of the residents who just seemed to disappear."

"You do know," said Katie. He had to know the circumstances at least. "Tell us what you know and what you think."

"I don't think that would help you."

"We'll be the judge of that. What do you know?" They were finally getting somewhere. Whatever caused Ivy to be murdered had something to do with her mother.

He leaned forward in his chair and Cisco jumped down and sat in front of him.

Thunder rumbled in the distance as the storm moved away.

"The only thing I know for sure is that Rebecca Miller left and hasn't been seen since—that's been about two years or so."

"What do you think happened?"

"I can't speculate on that."

"Tell us."

"There are things that you're not privy to."

"So tell us." Katie pressed him.

"She was naïve and mixed with the wrong people. And she left."

"She wouldn't leave her daughter behind."

"I don't know."

"You do."

He stood up and moved into the kitchen as Katie followed. It was clear that he knew something and it wasn't good.

"Joshua, does it have something to do with all the surveillance cameras all over town?"

"Yes."

"They're watching us, aren't they?"

"Most likely."

"Whatever it is, we can help you and protect you," she said, softening her approach. She liked Joshua but she had a case to solve and that meant unpleasant things coming out—and things that they weren't prepared for.

The old man turned to her. "I know you mean well, but I've lost everything I love and I'm too old to change or move from here. This is where I'm going to die."

"You don't strike me as someone willing to let a killer get away with it," said McGaven. "We're here now and we can help you in whatever you need."

Katie didn't mention anything about the unknown man that she had had contact with twice. She knew that there still was the slim chance that Joshua was under the control of who they were trying to fight against.

"You two seem like honest detectives—hardworking, dedicated. And I know you're trying to find the killer. I can see the hunger in your eyes of wanting to find justice. But the only thing I can tell you is that you're on the right track. Don't let anything or anyone sway your judgment."

"Please, Joshua," said Katie.

The old man studied the detectives, but he remained quiet. It was clear that he was done talking, either because he didn't know anything more, or because Katie and McGaven were on the right track. Or maybe he was afraid.

Katie put down her mug on the counter. "Thank you for your time, Mr. Kimball. You know how to contact us." She slowly shook her head. "C'mon, Cisco."

"We're here in town, don't know how long, but you can call us anytime. We're staying at the cottage on the south end," said McGaven. He rested his hand on the old man's shoulder. "Take care."

McGaven followed Katie and Cisco out the door.

Joshua went after them. "You're on the right track. I know you will find the answers you're seeking, but you will not like what you find. But please take a word of advice. Stay vigilant. Watch each other's back. Be careful and don't ever let your guard down."

Katie and McGaven continued their walk down the path.

Katie could see the clouds moving away and there was some sunlight peeking through. The forest seemed different now—new and cleansed. She ran the conversation through her mind as she moved faster down the pathway. There were places they needed to be.

*Stay vigilant. Be careful and don't ever let your guard down...*

# THIRTY-EIGHT

*Friday 1525 hours*

Katie remained quiet the entire trek back down the trail. Things around her didn't seem so dire and potentially dangerous as she gazed at the deep green groves of pine and oak trees. There was a renewed strength in her body and it wasn't the strong coffee she'd had at Joshua's cabin, but a sense that they were on the right track, just as the old man said.

Just before they returned to the Jeep, McGaven said, "I believe what Joshua told us and I also think we need to plow ahead with our plan."

"I agree."

Katie drove into the downtown area where there were more cars and people to give them cover so they wouldn't be spotted as easily. There were townspeople going about their errands and coming and going from work.

Katie decided to drive toward the police office and see what the chief and his officers were up to. There were two cars parked out front; the chief's and part-time Officer Brock

Daniels'. They hadn't seen much of this officer except on Monday when he had driven McGaven and John to Ivy's crime scene. It was unclear why he was on part-time duty.

She eased the Jeep into a parking place a couple doors down from the police office. It blended in with many other vehicles during the afternoon hours.

McGaven took his small binoculars and swept the area, looking for anything that might be suspicious or unusual.

"Can you see any of those surveillance cameras?" she said.

"Not yet." He swept the street area, buildings, and trees that he could see from the car.

"If I had to guess," she said, "they would be up there." Katie gestured to the small park that had big trees. "It would be a perfect place to camouflage cameras. No one would notice them."

"Wait. Here comes Chief Baker," said McGaven.

They watched as the chief and Officer Daniels came out of the office. They appeared to be deep in discussion. Finally, Daniels left and got into his car. The chief waited and watched the officer drive away. He got into his own car and pulled away from the curb.

"Do you think that the chief has an assistant or someone answering phones and doing the filing?" said McGaven.

"Probably not. I couldn't tell if he locked the door or not." Katie pulled away and got in two cars behind the chief.

Chief Baker drove slower than the posted speed limits. He slowed almost to a stop and then sped up again.

"What's he doing?" said McGaven.

"I don't know. Looking for something?"

"You don't think he sees us?"

"I don't think so. His personality and how long he's gotten away with whatever it is he's doing—he seems to think he can't be touched by his actions."

Katie kept the car in view until the chief pulled into a shopping center. He drove around to the back of a grocery store where deliveries were unloaded.

"What now?" she said.

"Go across the street to where that truck is parked," he said. "There's partial cover and we can still see what's going on."

Katie turned around and parked where McGaven had suggested. "There's the chief."

McGaven peered through the binoculars again. "And he's talking to Max Torrez and two other guys. I'm assuming that's Max's buddies."

"Are they getting their orders?" said Katie. The thought disgusted her. She wondered if someone saw her and McGaven visit Joshua. With everyone they had talked to—were they putting people in danger every time they interviewed someone?

"What if they're talking about us?" said McGaven.

"I was thinking the same thing."

"This investigation is like walking a tightrope—one wrong move... and..."

"I think you're right. Let's go back and work on research and digging for more information." Katie looked around the street and at the shopping center, trying to see if there were any cameras. Suddenly her anxious feeling cropped up. "We need to leave."

"You okay?" said McGaven.

"Yeah, but I'm beginning to feel like a rat in a maze—no matter where we go we could be watched." People she saw walking or getting into their cars seemed like potential agents watching them, but she knew that was her anxiety rising up.

McGaven didn't say anything, but must've sensed her instincts and scrutinized the area himself.

Katie had been rarely spooked by a situation or something dangerous she had to do. But by this stage in the investigation she felt trapped in a strange town with secrets worth killing for with no way to know who the good guys were.

She drove back to the cottage, where they had a mountain of paperwork to sift through and computer databases to search. When she reached the winding driveway, she noticed that there were deep tire tracks in the gravel as if a large truck had driven up or down it recently. She slowed the SUV and then stopped.

Cisco alerted, standing up looking out the windows.

"What's up?" McGaven said.

"I'm not sure. But those tire marks look recent."

"Maybe a delivery truck at the wrong address? Or someone who booked the cottage on a wrong date." Both of these were possibilities but she knew in her heart there was a better explanation.

"Or maybe someone else..." Her words stayed in the air. Katie's nerves were tingly and that sudden coolness filtered through her body.

*Stay vigilant. Be careful and don't ever let your guard down...*

"There's only one way in and out," he said. "I'll take a look at the camera views." He accessed them from his cell phone.

"Anything?"

"Not sure. They don't seem to be working correctly. Could be a glitch? What do you want to do?"

"Go straight ahead."

McGaven pulled his semiautomatic and prepared himself for anything.

"Cisco, *platz*." She ordered the dog to down in the back seat. At first, he hesitated, sensing the concern between both detectives, but then he obliged and downed.

Katie didn't speed up the curvy driveway but kept the vehicle at a moderate consistent pace. As she rounded the last corner, she was almost expecting to see Max and his men waiting with automatic weapons, ready to shoot them—her imagination working overtime.

There was nothing.

No one was there.

No car.

Katie stomped the brakes and they abruptly stopped.

Dust floated in the air. The Jeep sat in idle.

"This case is getting to us, to me," she managed to say. "I'm sorry for being so paranoid."

"You don't need to apologize. I was one hundred percent on board with you."

Katie cut the engine and got out. Cisco jumped to the front seat and followed her.

McGaven holstered his weapon and followed Katie to the front door.

Katie took out her key and just as she was about to unlock the door, she looked down. There was a black lid to some type of can. "Gav," she said, looking down.

He bent down and picked it up. "This wasn't here when we left this morning. I'm absolutely positive."

Katie backed away from the door, pulling her Glock. McGaven retrieved his weapon again. He nodded to her. Katie slowly inserted the key and turned the lock. She was the first through the door with Cisco moving in sync next to her.

As soon as Katie and McGaven entered the cottage, they stopped and gaped in disbelief at the inside. There were large words spray-painted across the walls:

*GET OUT NOW! OTHERWISE YOU ARE DEAD! LEAVE!*

Their files, computer, and investigative board were shredded, smashed, and torn up.

They searched the cottage and cleared it for anyone who might have been inside.

"Katie," said McGaven from her bedroom.

When she reached the room she saw that her clothes were shredded and there were three words on the wall that sent chills down her spine:

*MORE, NEVER, FOREVER. AND NOW YOU'RE NEXT...*

# THIRTY-NINE

*Friday 1745 hours*

Katie looked at her shredded clothes—even her undergarments —in disbelief. Then looking at the wall she knew that the killer was taunting them as if he wasn't ever going to be caught. She ran out of the room.

"Katie! Katie!" said McGaven as he raced after her. "Wait. You can't do this." He knew her weakness to be impetuous and wanted her to focus and calm down.

"Oh really? And who's going to stop me?" Her heart raced and she could only see the shadow man in her mind. She wasn't going to be caught off guard again. Not this time. Huge waves of frustration and anger rolled through her mind—feeding her rage. She knew that she sounded more like a spoiled child not getting her way—but this incident had taken it too far.

"Katie, you need to rethink this." McGaven's voice was calm and he had a way of making her listen to him even when she was angry.

"There's nothing to rethink. I've had enough."

"You're letting them get to you—that's exactly what they

want. They're trying to play us into making mistakes. Compromising the investigation—*our* investigation. Think of the victims."

"I don't care. This is ridiculous. They come into where we're staying, they spy on us everywhere we go, and they destroy our investigation... and..." She stopped abruptly and could feel a panic attack coming on—shortness of breath, head pounding, tingly limbs, and her vision becoming blurry. The room looked skewed, strangely like the funhouse in an amusement park. She thought she was going to pass out.

"Katie, you okay?" McGaven steadied his partner and directed her to the couch to sit down. "You have to calm down and breathe."

She nodded, trying to concentrate on this single most important task—breathing.

Cisco pushed his way onto the couch next to her, trying to comfort her.

A few minutes later the room had taken on its normal shape again. Katie looked around at the ransacked mess. Its disarray echoed how she felt right now: discarded, torn up, and frustrated. She wished that they had never taken the shortcut through Coldwater Creek. Looking down, next to her foot was a torn photo of Ivy Miller, staring at her as if pleading her to find the killer. She picked it up.

"You feeling better? You have color back in your face." He gently squeezed her arm for reassurance. Looking around he said, "This makes me angry too. But we need to be organized, smart, and ready to anticipate their next move. You have to admit this is juvenile and desperate behavior."

"I know you're right."

"I am."

Katie felt calmer presently. She didn't feel lightheaded anymore. Her body was weak and tired, but she began to regain her focus. She knew that McGaven was right and was glad that he was there for her, because she would have gone out loaded for bear and ended up making a fool out of herself—compromising the homicide investigation irreparably.

"You still have your laptop?"

"It's in the bedroom closet," she said. Her voice was still shaky. She kept her hand on Cisco, which helped her nerves and blood pressure to stabilize.

"I'm going to salvage what we have." McGaven began picking up papers and putting them in stacks on the table. He looked at his cell phone. "It looks like they destroyed the video cameras on the house."

"Gav, Max Torrez and his two buddies couldn't have done this. They didn't have time from when we saw them. Did they? So who did?" She focused on their day and realized that the destruction must have been done when they were up the mountain talking to Joshua.

"I don't know."

"Lenny?" she said.

"Maybe."

"Someone who isn't on our radar right now?"

"Could be," he said as he tried to put together his smashed laptop.

"Now we have to figure out who is really who they say they are—and who isn't. Everything makes me dizzy thinking about it." She stood up from the couch, making sure her legs weren't going to give out, then went to the kitchen and tried to reorganize the sticky pieces of paper.

"It's not as bad as it looks," he said.

"Gav, they shredded my clothes. I have nothing to wear except what I have on. I saw a place near the grocery store that had T-shirts and hoodies." Katie took her keys from the door. "I should go grab a few things before it gets late. I'll get food too."

"I'll go with you."

"No, continue with what you're doing. I'll leave Cisco here in case they try to come back."

McGaven was about to insist that he should go with her, but he gave up. "Just hurry and get what you need. If you're not back in half hour, I'm sending out the Marines."

"I'll be fine. It'll allow me to clear my head. I'll be back in the game when I get back. And we can figure this whole thing out together."

"Should we report this to Chief Baker?" he said.

"And then what? It won't help—at least not right now. We need to stay away from him and his officers. But we should date and document this."

Katie left the cottage. She was still trying to get her symptoms of anxiety to dissipate, and running errands would give her some time to think about what they were going to do next. She drove the Jeep down the driveway and headed to the small shopping center not far away.

She pulled into the business area and was relieved that the tourist store with some clothing was still open. She found a place to park at the southern end. Just as she stepped out, a strong arm grabbed her around the waist with a hand over her mouth, pulling her into the trees.

# FORTY

Katie tried to fight her assailant, but her exhaustion kept her at a disadvantage. She tried to free herself from his grip as she was pulled farther into the trees and away from the shopping area. Her gun was holstered and her cell phone was in her pocket; she couldn't reach either one. The only thing she could do was keep her attacker off balance by moving her body and flailing her legs.

"Shhh. Be quiet," the person whispered. "I'm not going to hurt you. Please be quiet."

Once they were far enough away from the populated area, the person released Katie. She spun around, grabbing her weapon in unison. Stepping back, she was surprised. "You?" she said, still directing her Glock at the assailant.

Officer Brett Lane stood in front of her. His expression was scared and he cautiously kept looking around. "I had to talk to you."

"There are better ways than this. I could have shot you," she said. She still couldn't believe the young officer had got the upper hand on her and she didn't see him following her.

"This is a place where there aren't cameras watching us." He looked around again. "I only have a short time."

"What is going on?"

"We don't have enough time for me to explain everything. You and your partner need to leave."

"Why?"

"For your safety. They'll keep trying to derail your investigation—but there will come a time when they will make sure your investigation stops permanently—understand?"

Katie saw Brett was genuinely scared. His eyes were wide and he had dark circles underneath, indicating he wasn't getting much sleep. "If anything happens to us, this town will have an entire department coming down hard on it."

"It won't matter—there won't be any evidence of what happened to you."

"Who is doing this?"

"It's complicated."

"No, it isn't. Who? Who is it keeping this town hostage? Who killed Ivy? Tell me! This has to stop right now." Katie felt the anger begin to rise in her body again. She knew the officer was telling the truth—she had interviewed enough suspects who were lying and it had trained her to know when someone was being honest—the subtle ways of eye contact, body language, and body positioning. She holstered her weapon.

"I can't do that."

"Why?"

"Someone else will die."

Those words hit her hard with a stinging type shock. "Who?"

"I can't say."

"Can't say or won't?" Katie suddenly realized. "It was you."

Officer Lane's build and strength fit the stature of the unknown man she had tried to catch.

"What do you mean?"

"You're the guy who was at Ivy's crime scene and at the shoreline near the cottage. You tried to kill me."

"No, I stayed at the creek shore to make sure you were okay. I couldn't let you see me."

"How do I know you're not the killer?" she said.

"I would never murder anyone," he said with conviction. "Ever. I knew Ivy... and I would never hurt her—ever. I tried to protect her, but she kept digging for more information about her mom after she found that flash drive in her grandmother's things."

Katie paced, trying to make sense of everything. "Then who killed those girls?"

"Look, I'm risking a lot talking to you. But you have to leave now." He glanced behind them.

"There wasn't a text message about Nikki and Dawn, was there?" Katie started putting the pieces together and it began to make sense.

He remained silent.

"There wasn't a text message, was there? You made it look like it." Katie kept her emotions in check, but she was losing patience. They were losing time as well. "Was there?"

He shook his head.

"We've been trying to solve these murders—but everything, mostly everything, has been orchestrated. Is that what you're saying?"

"Yes."

"We're not leaving until someone gets arrested."

"Detective, *please* leave."

Katie stared hard at the officer. She had thought about packing things up, especially after the break-in at the cottage, but there was no way they were leaving now. Ivy and her friends deserved better. Coldwater Creek deserved better. Her worst fear was more victims. She knew that Brett wouldn't tell her the names, but she would ask directly. "Is Chief Baker part of this?"

He nodded.

"Who else?"

"I can't say, but they're usually around him."

Katie was frustrated. "Who controls the cameras?"

"They are monitored and controlled from a certain building."

"Around the clock?"

"No, the data is picked up once a day."

"Is it accessible?" she said.

"Yes. It's in plain sight, but still takes a key to open the office."

"Where is it?"

That question seemed to make Brett even more terrified. "You've been there." His voice lowered into a whisper. "It's a place that no one would think to look."

"I'm not in the mood for games."

"Think."

Katie recalled everyone they had interviewed and places they went. "The medical examiner's office?"

He nodded.

Of course, she thought. A building that was cement, only one door in front and one entrance in back, it made perfect sense. But that still didn't tell her what Coldwater Creek was doing.

"Please," she said. "What is the operation that's going on here?" She began to think that this town was like one of the ops she worked in the army.

Brett fought whether or not he should say anything. He paced, clenching and unclenching his fists.

"What?"

He moved closer to her and whispered, "It's a clearing house for anything from trafficking to drugs to guns. Baker and his crew get kickbacks."

"Who?"

"There are syndicates that require places to keep things until their situation cools off."

"Mob?"

"Of sorts."

"So Ivy must've found something out when she was trying to find her mother." Katie was thinking aloud instead of making a statement.

Brett looked back and saw something. "I have to go."

"Wait."

"No, I've been here too long."

"Wait..."

"Look at the words from the crime scenes—they are not words... not what they seem."

"We need to meet again."

Brett hesitated. "I'll contact you. Watch your backs."

He disappeared.

Katie wasn't sure where Brett had parked or where he disappeared to now, but it made her remember what Joshua had said to them earlier.

*Stay vigilant. Be careful and don't ever let your guard down...*

She needed to get back to McGaven and fill him in on what Officer Brett Lane had told her. Her mind spun, her obsession with the investigation rekindled. The list of suspects took a sharp turn as everything seemed to go sideways, but no matter what was going on, she wasn't going to allow another murder. She would find the girls' killer.

Katie quickly bought two shirts, underwear, a pair of khaki pants, and picked up chicken dinners. Walking past an office for Animal Rescue of Coldwater Creek, she saw photos of dogs and cats available for adoption. Despite the situation, she paused and looked at the photos of all the cute faces of all sizes and breeds of dogs.

When she got back to her Jeep, she took a nonchalant look around and spied where the cameras were placed, facing the shopping center. Driving back to the cottage, she vowed that the people involved in this scheme—one where you were killed because of what you knew—were going to pay.

# FORTY-ONE

Katie hurried into the cottage carrying her clothes and two bags of food. Cisco immediately was interested to what was in the bag. She dropped everything on the kitchen counter.

"What took you so long? I was working out a SWAT detail trying to figure out where you were," said McGaven as he approached his partner.

"I was accosted by the unknown shadow guy," she said with a slight smirk on her face.

"What are you talking about?"

"I was getting out of my car when I was dragged into the bushes."

McGaven looked at her with disbelief, clearly not knowing what to say.

"I'm fine, but had an interesting conversation with Officer Brett Lane."

"Brett, the guy who helped us at the crime scenes? He's the guy who pushed you down—twice?"

"The one and only." Katie began unloading the food. "He was warning us to leave."

"Just like the spray paint on the walls."

"Grab some drinks and I'll fill you in on what he told me and some things that became clear to me."


Katie finished telling McGaven everything and waited for him to respond. She polished off her chicken—saving some for Cisco—and waiting for her partner to say something.

"I'm speechless," he said.

"I know how you feel."

"But, Katie, this is way outside what we can do here—and beyond the scope of the investigation and what we're sworn to do."

"Yes, and..."

"And we need to talk to the sheriff and probably abort this investigation."

"I knew you would say that, but listen for a minute. First, the situation is still the same; we are here to investigate these murders, and we are getting closer to the killer. We don't know what Officer Lane told me is the truth; it could still be part of the so-called mirage that they are trying to create."

"Okay, but even if half of what he said is true, it means we have a problem—a very serious problem."

"I agree. But we need to find out more before we report anything. Personally, I believe that Brett is telling the truth—you can't fake being terrified the way he was. He was really trying to save us by telling us to leave."

"I'm not going to change your mind, am I?" he said.

"We have to play the cards we've been given."

"Don't use card analogies."

Katie smiled. "Okay. But if we leave, then we're leaving innocent people behind us. But he made mention that if we kept pursuing this investigation, then there would be another murder. I keep running through my mind about another girl—we can't let that happen." She felt her chest compress, heavy with dread if another girl was murdered.

McGaven stood up and cleared the wrappers and containers. "I've known you long enough and I have an idea of what you want to do."

"You should by now."

"I still remember vividly when I first met you and had to be your handler because you weren't a detective. You remember?"

"Of course."

"And I also remember that you left me behind at the coffeehouse because you wanted to follow a lead that I would have protested against."

Katie stared at what was left of the paperwork on the table —stacked in neat piles, some taped back together.

"Your instincts are usually right—and you know that I have your back no matter what."

"So we wait to report to the sheriff until we substantiate the evidence?"

"Yes and no."

"What do you mean?" Katie was impatient and a little surprised by McGaven's answer.

"Yes, let's move forward to verify the information. But I have a few alterations."

Katie patiently waited—her curiosity escalated.

"I know we haven't nailed down our next move—but I'm assuming, knowing your thought process about such things, that you want to get inside the medical examiner's office."

"Yes."

"I think we need some help."

"Help?"

"I think we need another person to help us who's capable even if something goes spiraling down or sideways."

"And that would be John, right?" She knew that he would be the only person who was qualified and able to handle the situation they were considering.

He nodded. "We also need some serious backup in case this situation turns ballistic."

"But that would mean we have to get that permission from the sheriff."

"Not a formal written order, but a heads-up. I don't like it, but it would suffice."

"It would be just a conversation with SWAT. Nothing more that would jeopardize our sworn oath and chain of command."

"Nothing more," he said.

Katie noticed that Gav was tense. His jaw was clenched as he spoke about the plan. "First, we have some planning and research to do."

Katie and McGaven spent the next two hours searching the background and property of the town—buildings, police department, missing person's cases, accident reports, witnesses, and suspects. There was no doubt that the homicide investigation had been ratcheted up to an all-time high and they had to know who and what they were dealing with.

Katie studied the remains of her initial killer profile; most of it would still be applicable for the new challenges they were currently facing. Dividing the real evidence was a simple way of putting their priorities at the center of their investigation: primary and secondary evidence. One wasn't any less important than the other, but rather, it streamlined what they needed to concentrate on immediately to get to the source—only then would everything fall into place.

Katie made two lists on her notepad, a method unlike any previous records she had made for an investigation. She named them primary and secondary categories, and arranged her evidence accordingly. She studied each entry and the same things came back to her every time.

What did Ivy find out? Was it something about her mother? Was it about the town itself?

Katie sifted through the information about the cement building in the woods. It seemed logical to her that it was the center of criminal activity—a plausible place to store anything that needed to be hidden or laundered. The fact that the building was supposed to have been demolished years ago yet it somehow managed to still be standing in the woods was a mystery to her. She found documents supporting its demise, but then others contradicting the previous memos.

She looked at her notes and then thought about the conversation with Brett. He said something that raised some questions.

*Look at the words from the crime scenes—they are not words... not what they seem...*

Not what they seem? They're words—what else could they be? They represent something else? A code? Numbering system?

Katie heard McGaven talking with John on the phone. He was explaining what they were up against and they were creating a plan of action. She felt more at ease with John coming to help—he would have a perfect pretext regarding the forensic evidence and all they had to do was devise a plan to get a peek at the surveillance room at the medical examiner's building.

*More...*

*More...*

*M O R E...*

It was such a simple innocuous word. It simply meant a greater or additional amount of something.

Katie let the word rattle around in her mind. She knew that Brett was giving her a huge hint. But what? She glanced at the bag with the newly bought clothing. On the receipt it said "Give today to ARCC," which was the Animal Rescue of Coldwater Creek. Many companies, whether nonprofit or not, used acronyms to shorten the length of business names.

*More?*

Katie borrowed her laptop from McGaven on a hunch. He was still talking to John about details in the investigation.

She sat at the dining table and began a search of M.O.R.E. as an acronym. There were more than she realized—around fifty to a hundred. She began scanning down the list. Most were various business names for schools and government. She toggled back and forth from website to website—and kept digging. A half hour passed. But a few caught her attention because they had to do with research and enforcement, which was sometimes connected to compliance:

*Mindfulness Oriented Regrouping Enforcement* and *Maximizing and Optimizing Research Environment.*

What was enforcement and research? They sounded more like names for cover businesses that really didn't want to reveal exactly what they did.

Katie ran the names through the database of business lists and licenses in Sequoia County, secondary Coldwater Creek in California. She got a hit on Maximizing and Optimizing Research Environment. The mailing address was 1707 Cypress Lane, Coldwater Creek, California.

"Gav, I got some information that backs up what Officer Lane told me."

McGaven was immediately at her side reading the computer screen.

"'MORE' is an acronym for Maximizing and Optimizing Research Environment, and the mailing address is the medical examiner's building right here in Coldwater Creek."

# FORTY-TWO

*Saturday 0645 hours*

Katie tossed and turned during the night. Her mind went through scenarios of catching the killers, both in her dreams when she dozed off and then when she lay awake again, thinking through everything. In the early hours of the morning she finally relaxed enough to gently fall asleep again.

"Wake up, babe."

Katie was enjoying a wonderful dream where she was with Chad and they were out in the country enjoying the weather and the tranquil solitude. She could feel him nuzzle her neck.

"You have to get up. We have to go."

"Go where?" she said groggily. Suddenly she realized that it wasn't a dream. Her eyes snapped open and she saw Chad sitting on the bed leaning over her. "What are you doing here?" She was completely surprised but so happy that he was with her. She hugged him tightly. "I don't care how you got here, but I'm so glad that you're here."

"Hey, you okay?" he said.

"Yeah, I'm okay. It's just been a really tough investigation."

He held her close.

Cisco came into the room and bounced on the bed.

"Hey, buddy," he said.

The dog pushed in against Katie and licked her face.

"Good morning to you too, Cisco." Turning to Chad, she said, "You still haven't told me why you're here."

"When I couldn't get ahold of you, I called Gav. And well, he filled me in on some stuff and told me that John was coming to help. So... I hitched a ride and figured I could help too. I'm off for three days."

His blue eyes could have easily melted Katie's heart, but she soon became concerned. It was going to be difficult moving around town without raising suspicion. "It's too dangerous, Chad."

"I'm a firefighter who could've been a cop. I can handle myself."

"I know you can, but this crime web, for lack of a better description, that we're involved in now is different."

"Well, I'm here now, so I guess I have to stay." He shot her that boyishly handsome smile she admired since they were teens.

The door opened and McGaven appeared. "Ten minutes, we need to be packed and ready to go. I've already documented all the damage here." The door shut.

"What's he talking about?" she said, sitting up. "Why didn't he wake me sooner?"

"John and McGaven thought it best that we stay some-where else. We've got a two-bedroom suite at a motel just outside town."

"Oh." Katie thought that was a great idea. Out of the range of the surveillance cameras meant that no one would be able to find them immediately. Throwing back the covers, she got out of bed and began getting her things together.

"From everything I've searched around the cottage, there

aren't any of those cameras watching us. Maybe they didn't have time to implement them or this cottage wasn't in the original plans for us."

"I almost forgot." Chad picked up an overnight bag. "Gav told me about your clothes situation. We stopped by your house and I grabbed a few things for you and checked to make sure that everything was okay there." He went to the bedroom door and opened it. "I'll let you get things packed. See you out front." He shut the door quietly.

Katie could hear the three of them talking. Someone must've said a joke because she heard laughter. She remembered before her missions in the army that the morale was high and there was joking and laughing. It was a way to release stress before an important operation.

After everything was packed, the four of them left the cottage to head to the motel. Chad rode with Katie, leaving McGaven and John riding together. Katie didn't feel much like talking so Chad filled the silence with fun stories of what had been happening at the firehouse. It was obvious that he was distracting her with lighthearted stories because he knew that things were going to get dangerous.

It took fifteen minutes to drive from the creek-side cottage to get to the motel. It was in a good location and it would be easy to see if anyone was watching or coming to ambush them. Katie didn't want to think in those terms, but it was clear that whomever they were dealing with would stop at nothing—even murder—to keep their secrets.

The suite they'd booked was located in the ground-floor corner unit in the back. It was easy to enter and exit the locked hallways and had quick access to their vehicles. Cisco loved the suite and ran back and forth between rooms.

The large seven-hundred-square-foot room had two

bedrooms, each with a bath. In between them were the living room, small kitchen, and an eating area. The décor was tones of brown and beige to off-white. The sofa couch and two upholstered chairs were modest pieces of furniture and a bit dated, but comfortable. The artwork was prints of famous photographs from around California, scenes of beaches, mountains, and rivers.

John and McGaven moved the dining table from the small kitchen into the middle of the living area and used it as a makeshift command center. They organized the paperwork and set up two laptop computers. The mood was solemn and professional. It was clear that everyone knew what was at stake and that they needed to discover real evidence if the chain of command and proper authorities were going to get involved: sheriff's department, FBI, ATF, and special organized task forces.

John unrolled several maps of Coldwater Creek. The first one was of the town, which was notated where the cement buildings were located along with any other points of interest, including entries, exits, and other close buildings.

To Katie's surprise, there were two more cement buildings on a smaller scale than the one near Joshua's house.

"I was able to verify these structures through the planning department," said John. "They exist and they should be on record for demolition. They aren't necessary and are deemed too old and hazardous—you can see the double walls to the main building with various crawlspaces. It's like a fortress. Since Coldwater Creek encompasses two California counties, it can be confusing when it comes to properties. But... the paperwork gets murky. I called a friend of mine who works for the county and he said from their records they should have already been torn down."

"That just means that someone at the top was paid to lose

THE ROSE GIRLS    285

the paperwork," said McGaven. "Obviously they aren't a priority, so no one complains about it."

"Those buildings have been around for a while, so I checked the Sanborn Fire Insurance Maps to see if I could get more information for you, but no such luck," said Chad. "They do show these buildings verified with what's on the current map."

Katie pointed at the large building. "We checked out this one, but were only able to have access to the first floor. I know there has to be a way to get into the other levels—the second story was locked, and we didn't find the door to the basement."

"You didn't see anything on the first level?" said John.

"Nothing except a table and what looked like the stump of a burned down candle," she said. "It matched a photo that we found on a flash drive in the first victim's bedroom—that of Ivy Miller."

"Did you identify the woman?" said John.

"We think it's the missing mother of Ivy Miller."

"No luck on finding her or what happened to her?"

"No," she said.

"Okay," began John as he untied another roll that had the original building plans, electrical, and plumbing of the building where the medical examiner's office was now located.

McGaven took a red marker and began identifying what they had seen when they had visited. "Here's the main entrance, which is like an empty building: no reception, nothing on the walls and it leads to the elevator. Right here."

John and Chad compared the electrical plans to the main building area and it matched up.

"Since the building wasn't designed to be a morgue, they had to put in extra power for the refrigeration. Junction boxes that would be located here and here," said Chad.

The group spent time examining the maps and labeling the areas until they were left with a space where the offices of

MORE must be located. It was near where the main exam autopsy room was situated and would be easy to find.

As the guys were scrutinizing the maps and the buildings, Katie took her notebook, along with McGaven's notes about the messages, and the stacks of information and research, and sat down in a big chair to skim over everything. She didn't let the rest know her thoughts. This mission of gaining access to the medical examiner's building was so that they could collect enough information to prove the surveillance cameras weren't just for security for the town—but to keep the town under constant scrutiny. But for Katie, it was more important that the killer was found, arrested, and prosecuted for killing Ivy Miller, Nikki Prager, and Dawn Cromwell. To her, that took precedence. That was why they were in Coldwater Creek. It may have been a coincidence that they happened to break down here, but now they couldn't leave until the killer was identified.

Katie reread the statements and the list of places and people of interest. She now knew that Officer Brett Lane was an accomplice to the crimes in the town, but she believed him that he didn't kill the girls. He also confessed to being the unknown assailant who tried to scare them away—to get them out of harm's way. He still would have to pay for his part in the scheme—whatever that was.

Katie read McGaven's notes about "more," "never," and "forever" and she found it interesting that these words were extremely common in books, blogs, podcasts, and news articles, but there was no combination that seemed to indicate why they would be used at the crime scene. The words were used on a regular basis. She read notations that all three words were mostly used in fiction stories. There wasn't anything nefarious about them, making her wonder if they were just all about show at the crime scene. McGaven had had Denise check out *The Mystery of the Secret Room* by Margaret Brand that was found in Ivy's room and the words showed up all throughout the novel. There was no specific meaning or words strung together in an order in any way that could provide clues into the words carved on all three victims.

Katie was beginning to think they were random unless they meant something personal only to the killer than just a name for a company. "More" referred to a greater amount—maybe more victims? "Never" meant "not at all"—was it telling about the victim or were there going to be no more victims? "Forever" meant "lasting or permanent"—were the victims forever in the mind of the killer? There were many ways to look at the common words—but Katie felt that it was a puzzle meant to send them in circles.

*Three girls...*

*Three messages...*

Thinking back to the interviews they had conducted, Katie focused on the suspects they had listed on the board. Lenny came to mind. She remembered how helpful he had been when they borrowed the old police vehicle. His reaction made them believe that there was something in that car. He had also been at the inn when they were staying there—and when she discovered that her stuff had been moved in their room. It made sense that Lenny had been snooping. Why? Then when they had spoken to him when he was working on his car—the one that fit the general description of what Joshua saw that night—it set a chain of events in motion. It was circumstantial, but enough evidence to infer his guilt.

Katie knew the type of personality that Lenny conveyed. His reactions and answers seemed to tick off a fair number of boxes for the psychopathic behaviors that led to his actions. It was early in her hypothesis, but she had investigated so many like him that it seemed to fit into what they were dealing with.

*What was Lenny looking for in the old police car?*

*Evidence?*

*The knife used to kill Dawn and carve the messages on each victim?*

*If so, did he stash the evidence or destroy it?*

Katie knew statistically most criminals hide their evidence rather than completely destroy it. It made her think about the knife. If they could get the weapon linking all three murders, Lenny would most likely crumble and spill everything about what was going on in town to get a better sentence.

"Katie?" said McGaven. "You okay?"

"I'm fine. Just looking over some notes."

Her partner stared at her a moment as if trying to figure out what Katie was struggling with before going back to discussing details about the buildings and the town access without being seen.

Katie read the statements again and looked at some of the background information that Denise had pulled up for them. What caught her eye was that Sadie Ramos, aka Mama, not only owned the Wild Iris Inn, but she also owned a small fishing cabin near the Oak Valley Creek. It was a long shot, but Katie needed to cross it off the list. She needed to search the cabin and area to see if Lenny had disposed of the knife or anything else connecting him to the murders there. It would be a prime place to do that and she knew that so often criminals not only committed their crimes in places they felt comfortable—but they hid or discarded damning evidence there too.

Katie took one of the laptops from the table and did a quick search for 221 Creek Way, Cabin 14, and memorized the directions. She deleted her search and put the laptop back on the table.

Grabbing her things, including Cisco, she said, "I just realized that Cisco is down on his food. I saw a feed store about a mile from here. And it looked like there was a big field behind the building so I can run this guy." She hated lying to them, but she didn't want to take them away from the plans and she was only verifying if any evidence might be there.

"You want company?" said Chad.

"No, that's okay. We're only going to be about a half hour."

"Okay, stay safe. Call if you need us," said McGaven.

"I will," she said, closing the door behind her.

# FORTY-THREE

*Saturday 1030 hours*

Katie drove fast, estimating that it would take about fifteen minutes to get to the fishing cabin. As she finally reached Creek Way, she discovered that there were many one-room fishing and hunting cabins, and they weren't numbered in consequential order. There seemed to be only a few people staying there as she saw very few trucks and SUVs along the way.

Katie finally saw a crudely painted sign indicating 221 Creek Way, Cabins 1–15. She took the turn, noticing that the road narrowed until it was barely wide enough for a vehicle to pass. The huge pine trees seemed denser and darker than the previous area. She finally saw the address #14 and turned into a small half-circle drive.

Cisco whined from the back seat, sensing something fun was afoot. He panted in between whines, pacing back and forth.

"This is it," she said.

Before getting out of the Jeep, Katie studied the area and came to the conclusion that no one was there—or in the cabin next door. She felt assured that no one would see her snooping around. She inspected the eaves of the cabin and surrounding trees for any cameras, but couldn't see any. She let out a breath of relief as she opened her door and walked toward the cabin with Cisco.

The sky was dark. There had been a few showers earlier in the day and the gray clouds that moved overhead gave the air a gloomy eerie feel. The humidity level was high. Water dripped on the side of the cabin around the windows, making a steady beat of droplets.

The small dark cabin was the size of a motel room, the type mainly used for those who wanted a fishing or hunting week-end. They were popular at certain times of the year.

She wanted to get a firm grasp of the cabin's situation so she walked around it looking up, around, and even down at the ground level. Nothing indicated that there were any traps, no cameras, and it didn't appear that anyone had been there recently. Studying the ground, she couldn't tell if there were any footprints—but nothing looked fresh.

Katie checked out one of the windows, which had broken seals, but the glass was still intact. She peered inside. There was a bunk bed and a twin cot with blankets tossed back, small table, two wooden chairs, mini refrigerator, and a hotplate. There was a small bookcase in the corner, where there were stacked papers and several shoeboxes. It seemed safe, so she made her way to the front door and put her hand on the knob. It was locked. She had hoped it would be easy, but of course, it wasn't.

Cisco was checking out something interesting in the bushes near a group of trees. A heap of discarded garbage of cardboard, old buckets, and a tire on top.

Katie kept her focus and hunted around for a key, looking under the small doormat, under a couple of empty terracotta planters, and above the door along the frame. Her fingertips touched a key on the latter, which she quickly retrieved.

"We're in luck, Cisco," she said and the dog came instantly to her. She opened the cabin door and quickly slipped inside. It smelled moldy and musty with a trace of rotten garbage. The bedding was wadded up and hadn't been laundered in quite some time. She wrinkled her nose in disgust, not wanting to touch anything.

Katie snapped to her mission. She looked for anything that might have been connected to the crime scenes. After standing for a moment in the middle of the smelly room, it seemed success was probably doubtful. Her hope of finding anything that would prove her theory dwindled.

She looked at the papers. They were just various fliers, bills, and miscellaneous receipts for gas and fast food. She opened the mini fridge but it was full of rotten food. Looking around, she didn't see anything that would have something incriminating hidden beneath.

Cisco went to a corner and began scratching at the paneling. His nose went down and then he sat staring at Katie.

"What do you have?" she said.

She went to the corner but didn't see anything. Her first thought was maybe Cisco caught a scent of a rodent or remnant of old food. The entire room was an absolute pigsty and she wanted to leave immediately—but her curiosity began to gnaw at her. What was so interesting to him?

She didn't want to touch anything or kneel down on the floor, but instead, she squatted down to look closely at the corner wall. That's when she saw it—faint at first—but if you knew what you were looking for, it made it easy. There was a secret compartment.

"What do we have here?" Katie's pulse quickened.

Cisco sat patiently next to her tilting his head slightly.

She took a photo first on her cell phone, then, using her thumbnail, she tried to pry the cheap plastic paneling piece away from the wall, but it wouldn't budge. Looking around at the room, she spied some dirty pieces of silverware and grabbed a knife.

After a few minutes, the paneling popped open easily. Inside were some plastic bags and two envelopes. After taking another photo, she pulled on a pair of gloves and retrieved the two plain brown envelopes—there was something squishy inside like a towel. With the parcels in hand, she stood up and laid them on the table. Carefully opening one, she pulled out a piece of chammy cloth, the kind of soft fabric used to buff car wax, and it revealed a thin-bladed knife.

Katie took in a breath and stepped back, glancing out the window expecting someone to come barging into the cabin—but of course, no one did.

*Could it be?*

She used her phone's flashlight to highlight if there was any blood residue, but there was none. Using part of the cloth, Katie turned the knife over and there, stained on the fabric, was blood. There was no doubt in her mind that it belonged to one of the murder victims—but it would need to be tested after a search warrant was executed. No one would hide a knife that they had used to skin or bone a fish—there was no other explanation.

Taking a couple of deep breaths, she checked the other rolled up chammy cloth to find another knife. There were two knives used—similar to each other—if she had to guess, most likely one used on Ivy and the other on both Nikki and Dawn.

Katie quickly rolled the knives back in their soft cloths and took a moment grasping what this meant. She didn't have permission to retrieve the knives, but given all of the circumstantial evidence it would be easy to have a judge sign off for a search warrant for the fishing cabin belonging to the Ramos family—specifically where Lenny often stayed. Unless other people stayed there or they rented out the cabin, there was no one else the evidence pointed to except Lenny. He must've hidden the knives in the old police car at first, never suspecting that anyone would need to use it—especially police detectives.

She didn't want jeopardize the case. After she quickly photographed the knives, she returned them, making sure the clever secret compartment was exactly the way she had found it. The killer had probably been identified and they were moving in the right direction. It was the best news yet.

Katie double-checked the area before she and Cisco left the cabin, feeling comfortable that no one had seen her enter it. Things were closing in on the nefarious dealings in Coldwater Creek, but now, she needed more evidence to prove why Ivy and her friends were murdered. And Katie knew what she had to do next.

*Three girls...*
*Three messages...*

# FORTY-FOUR

*Saturday 1330 hours*

Katie opened the motel door and was immediately reprimanded by McGaven and Chad.

"Where have you been?" said Chad. "We tried calling and texting."

"I'm sorry. I guess I was out of range."

"What took you so long?" said McGaven.

Katie glanced at her watch. She had been gone more than an hour and in hindsight she should have called to let them know everything was okay. But she kept the smile on her face because she couldn't wait to tell them the news.

McGaven softened his tone and realized his partner had some news. "Why am I getting the feeling that you didn't go to the feed store for Cisco?"

"Again, I'm sorry. All of you were working so hard on the buildings and the best way to access them that I felt my efforts should go way back to why we were called to investigate these crimes in the first place." Walking farther into the room, she continued, "I went over everything we had and what was on our lists before they were destroyed. Our suspects were Lenny Ramos and Tyler Rey. I wanted to dig a little more into their backgrounds."

"Lenny seems the most likely," said McGaven.

"I agree, but we didn't have any solid hard evidence, just circumstantial—and theories."

"And what did you find?"

"When we spoke with him behind the inn as he was working on his car, remember he started getting mad when I accused him of hiding something in the old police car?" Katie went to her paperwork and pulled the background information that Denise had done. "I found that Lenny Ramos, namely his mother, owned a small fishing cabin in addition to the inn."

"So you decided to check it out by yourself," said John who had been quiet. "You should have had one of us go along with you. Especially after all the encounters you've had here."

"It may not have been the best move, but I was extra cautious and had Cisco with me. I wasn't going to get out of the Jeep if anything, *anything at all*, looked suspicious."

"What did you find?" said McGaven.

Katie swiped her phone and showed them the weapons and blood.

"You found the murder weapons?" said John.

She nodded. "I know statistically criminals only completely dispose of their weapons about thirty or forty percent of the time. Many psychopathic behaviors are complemented by the fact they like to keep the murder weapon so they can revisit it and the crime scene in their minds whenever they want. I reckon he hid the knives in the car, but then he had to move them when we needed transport." She watched all three of them stare at her with some concern.

"You took quite a risk," said Chad. It was plain to see that he was deeply uneasy for Katie's safety.

"Yes, you did," said McGaven.

"But you replaced the evidence?" said John.

"I did what I had to do to prove that Lenny Ramos is the killer of those girls. But, I know that we will have to get a search warrant so that it will be used to convict him of first-degree murder times three. And I think, based on our theory, conversations, and his lack of alibi, there's enough to convince a judge for a warrant."

"I see where she's going with this," said McGaven. "If we show our cards now, then we take the chance that other evidence will be destroyed—namely the linkage evidence against Baker and his crew."

"The way I see it," said Katie, "we have only one chance to get this right. I had to check out this information—and it paid off."

Everyone seemed to see her point. They were all energized that there was actual hard evidence that hadn't been destroyed. Katie could still see concern that she had been impetuous and her actions would probably end up in her personnel file as a disciplinary action once the investigation had been completed. To be able to solve these homicides and free a town of a criminal enterprise, was worth the risk to her.

John looked at his watch and reminded the group, "We have a special forensic meeting with Dr. Deborah Sanders in the ME's office in about an hour."

"We'll fill you in on the details," said McGaven to his partner.

For the next half hour, they explained the plan to Katie, where everything was located and how they planned on completing the task. It would be her job to find the surveillance room and document it for proof, leaving it fully intact and not disturbed—but creating evidential links that would generate a major investigation on the town of Coldwater Creek.

# FORTY-FIVE

*Saturday 1450 hours*

Katie and John arrived at the building of the medical examiner's office. It was unlike Katie to feel nervous, but there was so much riding on every move they made. The main objective for her was closing the cases for the murdered girls. They were never far from her mind.

"You okay?" said John. He had been quiet during the ride.

"I'm fine. I'll be better when we leave this town."

John gathered his briefcase, which held forensic containers and his digital camera. "Dr. Sanders wasn't too pleased to come in on a Saturday, but I convinced her that we needed additional information on Dawn Cromwell's body." He looked as stressed as Katie felt.

"John, we really appreciated you coming back here to help us—to help this case."

"There was no way I wouldn't help out—three homicides and a criminal enterprise."

Katie adjusted the small video camera on her jacket. "Can

you see and hear clearly?" she said into her discreetly hidden microphone. She adjusted her earpiece as well.

"Ten-four," said McGaven.

Katie was relieved to hear her partner's voice.

John looked at her. "You ready?"

"Ten-four," she said and smiled. Her nerves were tingly and she had to concentrate on breathing normally. She pressed her fingers into her palms to steady her hands. Feeling a bit off balance would help to sell her pretext.

Katie and John got out of her Jeep and headed for the main entrance. Katie knew that they were being watched and scrutinized, so she made sure she projected the professional business-as-usual demeanor. She remembered the first time they had entered the building, not knowing what to expect. The plain exterior without any identification or numbers made it appear to be more like a bunker than a working morgue. No landscaping or interesting focal points around the entrance gave the impression it was abandoned—unless you saw cars in the parking lot. There were only three other cars. Katie assumed it was one morgue technician, one security guard, and Dr. Sanders.

They didn't have to wait long before the security buzzer sounded and the door unlocked. They entered and continued down the long hallway. Katie couldn't tell if John was uncomfortable or surprised by the nondescript interior, but he didn't let it show. His manner was calm and alert. He knew well how to show resilience under pressure—as a retired Navy Seal. He had worked many missions but had decided to pursue his passion and expertise to run the forensics division at the Pine Valley Sheriff's Department nearly eight years ago.

Katie was keenly aware of their surroundings; there was no music piped in and no sign of anyone working in the main area —just white walls, ceiling, and shiny floors. It was a ghost of a building, intentionally conveying that it did not have any identity. It was a mere front to the inner workings housing the central town surveillance, with some areas recorded that were clearly a violation of privacy.

Katie was relieved when the elevator doors opened, beckoning them to enter. Stepping into the box, she knew it was the point of no return. The con was officially on as she watched the two doors slowly close, trapping them inside.

She glanced at John. He gave a faint smile and nodded, giving her the heads-up that it was a go and that he had her back.

Katie heard a whisper in her ear, startling her. "Stay calm. We have your backs," said McGaven. She knew that he fully understood what they were potentially walking into. Katie was specifically chosen for the task instead of McGaven, both to give their visit more credibility and because of her previous experience in military covert activities.

The elevator pulleys ground and slowly dropped them to the basement floor. They could feel the air being pumped in, blowing lightly from above. Katie kept her vision fixed on the doors, not wanting to think about being trapped in an elevator or basement.

The doors slowly opened, pushing them into a long, deserted hallway. Katie took the lead since she had been in the building before and headed down the hallway. Unidentified doors were shut and there were no noises to indicate any employees were present. She kept walking until they reached the main examination room.

Katie paused.

"Is this it?" said John calmly.

"It was where we met previously." She looked around and didn't see Dr. Sanders. Her suspicious mind jumped to the thought of a trap—and they would be walking right into it.

Katie walked a bit farther to the smaller examination and autopsy room. There was a covered body on the stainless table. She assumed it must be Dawn. Remembering the excessive and rage-fueled damage done to the girl's body made her deeply troubled. She ran through various scenarios of why Dawn might have received the harshest and most violent death. The only situation that made sense was that she must've had a relationship with Lenny—and that something unexpected had happened. Maybe? Perhaps she had been part of the murder plan and had had second thoughts about the murder of her friend Nikki. Katie found it troubling that Dawn could be a part of the murders—but she couldn't rule anything out at this point.

"Detective Scott—and this is John Blackburn, I presume," said Dr. Sanders. She came out of an office smiling broadly, casually dressed in jeans and T-shirt with boots. Her short hair had been backcombed and hair-sprayed into place.

"Dr. Sanders. It's nice to meet you," said John as he shook her hand. "Thank you for coming in on a Saturday."

"My pleasure. Nice to see you both." She entered the autopsy room and uncovered the body. "Anything I can do to help you solve these cases. Such senseless tragedies."

"I need to take another sample from around her neck and some photographs. We are getting close to identifying the knife," said John.

"Please, take your time," she said as she pulled down a light and directed it at Dawn's neck.

Katie found it incredible that the medical examiner could host the surveillance headquarters in her building and yet stand there talking about one of the dead girls as if she knew nothing about what was going on. She may not have known who killed the girls, but she certainly knew there was something going on in Coldwater Creek—and who was behind it.

"Detective Scott?" she said. "Are you feeling alright?"

"You do look a bit pale," said John, selling the act.

"I'm sorry, I'm not feeling well. May I use your restroom?" Katie's dislike for the medical examiner and the fact they were getting close to teetering on an unlawful act made her feel unwell. It was making the ruse believable.

"Of course. It's right down that hallway, third door on your left," she said and indicated the hallway they had studied.

"Thank you." Katie quickly walked away, leaving John to perform his forensic activities. She hoped that he would keep Dr. Sanders busy.

As Katie moved quickly, she was surprised to see that the doors had black letters and last names on them, unlike the previous one. It was definitely the right place. She ducked into Sanders' office, quietly shutting the door behind her.

Without wasting another minute, she searched for keys. The office was small with a nice walnut desk and expensive office chair. There were two bookcases with binders and a tall filing cabinet, which was locked.

Katie opened the desk drawers but couldn't find any keys.

"You in?" said McGaven.

"Yes," she whispered. "Can't find the keys."

She looked at the door where there was an ornate coatrack with Dr. Sanders' white overcoat hanging. Instantly, she searched the pockets and found a set of keys.

"Got 'em."

Katie hurried out of the office and went down the hall until she saw a door that read: *M.O.R.E., Incorporated.*

Looking up and down the hallway, she tried the first key, then the second, and then several more until she found the right one. She could faintly hear John and Dr. Sanders talking. It seemed friendly and professional.

Pushing the door open, she half expected to see a security guard sitting there waiting for her. But the room was empty, except for three tables with computers. The corresponding monitors were large, some of the screens divided into four and six sections. She recognized areas of town and of where they had been, but studied the other areas too. It would be difficult for anyone to skirt around the cameras and leave town or go somewhere without being watched.

Katie glanced at her watch. Two minutes had already passed. She had to hurry.

She saw large computer storage backups. It had files with titles: *North Section, Main Street, South Section, Investigation.* The label with "Investigation" neatly typed on the top caught her attention. She opened the file and there were detailed pages of their investigation of Ivy Miller, Nikki Prager, and Dawn Cromwell. There were photographs, video screen grabs, and times and dates of various people around town—she recognized some: Mama Ramos, Officer Lane, and various other people. She held her breath when she saw surveillance photos of her and McGaven when they went to see Sydney and Tyler Rey. Some of the images were close up. Goosebumps scuttled up her arms. Everything about the town unnerved her and she knew now more than ever she needed to free the citizens of this control.

"You seeing this?"

"Affirmative," said McGaven.

"I'm going to photo what I can."

Katie took out her cell phone and photographed the file contents, the room, the computers, and the name of the company, M.O.R.E.

"Get out, Katie. You've been gone too long," Katie heard in her ear, but she got everything she could before leaving the room, and then stealthily returned the keys and made it into the hallway.

She stood for a moment composing herself; she knew that

she was perspiring from the adrenalin surging through her veins making her head pound and her hands shaky. She started walking back toward the exam room and was relieved to see that John was still talking with Dr. Sanders. They turned to look at Katie.

"Feeling any better?" said John.

"Not really. I guess I need to lie down for a while." Katie knew that she looked believably ill as her pounding heart began to slow down.

"I'm sorry to hear that," said Dr. Sanders. "I'm sure you've been working so hard on your cases—it doesn't surprise me that you need some rest."

"We're done here, I think?" said John. He put his digital camera away.

"Yes. Thank you for enlightening me on the different puncture and slicing wounds. I will keep it in mind." She turned to leave. "Will you be able to find your way out?"

"Yes. Thank you, Dr. Sanders," said John.

She smiled and stepped closer to him. "My pleasure. Oh and, Detective Scott, I hope you feel better soon."

Katie and John retraced their steps and went back the way they had come down the hallway, up the elevator, and out the front entrance.

Katie didn't say a word until they were in the Jeep. "That was fun." She breathed a sigh of relief.

"What took you so long?" said John. His voice sounded tense, unlike his usual calm self.

"I found more than I imagined, more than all of us imagined, and it's on video as well as photos on my phone."

"You guys did a great job," said McGaven in her earpiece.

"Really?" said John.

"Yes." Katie was relieved that the pretext was over and it was a huge building block for the investigation. "Thanks, guys," she said in the microphone. "We'll meet up back at the room."

She started the Jeep and backed out of the parking place when her cell phone chimed with a text message:

*Meet me at the rural cement building near the south side 1630 hours.*

It was from Officer Brett Lane.

# FORTY-SIX

*Saturday 1550 hours*

Katie and McGaven studied the map of the cement building near Joshua's property. John had been able to gather several maps of Coldwater Creek that had the rural building on them.

"Are you sure the text was from Officer Lane?" said Chad.

"As sure as I can be. He's trying to fight this operation and confided in me, taking a huge chance of being seen. He's scared, but he wants this all to end—as much as the rest of us. He wants to give us information—the cement building is a good place to stay hidden." She could see that Chad was concerned, but trying to maintain his objectivity.

"We'll be backup, basically lookout, while Katie and McGaven go see what Officer Lane has to say," said John.

Chad nodded but still didn't seem convinced.

"We're going to be in a better place to see anyone coming and going from that area," said John.

"I'm not worried about that—what if someone is already there?"

"We're going to do a general sweep of the area and near the

building with Cisco—if anything seems off we're coming right back," said Katie. "No problem. I'm interested in what Officer Lane has to say—I believe it's important enough for him to take the chance of meeting with me again."

No one said a word. Each was left to their own thoughts of what they'd learned so far and what the local officer had to say.

"We need to get going to have some time to do a sweep," she said to McGaven.

He nodded. "Everyone gear up."

"You sound like we're getting ready for a military maneuver," said John lightheartedly.

Chad pulled Katie aside. "You okay? You seem a little out of sorts after the medical examiner's office."

"I'm fine. It's just been a long week."

"You don't have to bear all the weight of this by yourself."

"I know. That's why I have all of you." She forced a smile, trying to make Chad's burden of not knowing what was going to happen a little bit lighter. "This wouldn't be something that I would take on—but if we don't, the bad guys will cover their tracks and slip away. I can't allow the murders of those girls to go cold."

Chad paused. He knew that she had to do this. "I'm here for you—and I'll help with support in any way."

Katie leaned in and kissed him. "Thank you. We'll know more after Gav and I talk to Officer Lane."

Chad joined McGaven and John, making sure that the technology was in working order and inspecting their weapons.

Katie checked and secured her weapon before fitting Cisco with his tracking harness.

The room became quiet except for the sound of everyone checking and double-checking their equipment.

Again, John and Chad would be in John's truck and taking position near the entrance where Katie and McGaven were headed up the mountain. Katie, McGaven, and Cisco were in her Jeep and would park in a secluded location different from before.

"Ready?" said McGaven.

"Ready," said John.

"Me too," said Chad.

Katie looked at her fiancé and her two co-workers and thought what an amazing group they were. How lucky she was, personally as well as professionally. Her nerves settled and she found herself more than curious as to what Officer Lane was going to tell them.

# FORTY-SEVEN

*Saturday 1615 hours*

Katie made good time getting to their location. They had discussed whether or not to drive up the old SWAT road because the Jeep could easily handle the terrain, but decided against it. They made the decision instead, an extra precaution, to stay as covert as possible when they were within the town's boundaries.

Katie recalled the conversation that she and Officer Lane had at the shopping area. From what he had said to her, and the real fear that was apparent on his face, there was no doubt he was scared. She knew that he wasn't lying, but he was still trapped in a situation that didn't have an easy resolution. But in the back of her mind, she still wanted to be sure—that was why they were going to sweep the area with Cisco. It might make them a few minutes late—but at least they would know that it wasn't an ambush.

John and Chad followed them for the first few miles. Then she could no longer see them in the rearview mirror. They were taking another route to get to their vantage location.

Cisco sat up straight in the back seat, staring straight ahead. Whenever he had his training vest on he knew that they were headed somewhere so he could work—and he was ready for it. No whines. Just soft panting. His intense eyes watching. Waiting until it was his turn.

Katie made a sharp right turn before the Bates Hiking and Camping area. There was a utility road that paralleled the hiking areas, which held the water mains for the fire department in case of a fire. Utility roads were great places to stay hidden or to shadow someone by staying just out of sight but close enough to observe what you needed to see. She easily pulled off the narrow road into a group of trees. The Jeep was a perfect fit and even if someone happened along this road they wouldn't instantly see the SUV unless they were looking for it.

Katie turned the car off but sat for a moment.

Cisco whined, pacing back and forth in the back seat.

"You okay?" said McGaven.

She turned to him and saw that he, too, had a haunted look upon his face. His eyes seemed tired and his complexion was pale. "I'm fine. What about you?"

"You know me."

"Yeah, I do. And you look like you're carrying the weight of the world right now."

"I think I'm at where you were coming from earlier today."

"What do you mean?"

"I keep thinking about those girls and the crime scenes." He looked out the side window at nothing in particular. "I agree with you. We came here to investigate the murders and find their killer."

"And you now feel that things have shifted direction." She felt it too.

"Something like that. But, it's clear that we need to finish this."

"Are we good?" she said.

"More than good."

"Let's go then and see what the local officer has to say."

Cisco, using his heightened sense of smell, led the way. They chose to hike the old road. It was the most direct and strategic way to go—they could watch both sides of the area while Cisco searched.

The sun had shone brightly most of the day, but now as it passed 4 p.m. it was becoming darker and threatening to rain again. Moving up the partially overgrown back road slowed them down, but they forged ahead as quickly as they could.

Katie half expected to see Officer Lane, but she was sure that he was already waiting for them. She watched Cisco's posturing. He seemed relaxed and eager to get to where they were going. The dog would keep his nose closer to the ground, but at other times, he did an open-air sweep, positioning his nose higher than normal. She knew that he was cataloging familiar smells, like the environment around them, forest critters, bird activity, and even who might have passed through the path in recent days.

Katie stopped, seeing the north side of the cement building —they needed to reach the south side for the meeting. She turned to McGaven and alerted his attention. He had already noticed it too.

"Let me take Cisco around the area and the building," she said keeping her voice low.

He nodded and took up a cover position behind them; he would be watching for anything moving or approaching.

Katie directed Cisco for his track and they moved quickly through the brush and in between the trees. The breeze blew from behind them, making it more difficult for the dog to catch a scent out front and follow it, but Cisco kept his focus as they worked their way to the south end.

Katie moved along the back of the building, which they hadn't investigated before. She noticed vents and areas where the material had weakened. Looking up at the second floor, she saw small, barred windows. It was hard to differentiate between the shadows from the trees and what was behind the glass.

Cisco growled and went into a down position.

Katie halted, looking around, but didn't see anyone.

"Detective Scott, I'm here," said Officer Lane. He emerged slowly with his hands where Katie and Cisco could see them.

"Good boy, Cisco," she said, bringing the dog close her side. She looked at the officer. He looked exhausted and probably hadn't slept in a while.

Officer Lane moved close to a zombie pace as if he would collapse any moment. His clothes appeared to be the same ones he had been wearing when they were at the shopping center.

"Brett, are you alright?"

"I'm fine."

He went across to the south side where there was an entrance with a wooden door and a heavy-duty outer door of cement. It resembled an ancient doorway going into a temple, but with the extra enforcement it would be almost impossible to penetrate.

McGaven approached them. "All clear," he reported.

"I thought you were coming alone?"

"This is my partner. I trust him," she said.

"There's too much craziness coming in all directions. I wouldn't let my partner come out here alone." McGaven scrutinized the young officer. "How do we know that we can trust you? Did you lure us here? Are you the one who set those traps in the trees?"

"Wait," said Katie. "Brett has risked a lot to come here. It's one of the few places where there aren't those MORE surveillance cameras."

"You know about that?" the officer said. The look of dread overcame him. "Did you find them at the ME's office?"

"Yes, I saw them."

"You went inside there? This is bad, very bad. They are looking for me—and now you too."

"Who?" she said.

"*Them.* We need to get some cover. They use technology, cameras, drones, anything to watch over us. I've been too careless now."

Katie thought the young officer sounded as if he was under such duress that he was becoming paranoid. Maybe they didn't understand what they were walking into. "Wait a minute. You asked us here. What did you want to tell us?"

The officer began to pace back and forth. "You really don't understand."

Katie remained calm. "Why don't you tell us what's going on?"

He looked up in the trees and then behind him, shaking his head.

"Brett. Why don't you calm down, take a breath, and tell us what's going on?" she said.

Cisco's body began to stiffen as if he had caught wind of something he didn't like.

Katie watched the dog as she scanned the area. She now believed that Brett wasn't imagining the dangers. "I think we need to go—"

Two shots blasted against the side of the building, causing chunks of cement to explode in a powdery dust around them. More bullets followed, hitting too close to them.

Cisco began rapid barking.

"Take cover now!" said McGaven. He pushed Katie through the timeworn doorway. Brett was right behind them.

Once inside, Brett and McGaven tried to push the first wooden door, but it wouldn't shut. They struggled. McGaven pulled his weapon, trying to cover them until they closed the door.

Katie dialed John immediately.

"Katie," John immediately answered.

"We're under attack. Can't see who. I'd estimate three, maybe four, with guns. We're inside the first floor of the building on the south end—there's an old wooden and cement door and..."

The phone lost the signal.

More gunfire erupted. This time it was closer—they were coming.

She looked deeper into the first floor and there was a solid wall twenty feet in—there was no way they could escape through the other side. They were trapped.

"We don't have a signal here," she said.

"We have to hold them off until John and Chad can figure out how to rescue us," said McGaven. "We're outgunned."

Brett was trying to move the door to shut it completely when a bullet ripped through his left shoulder, dropping him to the ground. Blood immediately oozed from the wound.

Katie pulled the officer's body farther inside so McGaven was able to push the door shut, cutting out most of the light.

They heard more gunshots pummel against the door, but nothing would penetrate through the thick wood.

Katie knelt down and began applying pressure to Brett's shoulder. In an instant, she was catapulted back in time to the battlefield, attending to a fellow soldier. The familiar smell of gunpowder and dust slammed into her face. She knew it wasn't there but it felt more real than anything that was happening at the moment.

Cisco took his usual combat position and kept next to Katie until she might command otherwise.

Breathless and covered in dust, McGaven said, "How bad?"

"Bad... if I can't stop the bleeding..."

McGaven tore part of his shirt and tossed it to Katie. She immediately used it to press against the wound. "We're going to get out of here—all of us."

Officer Lane's complexion was white, perspiration ran down his face, and he grimaced in extreme pain. "I told you," he barely whispered. "I... told... you..."

"I lost a signal talking to John, but I think I was able to give them the information they needed."

"Whoever is out there is going to wait us out however long it takes," he said.

"And?" she said.

"They'll wait for as long as it takes for us to die in this tomb."

# FORTY-EIGHT

*Saturday 1710 hours*

"I would say this is worst-case scenario," said Katie. She wasn't a medic, but Officer Lane's wound was critical and they needed to get him to the hospital.

They heard pounding noises at the door.

Katie and McGaven pulled their weapons knowing it would only hold off the perpetrators for a short period until their ammo ran out. They waited with high anxiety.

The noise suddenly stopped.

"They sealed us in with the second door," she said. Her spirit sank. She tried not to focus on it: they wouldn't stop looking for a way out, but she didn't know how long they would have sustainable air.

McGaven searched every inch of their confinement. It was clear he didn't think there was another way out. He looked into corners and around the areas that should've led into the other part of the building.

"Anything?" she said.

"No." His voice was tense and it was clear that he was beginning to give up hope.

"There's a narrow passage..." whispered the young officer. He grabbed her arm.

"What do you mean?" she said.

He tried to sit up but winced in pain.

"Take it easy."

"There's... a passage that runs along the back wall."

Katie thought that this town must be full of secret rooms and passages. "Where?"

McGaven began searching closer along the back of the building. "Remember on the architectural drawings, there did seem to be some type of crawlspace? Like an area where it would support insulation or electrical components."

Katie did recall, but she wasn't sure if it was something that would be easily passed through even if it was cleared.

The room began to become warmer than it was only minutes ago, making the smell of an old building become stronger. The air would become thinner as time went on—making it difficult to concentrate or move around.

Katie stood up and paced around, taking some deep breaths. She moved her cell phone in various positions and it seemed to waver back and forth from signal to none. Finally balancing the phone, she was able to get one weak bar. She tried to call John again, but it wouldn't go through. Then she had a thought, she tried a text message:

*Did you hear the phone call?*

A moment later: *Yes. We're working on it.*

"Yes," she said. Relief filled her. "I have enough of a signal to send text messages."

*We're trapped in a small enclosed room. Lane was hit by bullet. Need medical attention.*

*Anyone else hurt? We're working on rescue.*

*Don't come near. Three maybe four shooters.*

*10-4.*

"I think I have something," said McGaven. He was at the back wall trying to dig into a loose area. "There is something back here. And it seems like it was roughly sealed recently."

Katie knelt down next to Brett. "How are you doing?"

"Been... better..."

Katie looked at the wound. The good news was that it had stopped bleeding, but the bad was there still was a bullet in his body and it could become septic. "Stay still, okay? We'll figure out how to get out of here."

McGaven gave a strong heave, releasing a smooth rock built into a frame. He was breathing heavily from the effort. He then pulled two more out. Using the flashlight on his cell phone, he directed it into the dark hole. It was indeed a space: thin, but it would be possible to pass through.

"What is it?" she said. Then looked inside. "I can feel air from outside, which means it has to lead somewhere—an exit." She leaned in farther; there was an obstruction in the way. It was impossible to ascertain what it was. "There's something in there." She climbed up and squeezed her lean body into the crawlspace. A smell like moldy garbage hit her senses.

"Wait. You don't know what will come crumbling down on top of you."

"Gav, this is our only chance to get out of here. Assess what's going on and get help. I have to try and somehow remove whatever that is blocking it."

McGaven was clearly against her moving through that crawlspace, but he knew they didn't have much choice as she was smaller than he was, and the chamber temperature rising. "Just go as far as that obstruction and then come right back. I would go, but secret passageways aren't made for my body type."

"She glanced at McGaven, Brett, and Cisco, trying not to think about what would happen if she didn't find a way out soon. They needed to get medical assistance as soon as possible.

Katie squeezed inside. It was tight, but she was still able to move easily. "Okay, I'll be right back." She continued to wiggle her way down and then the passage opened up wider making it easier to crawl, with only a few tight spots. She kept inching closer to the obstruction. There wasn't much air and she began to sweat and breathe heavier in short shallow bursts.

As she neared the blockage, it looked like some heavy rolled plastic. Probably some extra supplies being stored there. She inched closer and was about to reach out her hand to touch it when she realized what it was. Her stomach lurched, a sour taste filled her mouth, and her breath stopped. Her hand shaking and perspiration rolling down her back, her fears were realized when she pulled the plastic away and a skeleton bobbed forward, jaw slack. She could see brown hair still attached to some remnant of scalp on the skull. The body appeared to be a woman and she was wearing a rust-colored sweater. She knew where she had seen that sweater on a brunette woman. Even without DNA evidence, Katie knew that the skeletal remains hidden in the passage were those of Rebecca Miller—Ivy's missing mother.

\* \* \*

Chad paced back and forth, waiting for John to have some good news. He kept balling his hands in fists and then releasing them.

"Got it!" said John.

"What?"

"Everything is out in the open now."

"What do you mean?"

"I had to brief Sheriff Scott and SWAT Sergeant West on our situation."

"I bet the sheriff was angry."

"Not as much as you would think. He said he had a feeling something was going down that he wasn't aware of," said John.

"How long until we get reinforcements?"

"That's the problem. It'll take them more than two hours to get here."

"Two hours! Katie and McGaven don't stand a chance, alone and trapped." He secured his weapon to get ready to leave. "We're losing daylight."

"You can't do this. We need to stay put—for now." He took hold of Chad's arm. "They are safe in the room in the building. Katie will let me know if anything changes. Okay?"

Chad reluctantly nodded.

"We have to believe that they will either be able to free themselves from the building or they can wait until SWAT gets here." He relaxed his grip. "I know how you feel, but I also know Katie and McGaven. They've been in tight places before. They won't quit until they come up with a plan."

"I know Katie too, and that's precisely what I'm afraid of."

# FORTY-NINE

*Saturday 1815 hours*

Katie took a moment to process everything. The way she figured, it was Rebecca Miller who must've found out details of what was going on in town and it got her killed. The photos seemed to reveal that she was with people that she trusted—perhaps a secret meeting. Maybe she was investigating on her own. The scenario for her daughter Ivy was that she was searching for her mom—then what she found out got her killed. Her friends were most likely collateral damage to make sure Ivy hadn't shared anything with them. There was no intricate plot of a serial killer, but rather the crimes were centered around keeping any potential leak permanently quiet and a town kept hostage. In this case, three innocent girls had paid with their lives.

Katie closed her eyes for a moment, trying to calm her nerves and bring her breathing back to normal. The crime scenes flashed in front of her eyes, the innocent victims lost, no one there to protect or save them.

"Katie," said McGaven. His voice sounded eerie as it traveled down the passageway.

"I'm fine." She gritted her teeth, trying to keep her emotions in check and her creeping anxiety symptoms at bay.

"What is that?"

She didn't want to tell him, but there was no other choice. "A body."

"Body?"

"It's... Rebecca Miller." Their voices sounded like bodiless entities and it made her shiver even though she was sweating. It was possible that anyone passing by could hear people talking inside the building and believe that it was haunted.

There was a pause and McGaven didn't respond right away.

"I'm going to have to move it if I want to be able to get out."

"Can you do it?" he said.

"I'm going to try, but I'll have to pull it back to you."

Again, there wasn't an answer.

"Gav?"

"Do what you can. I'll be ready here."

Katie looked back at the body. Her first thought, even under the current conditions, was that she didn't want to destroy any possible evidence. She wanted to make sure that everyone involved would go to prison.

She grasped the heavy plastic, trying to make a strong handhold. There was very little bodily fluid, which told Katie that the body most likely had been put in the crawlspace a year or more ago.

She pulled the bundle and the body moved. Placing her hands, one about shoulder high and the other closer to the body's leg, Katie pulled and heaved. The wrapped body broke free from its final resting place and began its journey inching down the secret crawlspace.

The heat began to get to Katie as she kept a steady pace of

pulling the dead weight. Her arms grew weary in the awkward position and she had to change hands. The tighter areas in the crawlspace made her fight inch by inch, dragging the skeleton inside the heavy construction plastic.

"You okay?" said McGaven.

Katie was closer to the outlet and his voice sounded more normal. Turning her head, she saw that McGaven had leaned as far as he dared into the space with outstretched arms. Once she got close enough, she climbed back through the opening. Relief filled her as her muscles ached from the intense workout.

Together, Katie and McGaven maneuvered the body enough to free it from the space. Once inside the room, Katie felt a rush of air, which was a good sign that they wouldn't suffocate and they would be able to escape from the cement building.

McGaven carefully placed Rebecca Miller's wrapped body in the far corner of the room. His downturned mouth indicated that he was saddened by the turn of events.

Catching her breath, Katie paused a few moments, feeling the air wafting in and cooling her down. She looked at Brett, seeing that his eyes were closed and his breathing ragged. She immediately dropped to her knees to take a closer look. "Brett," she said. "Can you hear me?"

His eyes fluttered open as he mumbled some incoherent words before his head flopped to the side and his eyes closed again.

"Brett," she said. Katie checked his pulse. The beats were faint but steady.

"Is he...?"

"He's alive but I don't know how much longer he has." The thought of Brett dying made her deeply distraught but very angry at the same time. So many casualties. Too many deaths.

Cisco had moved closer to Brett, sensing his condition.

The air movement was better, alleviating the stifling warmth.

"I have to go," she said. "Send Cisco through when I get to the end."

"You want to bring him?" He seemed surprised.

"Yes. I don't know what I'm going to run into out there and Cisco knows when there's something bad. Including bad people. I'll get out and get help, and at least we'll know what and who we're up against."

"You know who and why."

"I know, but we have to outsmart them. I want them all to go down for everything that has happened here in Coldwater Creek."

She began to climb into the opening.

"Katie," said McGaven touching her arm. "Be careful. And don't try to take on all the bad guys by yourself."

She knew that McGaven worried about her, especially since they had encountered more than their fair share of dangers and precarious situations in their careers together. He was like family and she loved him too. "I will. Send Cisco in when I give the word."

He stepped back and nodded.

Cisco stood next to the opening, his dark body moving back and forth, agitated with low-pitch whines as he watched Katie disappear once more into the dark chamber.

# FIFTY

Katie turned her head toward where she was going after she progressed into the darkness. Watching McGaven and Cisco's faces in the dwindling light as she moved away from them made her heart ache. She was experiencing a seesaw reaction of both sorrow and anger. One would eventually win out when she found the crew that was trying to kill her and McGaven. They had already tried to snuff out one of their own as if it was nothing and they would not stop until any threats to them were extinguished.

She kept herself alert and active, trying not to think about the cramped quarters she was in. Her mind wandered back to the army. Several of her missions had to do with cramped quarters as they'd had to wait for further orders. It sufficed to say that most people were claustrophobic to a degree—but the trick was not to let it overpower you or then it would own you.

Katie passed the point where Rebecca's body had been lodged and she felt gritty and soft things beneath her feet. Forcing the terrible thoughts from her mind, she kept moving.

The old smoothed rocks and ancient cement at her back caused sore places along her spine as she pushed forward. She fought the urge to sneeze with the dust and mold festooned in front of her and inside the cracks, but in the dark it remained in her imagination.

More air rushed in and blasted her face.

She came to a section where it was narrower than where she had come from. Pushing harder, she gritted her teeth, making herself thrust her body forward. She stopped to rest as her chest became pressed against the cold deteriorating wall. The compression made her go into a head spin of anxiety.

*No, not now...*

She wanted to run, but she couldn't move forward. The next best thing was to move back and she couldn't—it was as if she had been poured into hardening concrete.

*No... leave me...*

Katie started to panic, which she hated. She'd had to learn to wait for it to dissipate by not fighting it. Her breath became shallow and fast. In the dark, she didn't know where her body ended and the building began. She could turn her head slightly and only saw complete darkness behind her. Her mind played evil tricks and she imagined something in the tunnel with her— something she couldn't see but could hear. The hammering sound she heard was her own heart.

Katie closed her eyes and literally saw no difference, but she did it anyway. She imagined something she loved and places she enjoyed: the beach, her farmhouse, and Chad. As she did this, her breathing slowed, still shallow, but reduced in intensity to a manageable level. Her head began to clear.

She pushed her body forward, but this time she moved with her breathing. Inch by inch. Breath by breath. Pieces of the wall ground away and she finally was able to keep going. More air greeted her. It wasn't pleasant-smelling air, but it still helped to relieve her angst and return oxygen to her body.

To her relief, the passage opened up wider and she could see some light from the outdoors. There was a vent almost two and half feet wide with a grille covering it, so she carefully pushed forward until she could see trees. Surveying the area, there was no indication of Chief Baker or his henchmen—or anyone. She listened. No sound from anything but a slight breeze. She wondered if they had gone back to what they were doing since they knew that she and McGaven were trapped, unable to get out.

*Would they just wait until they knew we were dead?*

*Then return and put our bodies in the crawlspace along with Rebecca Miller's?*

Katie pushed the vent and discovered it was loose. There were two small screws barely holding it in place. She pushed, twisted, and pulled it back and forth... until it released, leaving a decent-sized window. She cautiously put her face to the outdoors, finally smelling the fresh air of the forest.

Katie surveyed the area and listened intently again.

Taking a couple of steps back into the space, she called, "Cisco. *Hier.*" Katie knew that the dog wouldn't have a problem fitting in the crawlspace. His long lean German shepherd body would fit easily. He had been trained to go through tunnels, crawlspaces, across rooftops, up ladders, and high up in rafters.

She heard the clatter of Cisco's toenails hitting the cement and moving quickly toward her—varying at times. He didn't seem to slow down and didn't have any issue with the tighter areas. Not even a minute passed when Katie felt Cisco's nose touch her hand. "Good boy." She stroked his sleek coat.

Katie looked back at the window and made sure that nothing had changed. It was all clear so she readied herself to climb through the vent—there wasn't much of a drop because she was still on the first floor.

Once outside, Katie's senses and physical ability came back fully. She directed Cisco and he easily cleared the opening.

Immediately Katie jogged to the denser tree areas surrounding the building. She wanted to get some intel on who was at the location. Moving south, she heard voices. Carefully camouflaging herself in the brush, she could see Chief Baker talking to Officer Daniels. Realizing that the part-time officer was fully involved in the criminal enterprises, she watched the two men converse and laugh like there wasn't any problem with leaving people trapped inside a building waiting to die. They both carried automatic rifles in addition to their holstered semiautomatic guns. It was clear to Katie that they most likely had acted the same way when they planned to kill the three girls.

It was dark and the shadows cast an eerie light on the men, distorting them.

Katie inched forward, trying to hear what they were talking about. Cisco inched with her, remaining quiet and alert.

Another man emerged with a cigarette in his mouth, an AR-15 slung over his shoulder, and carrying a lantern light. It was Lenny Ramos. No surprise to Katie. His swagger and "don't care about much about anything" attitude, along with no remorse, made him a perfect candidate to become a successful psychopath.

"Where's Bob and Grant?" said Lenny.

"Taking care of business at the old man's house," said Chief Baker.

Katie's blood turned cold and her anger rose to a heightened level. She needed to get to Joshua's house immediately.

She took the time to text John and McGaven with the same message:

*I'm out. I'm fine. Five armed shooters: Chief Baker, Officer Daniels, Lenny Ramos. Two others at Joshua's house. When backup?*

Katie retreated back into the woods, making as little sound

as possible. She took a big loop and ended up at Joshua's cabin. Everything seemed fine and it was quiet out of doors.

She approached with caution with her weapon drawn. Sidling up to the kitchen window, she peered in then dropped down out of sight. She held her emotions. There were two men, the same ones they had seen at the shopping center with the chief, and now they were inside destroying the place. Joshua was on the floor in the living room and he wasn't moving.

Katie had the element of surprise on her side and she needed to get the men out of commission and see if Joshua was still alive. Staying low, she moved toward the front of the cabin.

\* \* \*

"What did they say?" said Chad. "I can't wait around anymore —we can't wait. They should be here by now."

"I can't believe this!" said John. "They're delayed and still more than an hour away."

"We have to go in as backup."

"Katie's text said there were five men—all with more fire-power than we have. We have to wait for tactical support. Now I have to update the sheriff." John was clearly agitated. "And tell him that his niece is out somewhere in the forest. His detective is still trapped inside a cement bunker, and there's a dying police officer with him."

# FIFTY-ONE

*Saturday 2045 hours*

Katie crept quietly toward the front door of Joshua's cabin. She could hear the two men laughing about something and then dishes breaking. Keeping Cisco on a down at the side of the house, she went to the area with the outdoor stove and large wind chime. She didn't want to alert the others with gunfire, so she chose her weapons carefully.

She crept toward the chime and carefully unhooked it. With a simple toss, she threw the chime against the door, scattered pieces sprinkled over the porch as it smashed. She heard heated voices as she hid behind a tree waiting.

"Find out what that was," said one of them inside.

"Fine."

The door opened and man came storming out, but he stepped on the broken glass pieces. "What the hell?" He looked down as the door shut behind him. Confused by the broken wind chime, he paused a moment.

Katie rushed him, kicking him in the stomach and dropping him instantly. He tried to get up, dazed by the blitz attack, and saw her. He clumsily got to his feet and immediately came after her but she swung one of Joshua's cast-iron skillets, dropping the man again. This time he was out cold.

Katie dragged the body to the side of the cabin. She found rope and a rag to gag the man. After securely tying him up, she waited for his partner to come looking for him as she took a hiding position.

It didn't take long. The other man, much taller and thicker, slammed the door open. "Where are you, Grant?" He stepped on the same broken pieces but didn't fall for it. "Grant, you taking a piss?" He seemed suspicious for some reason. He needed to take a couple more steps into the yard, but he waited. She didn't know if he was listening or sensed something was wrong.

Katie watched him and wondered if he was the one who'd ransacked the cottage and written on the walls with black spray paint. She was growing weary waiting—Joshua might need medical attention.

She stepped out with a rake in her hands. "Hey," she said.

Once the big man looked her way, she swung the rake, taking him instantly down to the ground. Katie made the mistake of not stepping back and he grabbed her ankle, causing her to hit the ground.

He then pounced on her, using his weight and keeping her pinned while he sat up and wrapped his hands around her neck. Katie was no match for the man as he wrestled her around like a rag doll.

"Cisco," she croaked and wasn't sure if the dog heard her or not. But it didn't matter.

Cisco jumped into battle, running full speed like a stealthy black blur and leaping into the air with perfect timing. As he came down, his jaws made a perfect hit onto the man's shoulder, taking him backwards. The dog continued his attack by viciously shaking him.

The big man screamed for Katie to call the dog off.

Katie caught her breath, still coughing from the lack of air. She got to her feet and pulled her weapon. "Cisco, *aus*." The command for the dog to release his bite. He did so immediately as Katie shoved her Glock in the man's face. "I wouldn't move if I were you." She smiled at the man. "Get over there with your partner."

She quickly secured him and double-checked their ropes and made sure they couldn't yell for help. There would be help arriving, she was sure of it. She had to keep moving.

Katie hurried inside Joshua's cabin and to her relief she found the old man sitting up nursing a cut on the side of his head.

Cisco ran to the man's side.

Katie knelt down. "Are you alright?" she said, examining the wound.

He looked at her. "I'm fine, but surprised to see you here. I thought all hell was breaking loose and was concerned about you detectives."

"You're partially right. We solved the three homicides but found out that there's an entire crime syndicate running this town—I'm still in shock over everything."

Katie helped Joshua to his feet.

"You look like you've been taking on an entire army of people."

She chuckled. "It feels like it, but I need for you to stay put and safe until this thing is over."

"Over?"

"Yes. I'm waiting for our backup to arrive. In the meantime those guys are tied up on the other side of your cabin."

"You can't go out alone."

"I'm not alone. We're just not all in the same place. Please... trust me?"

He looked at her and, for the first time, she saw deep into

the eyes of the kindest-hearted man. He truly cared about people and so it was a shame that he was living out here like a recluse. "I do. What do you want me to do?"

"Here, take this," she said, giving him her cell phone. "The last text messages are from my friends, so if you get a message respond to them. You text them telling them who you are if you need anything. Press this button, type your message, and hit send." She guided him to the back room as she quickly studied the solid architecture of the log cabin. "I want you to stay in here and barricade the door. I'm leaving Cisco with you."

"You can't leave me your dog and cell phone."

"You're just borrowing them." She smiled. "I need to know that you're both safe. Okay?"

Katie helped Joshua get settled in the back bedroom—it was smaller than the other and had only one window, which they could escape through if they needed to. He had two guns and Cisco. "Remember, if you need anything or someone else comes here—be ready." She went to the door and turned. "This will be over in a couple of hours." Cisco and Joshua looked at her. She knew she couldn't bear it if something were to go very wrong. She smiled once more and shut the door behind her, pausing a moment to breathe.

As Katie moved through the cabin, turning off the lights, she could hear Joshua move something heavy in front of the bedroom door. She quickly checked the windows and made sure everything was bolted and locked securely. The last thing was the front door. She stepped off the porch, looking back at the dark cabin and hoping this would soon be over.

Katie retraced her steps and cut over toward the cement building. She loved having Cisco with her, but it was too dangerous to have him beside her now without any backup. Her fear was that someone would shoot the dog, so the best place he could be right now was with Joshua.

She pushed through the forest at a slow speed, making sure

her footsteps were quiet. Doubling back around, she peered through some thickets but didn't see any of the men.

Maybe they'd called it a night and had gone back into town satisfied with the fact that they thought they had captured both detectives and their turned officer? Her next thought was that they might be looking for the other two men.

Katie decided to go back around to check on the cabin, making sure it was still secure. She ran scenarios through her mind of what she should do next—but it always came back to protecting the innocent.

Before she turned around, she was grabbed from behind, overpowered, and a plastic bag was forced over her head. Instantly clawing at it, Katie felt hands slowly begin to squeeze her neck tighter as the lack of air restricted her lungs. She fought with every ounce of strength she had, her body, her legs, but it was a losing battle. Her strength dwindled, her balance teetered and her head became dizzy as she gasped unsuccessfully—finally blacking out.

# FIFTY-TWO

*Saturday 2220 hours*

Katie woke up still gasping for air and instantly sat up, catching her breath. The cold evening air stung her throat and lungs. Her memory of having a plastic bag forced over her head had seemed real. She waited to clear her jumbled thoughts of what had transpired. The oxygen was returning to her brain and she felt stronger in her muscles.

She looked around and wondered why she was in the back of a tan truck, which was parked on the old access road that she and McGaven had hiked up earlier. When she tried to move, reality hit her. Her hands were tied in unusual knots so that every time she flexed them, it tightened the rope around her neck.

She scooted carefully to the open lift gate and pushed her legs to the edge. The pain was excruciating when she moved a certain way.

"You're not going anywhere unless you want to strangle yourself," said Chief Baker. He was now dressed in military fatigues and looked to be ready to start a war. He had since shaved his mustache and reminded Katie of those extremists living out on a large parcel of land plotting against the government.

"You might as well let me go," she said.

"Why would I want to do that?" He laughed. "I have to hand it to you. You and your partner were good, I mean really good. And I wasn't expecting that—no way. I should've asked for mediocre detectives." He moved close to her, leering, and she could smell his sour tobacco breath against her face. "You know no one can stop us. Oh, I know you must think that I'm a psychopath—but it's money—simple." He kept his close proximity. "Being a chief doesn't pay well so I recruited a few people while watching the rest of the town with cameras. It was quite brilliant, you know... anyone who happened to notice them were told that it was for everyone's safety. If that meant a few people had to disappear, then so be it. But, Ivy was another story..." His voice faded as if he was thinking about the crime scene. He finally moved away from her.

As she listened to his admission of killing, or arranging for the killing of, other townspeople to help him keep his money-making enterprise a secret, Katie wasn't going to show weakness or let him know she was terrified. Not just for herself but for McGaven and Brett along with Joshua and Cisco. There would be no excuses or apologies if anything happened to any of them. She wondered what John and Chad were coordinating and how long it would take—she gambled on them coming soon as otherwise her time was running out.

"There's the sleeping princess—now awake. I so wanted to snap her neck or crush her throat," said Lenny, appearing beside Baker. His creepy smile made him look like a crazed inmate who had just escaped a mental health hospital. "See, I told you she was going to be trouble—worse than the others."

"Simmer down. We had to let things play out." He turned to Lenny and said in a lower tone, "Since you didn't follow orders, we had to make it work for us. You better not have cost us our money or freedom." He clenched his jaw as it was clear that he was angry, at least annoyed, with Lenny for how the murders were executed.

"Play out what?" said Katie. "You seem very sloppy, to me, with your crime scenes and not initially answering our questions. I already knew who killed those girls. What went wrong— Ivy Miller was too smart and figured out your little enterprise here? A fifteen-year-old girl. Definitely not too smart on your end. Oh, that's right, you already killed her mother."

Baker grabbed Katie's hair and pulled her face even closer to him. "All you females think you're so smart, but look how that works out." He released her. "But you, you're different."

"She was in the army or something," said Lenny as he spat on the ground.

"You? A pushy little thing like you?" Baker looked her up and down. "What could you possibly do to help protect this country?" He deliberately spit to the side of the truck, missing her face.

"I knew you snooped through our things," she said to Lenny.

"So what?" He shrugged and took a step toward her with his head high like it was some kind of honor, rifling their belongings.

"That's why you had to get the knives back from the old cop car. Hiding the murder weapons there—that's real smart." Katie kept her emotions level.

"What's she talking about?" he said to the chief. "How'd she know that?"

"I told you and everyone else that we were in trouble with this one. Too smart for her own good. They should have left when they had the chance."

Katie rolled her eyes, trying to sell the fact that she was tough and their games didn't scare her. She watched Lenny move around. He was unpredictable—and now clearly matched her killer profile.

"I would bet that you, Lenny, killed Rebecca Miller," she said.

"What about it?"

"Looks to me that you had a thing for Dawn Cromwell. What happened, did you lose your temper or did she find out what a loser you really are?" Katie kept eye contact with both men.

Lenny slapped Katie across the face—she recovered from the stinging blow. He was going to unleash more violence, but Baker stopped him. "Now isn't the time."

"I take that as a yes," she said, keeping her voice even and surprising herself.

"That bitch didn't know what was good for her—defying me. The only girl that I ever confided in and she couldn't keep her mouth shut—she was going to blow everything we got going here." His rage mounted, causing the veins in his neck and fore-head to bulge.

"Lenny, take it easy, you're going to blow a gasket," said Officer Daniels as he walked up to the group. His dark hair mili-tary-cut, his posture, his carefully chosen words, his fit physique, Katie figured he had some military training besides the police academy—if he really attended. In fact, Katie didn't know much else about him except that he would make himself scarce every time she and McGaven were around. "Everything is in place. The extra vehicle with everything we might need is parked back a half mile. We'll be far away from here when they find the bodies." He smiled smugly.

"What's your role in this small-town scheme?"

"Detective Scott, you're not going to rile me with your obvious tough-guy attitude and some psychology classes behind you. I see your game and it's not going to work. You had your chance and we're in control now. Live with it... for now."

"So, you get put on the police department's payroll to make it seem legit? Makes sense, I suppose."

He smiled. "Something like that."

"Let's just gut her now and get it over with," said Lenny pulling a hunting knife from the sheath.

"Patience. Why don't you make your rounds?" said Daniels.

"Hard to get good help?" she said.

Daniels leaned in close, Katie could smell his sickening heavy aftershave. "Maybe I should cut out your tongue?"

"You don't scare me. You target little girls and murder them. The way I see it, that's pretty much a coward."

"We'll see about that when it's your time." Daniels said to Baker. "She said to wait. So we wait."

"Wait? For who?" said Katie. Her mind flipped through the catalogue of characters in the town.

*She?*

Her mind went through the women of Coldwater Creek: Dr. Sanders, Mama, and... then she thought of Sydney Barrett-Miller. *Of course.* It was the last piece to the puzzle. She had become aloof and distant as though she was grieving, but the entire time she had had her daughter and granddaughter killed for her own gain. The antiques and expensive décor, not to mention the most expensive house in town. Could she really be running things with these thugs? Not wanting to get her hands dirty. Her behavior ticking all the psychopathy boxes. Clever woman, but there had always seemed to be something off.

"Everyone's here, I see. I love this," said Sydney just at that moment as she appeared like an apparition from the forest. She seemed completely different than her persona had been at the house. She was dressed in hiking attire, and her previous, seemingly gentle, demeanor was nowhere to be found. "String her up," she said flatly. Her tone made Katie's skin prickle as she recalled her conversations with the woman.

"My pleasure," said Baker. He pulled Katie out of the bed of the truck.

Katie winced in extreme pain. She gasped for air. The sharp torturous pain shot up her back and to her neck. She could barely breathe as her vision became spotty.

"Sweetheart, just relax, it's only going to get worse," said Sydney as if she were talking to a child.

"How did you feel when you murdered your daughter and granddaughter?" said Katie, pushing through the pain.

"You didn't do your research very well. They were my stepchildren. I married into the family." She flashed a smile that matched her outrageous words and fire-engine-red fingernail polish.

"You know," said Katie trying to get air to her lungs, "I thought at first there was some type of satanic ritual going on here, but it's clear that there doesn't have to be when Coldwater Creek has its own demon queen like you."

Sydney's face turned sour and in the low lighting from the lanterns the creases around her eyes and mouth made her look like a creepy character from a horror film. "You think you're smart, figuring out your little clues, and yes, it surprised me that you uncovered our dirty little, but very lucrative, secret, but it doesn't matter now. You think you're going to shut me down? I don't think so. String her up, boys." A smile washed over her face. "Wait, better yet, she might be useful just in case things go sideways."

Baker and Lenny grabbed Katie, pulling her by her feet and ignoring Sydney's orders.

"We don't need her. Let's get rid of any evidence and witnesses," said Baker.

The ground ripped at her body, tore at Katie's arms, and back. She gasped for air as she wheezed trying to catch her last breaths. Everything faded away... She kept the constant image of Chad's smiling face in her mind...

The sound of a helicopter above with a deep thumping sound matched Katie's heartbeat.

Wind blew like a class-four hurricane.

Several spotlights lit up the forest like daytime.

Dirt, pine needles, and leaves picked up and swarmed around in circles.

"Drop your weapons! Let the hostage go! Now!" said a voice over a loudspeaker.

The shocked faces of the crime syndicate stared above in disbelief as red laser dots trained on them.

Reluctant, they dropped their weapons and let go of Katie.

Two SUVs drove up in a cloud of dust along with two sheriff's vehicles from the next county.

Katie lay there staring upward in a daze, still breathing shallowly and watching the strange lights. Her surroundings felt like a dream as she closed her eyes. She could hear voices yelling then turning into muddled sounds. Car doors slamming. It was like a movie reaching the end. She felt like she was lifted up and then her body floating into space...

"Detective Scott, can you hear me?" said a familiar voice.

# FIFTY-THREE

*Sunday 0130 hours*

Katie sat in the back of one of the SUVs as a medic checked her vitals. Chad never left her side. She watched as the investigation and arrests unfolded in front of her. Both counties were involved, the local FBI, ATF, and the Organized Crime Division. Everyone wanted to be a part of this.

"Detective, you should get checked out at the local hospital," said the medic.

"I'm fine, really."

"I'll make sure she does," said Chad.

Joshua and Cisco approached Katie. Cisco jumped up next to her, staying close.

"Well, Detective, you did it," Joshua said. "I never thought I'd see it in my lifetime."

"I'm glad you're okay."

"Cisco made sure of that," he said. One of the investigators asked to speak with him.

Sheriff Scott approached the SUV and it was difficult to

read his face, whether he was mad or relieved. Maybe a bit of both.

"You scared all of us," he said.

Katie jumped down and hugged her uncle. "I'm sorry, so sorry." It felt good to hug him amid the circus.

"I want you to get some rest. You're going to be debriefed and then we'll take it from there," he said. "You make sure she does."

"Absolutely, sir," said Chad.

Katie saw them wheel out Officer Lane and she was relieved that he was alive. McGaven emerged from the crowd and headed straight to them.

"Gav, you're okay?" she said, hugging her partner.

"Thanks to the SWAT team breaking us out of there."

Katie caught sight of Sergeant West; he made a salute motion as he went to coordinate his men.

"What a mess," said McGaven.

"It's going to take some time for everything to get sorted out," she said. "But for now, I'm thankful everyone is okay. And I want to go take a shower and sleep for two days."

# FIFTY-FOUR

## SEVEN DAYS LATER...

Katie and McGaven were wearing their police dress uniforms, sitting in a room in front of the Pine Valley Sheriff's Department's disciplinary committee. Sheriff Scott with his four lieutenants and sergeant from internal affairs faced the two detectives as they waited for their fates.

Katie knew that she wouldn't just get a warning. She stood a chance of getting fired or worse. She sat there, watching the sheriff, trying and failing to figure out what was coming.

She glanced to her partner, who remained solemn, looking straight ahead. The only thing she could do was count her blessings and let the rest fall where it may. There was no going back and changing anything, but she doubted she would've done anything different even if she could.

"Detective Kathryn Scott and Detective Sean McGaven," began Sheriff Scott. "We have gathered together for these proceedings in regard to the investigations you both conducted in Coldwater Creek. First, this has been the largest arrest and bust Pine Valley Sheriff's Department has ever been involved in. A total of seven arrests were made and others are pending the investigation. There was more than five million dollars' worth of combined drugs and guns recovered. The murders of Ivy Miller, Nikki Prager, and Dawn Cromwell have been closed, along with three other bodies that were found inside the cement structure. Officer Brett Lane will recover from his injuries."

Katie could barely breathe.

"You both will receive commendations for bravery and exceptional service to the community. However..." he said.

Katie tried to focus on her uncle, but what would happen was going to happen.

"You both have had a disciplinary action before and this makes your second. For not adhering to the chain of command and for conducting an additional investigation on your own, including bringing in two civilians for assistance, you will both receive suspension for one month. You will not have to surrender your shields and guns, but this will be reflected in your records."

Katie let out a breath.

"I hope I make myself clear. It had been the decision of this committee for this punishment, but I have to warn you: if there is a next time, it might not be as lenient. Do you understand?"

"Yes, sir," said Katie.

"Yes, sir," said McGaven.

"With everything aside, thank you, Detectives, for your dedication and service to this community. You are dismissed."

# FIFTY-FIVE

## TWO WEEKS LATER

Katie and Chad hiked back up the hill to Joshua's cabin in Coldwater Creek. Cisco stayed close to Chad as he held a leash for a beautiful sable shepherd.

"I never thought I'd come back here again," she said adjusting her backpack.

"This town is grateful. You're always welcome here," he said. "Are we almost there yet?"

"Almost."

"So this is officially our first outing since your suspension. And I was thinking that we need to book a private secluded get away—soon."

"That sounds fantastic. Count me in." She smiled thinking about how nice it would be to be alone with her fiancée.

Cisco ran ahead.

As Katie and Chad got to the cabin, they spotted Joshua hunched over a fabulous-smelling stew.

"Hello there, Detective," the old man said.

"I have a surprise for you."

"What kind of surprise?"

Chad moved toward the old man and handed him the leash to the new dog.

Katie watched the old man's face soften as he stared at the dog slowly petting her. It made her smile and she knew that they would be bonded. "In town, there's a dog rescue and this girl was definitely a special one. She needs a good home. It seems that she was found a stray, but no one has come forward to claim her."

"You're a beautiful girl," he said, petting the dog. There was a tear in his eye. "She's going to be a great comfort."

"I didn't think you should live out here without a best friend," she said.

"Thank you."

"What are you going to name her?" said Chad.

"I'm going to name her after a detective, of course."

"You can't name her Katie," she said, laughing.

"I think it has a nice ring to it."

She smiled.

"You two want to join me for lunch?"

"Thought you'd never ask," she said. She watched the new shepherd heel with Joshua.

"If that tastes half as good as it smells, you're never going to get rid of us," said Chad.

Katie and Chad followed Joshua and the new dog into the cabin.

Cisco ran circles around the couple and then rushed inside.

# A LETTER FROM JENNIFER CHASE

I want to say a huge thank-you for choosing to read *The Rose Girls*. If you did enjoy it, and want to keep up to date with all my latest releases, just sign up at the following link. Your email address will never be shared and you can unsubscribe at any time.

*www.bookouture.com/jennifer-chase*

This has continued to be a special project and series for me. Forensics, K9 training, and criminal profiling has been something that I've studied considerably and to be able to incorporate them into crime fiction novels has been a thrilling experience for me. I have wanted to write this series for a while and it has been a truly wonderful experience to bring it to life.

One of my favorite activities, outside of writing, has been dog training. I'm a dog lover, if you couldn't tell by reading this book, and I loved creating the supporting canine character of Cisco to partner with my cold-case police detective. I hope you enjoyed it as well.

I hope you loved *The Rose Girls*, and if you did, I would be very grateful if you could write a review. I'd love to hear what you think, and it makes such a difference helping new readers to discover one of my books for the first time.

I love hearing from my readers—you can get in touch on my Facebook page, through Twitter, Goodreads, Instagram, or my website.

Thank you,

Jennifer Chase

www.authorjenniferchase.com

 facebook.com/AuthorJenniferChase
 twitter.com/JChaseNovelist
 instagram.com/jenchaseauthor

# ACKNOWLEDGMENTS

I want to thank my husband, Mark, for his steadfast support and for being my rock even when I had self-doubt. It's not always easy living with a writer and you've made it look easy.

A very special thank-you goes out to all my law enforcement, police detectives, deputies, police K9 teams, forensic units, forensic anthropologists, and first-responder friends—there's too many to list. Your friendships have meant so much to me. It has opened a whole new writing world filled with inspiration for future stories. I wouldn't be able to bring my crime fiction stories to life if it wasn't for all of you. Thank you for your service and dedication to keep the rest of us safe.

Writing this series continues to be a truly amazing experience. I would like to thank my publisher, Bookouture, for the incredible opportunity, and the fantastic staff for continuing to help me to bring this book and the entire Detective Katie Scott series to life. Thank you, Kim, Sarah, and Noelle for your relentless promotion for us authors. A very special thank-you to my extraordinary editor Jessie Botterill and her amazing editorial team—your unwavering support and insight has helped me to work harder to write more endless adventures for Detective Katie Scott.

Printed in Great Britain
by Amazon

20789471R00212